BY: D.M. MEWHA

BEGINNINGS
BOOK TWO OF *BISHOP'S CROSSING*

RIVER CITY
SIREN PRESS

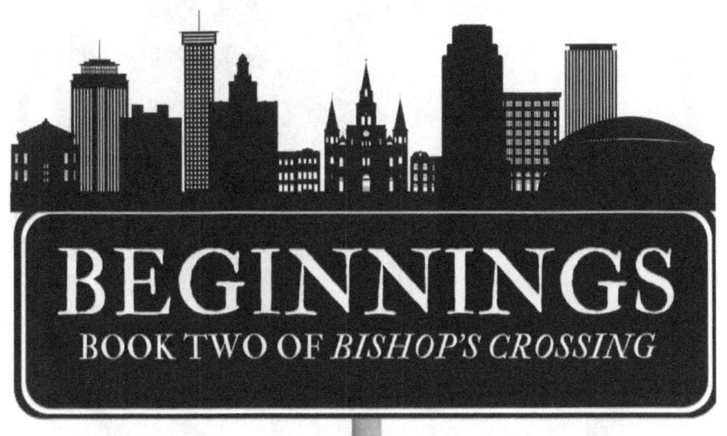

Hardcover ISBN: 978-1-964989-11-2

Paperback ISBN: 978-1-964989-10-5

For my grandmother, who was always my biggest fan. I miss you, Mom-Mom.

R eaders, please be aware of the follow trigger warnings found in this book:

- child abuse

- sexual exploitation of a minor

- cannibalism

- fast and loose Catholic doctrine

- monsters and horror-genre situations

- familicide

- incest

- murder

- attempted murder

- exploitation of the homeless

- body horror

- death of a parent

- possession

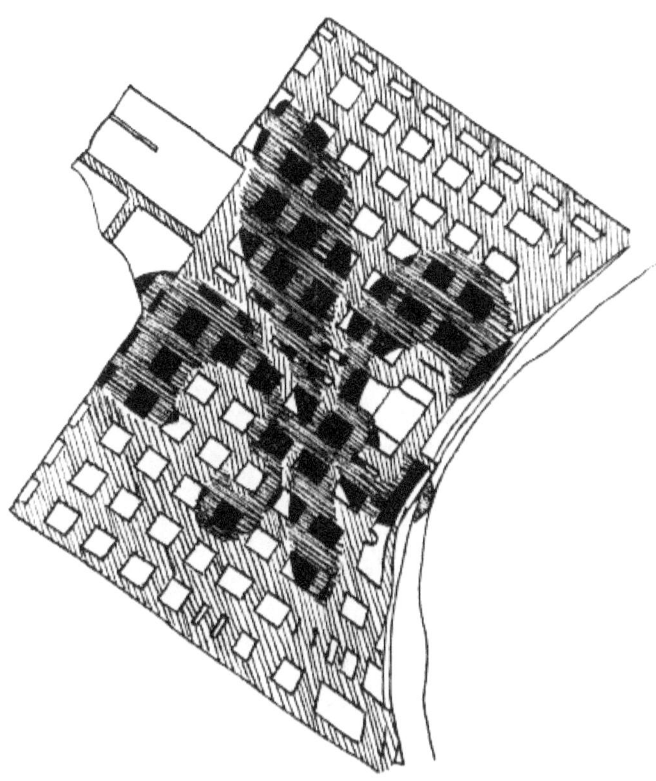

Thanksgiving has always been my favorite holiday.

Not what you'd guess, right? Most people see me and the sort of life that I've led, the work that I do, and assume that it's gotta be Halloween. But when you're waist-deep in creepy crawlies day in and day out, a holiday that plays on the sort of horror that you experience firsthand loses some of its shine.

Thanksgiving though? That I can get behind.

The last three months had been some of the happiest of my life, after over a year and a half of misery. After walking away from my friends–no–my family to try to prove to Jackie that I'm something I'm not, I was forced to re-insert myself into their lives when Father Raimond showed up on my door asking for a favor: track down Evangeline Grey, daughter of Papa Ivé, the Voodoo King of New Orleans, who'd gone missing not long ago to head off a supernatural gang war.

I almost have to laugh thinking about it. I turned Raimond down flat. I'd walked away. Gotten out. Then my daughter Mary started showing signs that she might have a touch of the supernatural, and Father Chase took an interest in potentially killing her, making a favor from Mother Church seem more pertinent to my day-to-day life. In a dizzying sprint, I met back up with Ava, Nero, and Nat, and we tracked down Evangeline while Chase made our lives harder every step of the way, shooting and nearly killing Ava in the process.

Like a bunch of big damned heroes, we pushed through and rescued the girl from a cult and handed her back to her dad, only to run into Evangeline Grey a short while later, this time without a pulse and sporting fangs.

Once we'd realized we'd been played, it was off to the races, going back to the cult's digs, where I found out my supposed-to-be-deceased father was behind a plot to shove a demon into Papa Ivé's body and had arranged the entire situation in some sort of twisted attempt to give me a chance to be a hero.

He was crazy, what do you want?

After a cathartic moment of shooting him in the forehead, we went back home to find out that my ex Jackie, her fiance Victor, and Mary had been taken by Father Chase to force a confrontation with me.

It turns out that getting into a fistfight with a former special forces guy isn't the best plan, even if people would describe you as "scrappy." The fight wasn't going well, Chase knocked me around, then was getting ready to kill Ava when Mary distracted him and Jackie put a bullet in his shoulder.

"More stuffing?" Mary asked from the other side of the table.

Bishop's Crossing was closed for the holiday; the staff were off with their families while I was here with mine. Ava sat directly to my right next to Nat, who was next to Dave, then Mary, Jackie, Victor, Nero, Aaron, and finally, Father Raimond.

We were a mismatched bunch, but we were here. Despite all the odds, we'd found one another (multiple times in some cases), and made a family of sorts. Every one of us was broken in our own way, but that was fine. We had each other and that made us whole.

We'd pushed a bunch of the tables in the restaurant area together, all in a long row then piled them high with food that Dave had been cooking since yesterday. Turkey, stuffing, mashed potatoes, corn, peas, homemade gravy, buttermilk biscuits, gumbo, jambalaya, shrimp boil, and a bunch of pies; Dave spared no effort. It was amazing. Laughter and warm conversation filled the room, working its way up into the rafters and leaving a pleasant, warm feeling wherever it passed.

It wasn't just family. It was home.

The late afternoon moved into dusk and the dark of night was starting to fall as the sun dipped further below the horizon. Dinner evolved into dessert and adults started to push themselves back away from the table, the universal sign of surrender at meals across the Big Easy.

Victor groaned as he leaned backward in his chair.

"That was amazing. I think I just gained six pant sizes, but totally worth it," he said through a smile.

"Praise is always appreciated." Dave beamed in return. "And I can say with happiness and pride that this was **not** an old family recipe."

His statement brought a round of laughter from me, Mary, Ava, Nat, and Nero. The others looked on in confusion.

"I don't get it," Victor admitted. "Is there some sort of story about Dave's family?"

"Lots of stories. Most of 'em are the type that tend to keep folk up at night," Dave replied with a shrug. "Was a long time ago. Different times and different places and a different me."

"Not all *that* different of a you," Ava corrected. "You never belonged there."

Dave smiled gratefully while Victor frowned.

"See, you guys always do that," Victor said.

"Do what?" Ava asked.

"That. You make a vague comment about how things have changed. Or family recipes, or dragons, then move on to the next thing like it's the most normal thing in the world," he replied.

"I don't think any of us ever said it was normal," I objected.

"Exactly, These little tidbits have me dying to know how all of you met," he said. "You have to admit, you're a bit eclectic, even for New Orleans."

"It's really not that interesting," I started, only to have Jackie chime in with: "Me too. I know that you knew Ava and Nero when we met, but Dave and Nat came later, and you never really talked about how you knew them except from 'the scene', whatever that was supposed to mean."

"It was him trying to keep you away from the Gloaming," Raimond offered with a half-smile. "For all the good that ended up doing him. Damage is done at this point, Bishop. You may as well come clean and just tell them."

"Yeah, Dad. I want to know how you and Miss Ava met. And Father Raimond!" Mary agreed, leaning forward and staring with rapt attention.

Raimond smiled, shaking his head.

"Your father and I met in Seminary. We were both studying to be priests. For that story your father is correct, there's really not much to tell," he admitted.

Looking disappointed, Mary's gaze shifted to the others around the table.

Ava and I exchanged an uncomfortable look as Nero shuffled his feet and avoided eye contact with everyone. Aaron looked confused while Nat stared at the rafters, clearly looking for tangible signs of that laughter from earlier. Dave poked at his apple pie ala mode, suddenly invested in mixing the ice cream in.

Taking in each of our expressions, Mary made a disgusted face. "Oh. They're all *those* sorts of stories? Yuck. I'm going to bed, then you can all talk about whatever inappropriate things you want," Mary declared, standing up from the table. "Pervs."

A guffaw escaped before I realized it was on its way out, drawing a frown from Jackie and a shake of Ava's head.

"Might be stories that are better for you to hear when you're older," I admitted to my daughter's retreating back.

"I'll never be *that* old, Daddy," she declared from the stairs. "Love you guys! Behave yourselves."

The thumping of feet on stairs traced her progress up and into the apartment above.

The night flowed steadily on, lubricated on its journey by copious amounts of alcohol.

"That's the great thing about doing holidays here," Nero observed. "We got a bar-sized supply of liquor."

This drew a loud round of cheers from all of us, and another round of drinks.

Jackie paused, staring around the room. "So spill!" she demanded. "What brought all of you together?"

"Well—" I started. "We all sorta trickled together over the years. After the whole seminary thing, I was kinda looking for purpose. Reading, studying, that kinda thing, then this letter showed up–"

"No way, Bishop. Nuh-uh. You're not gonna tell these stories," Nat interjected.

"Why not?"

"Because you'll tell them wrong. You make it sound like the case of the blah blah blah, and make it all about you, and it's clearly not."

"Huh?"

"The story of how I met up with the bunch of you is all about *me*, of course. I was the last one to hook up with everyone. The missing ingredient that made everything work I'm shocked you four survived without me for as long as you did. It was a minor miracle, really."

"I don't—"

"Stop. You're embarrassing yourself, old man." Nat declared and rose to her feet.

"If you want to understand how this group works, and how we all got together, you gotta start with the final and most important addition: Me!"

Book 1: Nat's Story

Chapter ONE

To understand the how and why of where I fit into our shared story, you need to understand what it was like for me growing up. I was always Daddy's Little Girl. As far as I was concerned, my dad was a rock star. He was not only a superhero, he was my *personal* superhero. I was convinced he was invincible, could do anything, and he could do no wrong. In return, I was his princess.

My mom was more artsy. A bit flighty. Dad handled the money stuff and Mom made our house a home. She made it beautiful. I don't remember a ton, but what I do remember was being happy. They were in love. It was...I mean...it was pretty close to perfect, or as close to perfect as a seven-year-old can understand. Until that day.

It was late afternoon, just before dinner when I heard some weird noises while I was playing in my room, so I went to investigate.

"Daddy?" I called out.

Nothing.

I opened the door to the room and saw him sitting at his computer, his back to the door. I remember the orange light from the window spilling into the room. I remember how I could see little dust motes floating, and the noise from the fan in his computer. It's funny the sort of things that stick with you.

"Daddy, what was that noise?" I asked.

Still nothing.

I took a deep breath and crept into the room, placing my tiny hand on his shoulder. It was the most delicate of touches. A butterfly kiss. It was enough.

My father went toppling out of the chair, hitting the floor and bouncing bonelessly.

I stood there in shock, trembling.

"Dad?" I nudged him.

"Dad?" I nudged him a bit harder.

"No no no no no no no..." My mind was blank with panic, refusing to latch on to the very real and very immediate fact that my superhero was gone. His body lay on the ground like someone dropped a toy, his eyes were open, and stared straight ahead. I remember he didn't blink. I really wanted him to blink. There weren't any warning signs that my dad had a grenade in his head that was just waiting to go off but that didn't change a thing.

"Mommy!" I shouted.

Anyway, Mom didn't take it great.

Like I said before, I don't remember a ton about her, except that she was shit at managing money, and no one had thought to plan for the only actual adult being taken out of the room. Before long, we had to sell the house and move from the suburbs into an apartment downtown, but even then, things were still kinda okay. 'Til she started dating again.

Her boyfriend's choices created a parade of alpha losers, each one worse than the one before. They wanted her for sex. For money. For—well...

It wasn't so bad when I was younger. Back then they mostly just resented me and looked for ways to keep me out of the way so they could get what they wanted out of Mom. My biggest interactions with them were stepping over passed out, drunk guys in the bathroom when I had to get ready for school, or asking my mom who the half-naked guy playing my video games was. When I got older, things got worse. I learned to keep an eye out. To recognize when they were looking at me in ways that would make me uncomfortable. To predict when they would try to get handsy to...well...you get the idea.

That was when I started staying away from home a bunch.

I was around thirteen, I remember waking up after I felt a weight shift on my bed. My covers were tight up around my neck, and I could smell the booze in the air. I didn't open my eyes, hoping that Derek, the alpha-loser du-jour, would just go away.

I screamed when his hand found my thigh, as loud and shrill as I could.

My mom was in the room a couple of seconds later. A long enough delay that Derek had moved to the doorway. I told her what happened. Tried to get her to believe me, but she didn't. She–

"Derek would never do that," she said. "You're just trying to cause trouble. To get attention. Why do you have to be so awful, Natalie?" she asked me.

I stared at her, stunned.

"How could you say that? I'm not making this up," I pleaded to her.

"I see the way you look at me, Natalie," Derek added. "It ain't right for a little girl to be looking at a grown man that way."

My mother gasped.

"Natalie, I know you want attention," she began.

"I don't want *his* attention!" I cried back.

"And those things have been hard since your father was taken from us," she continued, ignoring my tears. "But Derek is a good man. Now apologize for lying about him!"

Mom was standing between me and Derek, who wore a self-satisfied smirk on his piggy face. I balled up my fists and didn't say anything.

"Apologize to him, young lady. Right this instant," she demanded. Seemed like Mommy Dearest decided to try to pull her best June Cleaver impression and ignore the last five years.

I whispered a curse.

"What did you say?" she demanded.

"Fuck. You." I said, enunciating every letter, tasting the sound of the rebellion as it came dripping off my tongue. That's when she slapped it right out of my mouth, denying me the opportunity to savor it for long. Her slap came out of nowhere and spun me around, bouncing me off of the mattress and leaving me sprawled on the floor, more shocked than hurt.

"I said: *apologize,*" she repeated, just barely audible over the ringing in my ears.

I gritted my teeth and looked up at her from where I lay on the floor.

"And I said fuck you," I whispered. I hated the tremble in my voice. The way I knew it would make Derek smile. How it made me feel small. Weak.

It never even occurred to me that my mom would beat me. Even after the slap, it just wasn't something she'd ever done before, no matter how heated things got. No matter how disappointed in me she was. It wasn't part of our world. It was a line she had never crossed.

That night she crossed it with a vengeance.

I don't remember a lot of it. Not really. Just snippets. I remember the look on her face. How her normally pretty features twisted. The stark lines standing out on her forehead, catching the shadows in the room around us. How her hair broke loose from the bun she'd been wearing it in. It didn't want to be near her any more than I did.

"Please, no!" I remember begging. I recall trying to move my hand between the belt she was using to hit me and the tender flesh on the back of my legs. Her guttural voice while she muttered something about teaching me some damned respect, and the terrible moment when her face went from contorted in rage to just blank while she continued to beat me with the belt. I was crying so hard I could barely breathe. Any words or breaths were overpowered by shudders.

Huh. I guess I can remember most of it.

It took about fifteen minutes. Twenty at most. It felt like forever.

I like to think that somewhere in the middle of her rage, she understood she'd crossed a line. That she'd gone too far. Whether she did or not, the belt lashes eventually stopped biting. My legs and back burned red and angry from the beating. My throat was raw from screaming and my eyes were swollen and puffy from crying.

I curled into a ball on the floor, hugging myself tightly, my eyes closed against whatever was going to come next.

Footsteps.

Then my door opened and closed.

I don't know how long I lay there in the dark alone with my pain. Utterly abandoned by the last person I had in the world. However long it was, the next thing I remember was getting up in a haze, my legs were shaking as I began gathering clothes and a few belongings into my backpack, starting to leave, then going back to grab the silver unicorn necklace that my dad had gotten me for my last birthday before he died. Even if I was going to leave my mom, I'd still have my dad. Then I headed out the window.

I've heard people use the word *destroyed* to describe something bad happening to them, but I don't think they get what that really means. I feel like after that night, I might have understood for the first time. Everything that I thought was a constant was gone. My parents were the bedrock I'd built my life on. The star that let me navigate the world.

My father had been taken from me, and that was awful, but it wasn't his fault.

My mother chose someone else over me. Abandoned me. Showed that I wasn't enough for her. Wasn't important enough to her. And that was her fault.

I know it doesn't make a riveting story, and this sounds like a broken record, but I don't fully remember a lot of what happened next. It's like that sometimes, y'know? My brain just gets less sticky for the parts of life that are full of suck.

I was scared a lot, hungry too. Did a bunch of stuff I'm not proud of: I lied. Stole. Hurt people. Got hurt. I did the sort of things one thinks about when alone, sitting in silence, but had to so I could keep living. All of that stuff you're really worried about me telling you about right now? Yeah, it all happened. It doesn't make me a damsel who needed saving, it was something I had to get through to get to where I am now. Hell, it's a miracle I didn't end up in way worse shape than I did.

Probably has something to do with that whole latent willworker thing, right?

Yeah, I thought so.

Anyway, for the next two years that was my life if you could call it that. I avoided shelters because I was worried they'd try to send me back. I hurt a lot of people. Some of them wanted to hurt me. Some of them didn't.

Everyone is always curious about the details of what happened to me during that time. It happened. I got through it, and now I'm here. There are enough stories about little girls getting eaten up by monsters on the streets, human and otherwise, and I don't feel like that's me. I was adrift and if anything happened differently, I don't know how I would have turned out.

Dead, probably.

The real kicker in the entire thing was that as far as I could tell, my mom never tried to look for me. Not really. My face was never on a milk carton. Never had one of those alerts go off on a cell phone telling me to look for myself.

I was gone and she was good with that.

So fuck her all over, I guess

Chapter Two

Sometime during the year I turned fifteen is when things got interesting.

I was in an abandoned house doubled over, and I felt like I'd been stabbed. My guts twisted up inside me like they were gonna tie me into a knot. I was sweating, and I ached everywhere.

It gets that way sometimes when you need a fix.

I closed my eyes, willing it to stop. Trying to force my body to behave itself. This was a trick I'd taught myself. A trick that was my last line of defense when things got bad over the past couple of years, but today it was a trick that wasn't working.

"Fuck," I muttered and hauled myself off the dirty mattress in the flop house we were staying in. I stumbled past the arms and legs of other kids lying on the floor like a bunch of broken dolls. Discarded and forgotten.

Just like me.

I stumbled out onto the street and headed toward the Quarter. I held my hands out in front of me and watched them shake. Vibrate almost. Picking pockets wasn't gonna be on the agenda today, which left panhandling. I figured I could pick a public area down there and hope it took the cops a while to roust me out of it. I look younger than I am if I'm not all made up, even if fifteen is plenty young for most. Most but not all.

The air around me was hazy. People moved like ghosts in and out of my field of vision, and I tried to stay small. To not take up space. To not be noticed. Another one of the survival tricks I picked up in the past couple of years. Probably the one most responsible for keeping me alive. I somehow managed to weave and stumble my way to Jackson Square Park, right in the shadow of the St. Louis Cathedral. The artists and tourists made it a pretty safe spot. The cops had trouble distinguishing loitering, busking, tourists, and artists as long as I didn't look too fucked up.

I settled in next to a lady who did caricature paintings and a guy playing the trumpet. I had a hat out in front of me, hoping for the best. My brain was foggy, flitting from thought to thought, but unable to grab onto anything firmly. I felt the need in me growing.

God, I wanted a fix.

The sun was getting low and shadows were reaching their fingers further into the Square when he walked by. He was a tall dark-skinned man with flowing white, almost silvery hair, and pale blue eyes who looked like he was in his early twenties wearing a pair of painted-on leather pants and a midnight blue silk shirt which he hadn't bothered to button so it showed off his tight abs as it spread out behind him like a pair of wings. No, he didn't walk by. He sauntered, maybe? It wasn't a strut, he was way more fluid than that. I thought he moved like a cat, almost liquid with the way he slid around people, never quite breaking stride, but performing an intricate dance with the crowd around him as he moved. In his wake, he left a smell. No. Smell isn't quite the right word. You could almost taste him in the air.

For the first time that day, I stopped thinking about my fix. He was gonna be my fix.

I stood, willing the nausea back down and ignoring my screaming joints as I lurched after him. He moved through the crowd easily I struggled after him, stiff-legged and moving like a zombie.

"Fucking hell," I muttered, trying to close the distance. No matter how hard I pushed, he always stayed just ahead of me. Like I was on the verge of losing him. I tried running but quickly fell into a stumble before regaining my balance through sheer force of will. I needed him. Falling wasn't an option. He was the answer to everything.

The mystery man continued through the streets of the French Quarter, taking a turn here, an alley there, and a few side streets for good measure, moving with the careless grace of someone who has everything easy and not a worry in their pretty little head.

The beautiful, stupid fucker.

Despite my best efforts, I was still a good twenty feet behind him when we arrived in the parts of New Orleans that the tourists avoid. The transition doesn't take long, just a block or two and you go from Spanish moss-covered balconies and fleur de lis scattered in the architecture to row homes that look like they never quite recovered after Katrina did her number on the city.

My beautiful idiot just kept walking, oblivious to the three guys who nodded at each other and started following after him. He turned another corner into a smaller side street, inviting the *'he was askin' for it'* dialogue to pop into my head. I hurried after him as fast as my feverish, broken body would let me. I turned the corner to see him facing the three guys, a full, beatific smile on his face. By now, the sun dipped far enough below the horizon that we were bathed in shadow, but he still seemed to have a glow about him.

"Boys, come on now. We don't gotta do this dance. Why don't you just wander on off an' do your thing, that way I don't have to hurt you." the man drawled. His accent was hard to place. Texan, maybe?

"Fuck you and hand over your wallet," the largest of the three demanded. I thought of him as 'Lorge Boi'.

"Don't got one," the man responded.

"Liar," Lorge Boi spat back. "You stink like money, bitch. Hand it over." A knife appeared in his hand.

I gasped and pulled out my own rusty blade from its hiding place in my left sleeve and moved closer, hoping I could buy this beautiful alien enough time to get away while I–died horribly, I guess. I wasn't really thinking super clearly. I didn't even try to hide what I was doing. I just walked up behind the guy on the left and stuck the blade into his lower back five or six times.

Stabbing someone is a weird feeling. Blood doesn't come shooting out like it does in the movies unless you nick an artery, and that's not what I was stabbing at. It comes out darker than you'd think. And sticky. Stabbing with any sorta short knife means you're gonna get it all over your hand, and probably even more than that since you're so close

I was standing close enough to practically fall on the mugger with the pot beanie as the blade in my hand found purchase in his chest over and over. I might have been saying "No" while doing it. I know I was thinking it. We hit the ground and either the multiple and continuing stab wounds or eating pavement knocked the wind out of the guy.

There's all sorts of important stuff that a body needs that rests just above your pelvis in your back. Mostly spine and kidneys. You manage to cut into those things and it's pretty much game over. I didn't hit any of them cleanly, but what the stabs lacked in quality they were making up for in quantity.

"Da fuck? You're gonna die, you crazy bitch!" the mugger with the porn stache screamed at me. "You're gonna wish–gkkk–" his diatribe was cut off.

I blinked through the haze and wiped some of the blood off my face and tried to make my brain understand what my eyes were telling it.

Porn Stachi was dead. His head had been turned nearly completely around. Lorge Boi, the first one who'd talked, was hanging in the air, being held aloft by my mystery man's arm. But it wasn't his arm anymore. Where he'd stood there was a massive, monstrous beast. He was covered in silvery blond fur the same color the mystery man's hair had been. He was somewhere around ten feet tall as he stood upright on wolf paws that tapered up into a massive body topped off with a wolf's head.

"Nooo, please don't, I'll–"

I never found out what Lorge Boi would do as the werewolf leaned forward and neatly crushed his head in its jaws.

I knelt there for a moment, blood pooling around me and soaking into the knees on my ripped up fishnets. Then I opened my mouth and screamed.

It seems that seeing a gigantic monster eat someone's head finally breaks me out of whatever level of horny for him I was, which is sorta good to know. Unfortunately for me, I wasn't in any shape to outrun anyone, much less a giant predatory killing machine, and he was on me in like two steps.

He closed his massive paw over my head and then everything went black.

Chapter
Three

I was surprised when my eyes opened. Not surprised like '*what I'm seeing is really surprising*'. More like '*I thought I was a dead girl, and dead girls don't normally open their eyes and see stuff*'. That sorta threw me off for a second. I blinked. The ceiling was tall. A good fifteen or twenty feet up in the middle and maybe five feet less than that where it angled down toward the walls. I listened.

Nothing.

Taking stock of the situation, I realized my cramps and aches were gone. I wasn't sweating. Shit, how long was I out for? Riding the withdrawal train isn't a short process. I'd done it a time or two before, against my will, but this time felt different. Like I'd been flushed out. Cleaned? Cleansed?

I tried to stand up and found out that my legs had been replaced by rubber bands. Or so I assumed because they refused to listen to my brain or hold up my body, instead opting for wobbling a bit and tossing me unceremoniously onto the bed.

"Perfect," I muttered, rolling over onto my back and struggling upright again.

Looking around me, I became even more confused. I was wearing my clothes, but they were different. Wrong. They felt softer, and smelled like lavender.

Holy fuck, they'd been washed?

"Don't love the implications there," I said to absolutely no one. I was doing great.

I was sitting in what I guessed were barracks. It was very plain, and very long, with around a dozen beds running down either side of a central walkway. At the foot of each, there was a footlocker. I leaned over and saw one at the foot of the bed I'd been occupying.

I tried to gather my will and use the same trick I did to smooth over my withdrawal pangs, but my head felt fuzzy when I tried. Like it was stuffed with cotton. I put my hand back behind me for balance.

"You're awake!"

The voice flowed like honey, coating my brain and making me feel all sweet and numb, like chasing my high all over again. I looked over at the source, struggling to keep my eyelids from closing, and I saw my mystery man. He was resplendent in white linen pants and a matching jacket (no shirt, obviously), his silvery hair hung loose around his shoulders, and he was barefoot.

I tried to respond, but my tongue was too thick. Too awkward. I couldn't compare to someone like him. I blushed and looked at my Doc Martens.

"I–" I croaked in reply. He held up a finger toward my lips.

"Darlin' you don't need to say a word. I wouldn't be here if it wasn't for you chargin' in an' taking care of that mugger. Thought I was a goner."

That didn't sound quite right. I shook my head to try to clear the sugary haze that coated my brain. "No," I croaked. "I didn't–"

"Why, once those other two saw what you did to their friend, they just took off like you was gonna hit them next," he continued, ignoring my objections.

I frowned. "But I thought–" I said, trying to grab onto the memory that was sitting just beyond my fingertips.

"You thought they were gonna hurt me, an' you did somethin' about it. Least I could do is return the favor and do somethin' about what you were goin' through, right?"

I nodded vapidly, my eyes open wide like some sort of doll. "Least you could do," I mumbled.

Part of my brain was screaming that this isn't what happened, but the part that was in the driver's seat didn't care. I was willing to accept whatever story the man was spinning. I just couldn't force the thinky part of my brain back in control.

"Good girl," he said, cupping my chin. I shuddered in revulsion at his touch, flashing back to memories of that asshole Derek and a long line of assholes since. He frowned and cocked his head as he looked down at me.

"I'm—no one's—good—girl," I replied, forcing the words through gritted teeth.

"Oooh, you got spirit, kid. I like that. You'll do just fine," he drawled back, an easy smile settling on his lips.

Not his eyes though. They weren't smiling. The eyes that were boring into mine were off. Different.

He blinked and it was gone, replaced by normal, everyday baby blues.

"You see, you're not the only runaway staying with us. We've been pickin' up kids from all 'round Nerlins and helpin' 'em. Give 'em a place to get fed. Get safe. Get clean," he paused, looking at me meaningfully.

I looked back down at my boots.

"No judgment, darlin'. Whatever you went through out there is what you went through. What we offer here is a chance to get back to the way things were. Back to basics. Feel like you're part of the natural order again," he explained.

"How many?" I managed to ask.

"How many kids? Oh, I don't know…we got maybe a dozen here right now, but there's room for more an' we're always on the prowl for the right kinda someone. Someone with that spark and a need."

"Someone like me?" I asked.

"Someone like you," he agreed.

Look, living on the streets for as long as I had instilled a healthy paranoia in me and every alarm bell in my head was going off. The 'me' part of my mind was screaming to get out the door and put as much distance between me and this sex cultist as I could. Unfortunately, that part of my brain wasn't in charge. The part of my brain in the driver's seat was happy to be here. Happy at the very idea of someone…anyone looking for me without bad intentions was–

I wiped a tear from the corner of my eye.

He sat next to me and put an arm around me. I immediately stiffened.

"There, there, darlin'. You just let it on out," he said through a toothy smile.

I didn't want to cry in front of him. I hate crying in front of people. I pressed my lips together and fought back against it all: the haze in my brain, the sense of abandonment, the tears, all of it.

"I'm fine," I whispered, standing up and leaning on the headboard for support. "Just a bit tired and woozy is all."

A cloud passed in front of those baby blues, but was gone in an instant, replaced by that same friendly mask. "Not a worry, darlin'. You finish restin' up. You can meet the rest of the kids at supper in an hour."

"Supper?" I asked.

"Yeah, gotta feed ya'll. Plus what staff we got on site, of course. Can't have them goin' hungry, either."

"But where–what is this place?" I asked. The unease he triggered by putting his arm around me made it easier for me to control my brain to focus.

"A bit a' this, a bit a' that," he replied. "It's a farm and nature preserve about twenty minutes outside of the city. We find kids that are down on their luck. Special kids. An' we give 'em a place and a purpose."

"Purpose?" I asked.

"A purpose," he repeated. "We get 'em fed up, cleaned up, and sobered up, like I said before. Then we teach 'em what they want to learn and send 'em on their way into the world with some clean clothes and a little money in their pocket."

"Why? I asked, frowning.

"Can't a body do somethin' 'cause they got a callin'? 'Cause it's the right thing to do?" he asked.

"They can, but they don't," I replied.

"Well, in this case, we do," he said. "My name's Donovan. Donovan Morgan, an this little operation's my doin'. The camp's been in my family for generations an' I gathered a few like-minded individuals together to help with the cause."

I nodded, waiting for more. He didn't provide any. He rose gracefully to his feet and brushed off some imagined dirt from his pristine linen pants. "You must be famished. I'll get food out a bit early so you can get a good head start. New kids always get swamped when they first show up an' you look like you've skipped some meals."

I nodded again.

He shot me a wink, then turned and headed out the door, leaving me alone once again.

I immediately checked in my left sleeve for my knife. Gone. I checked the foot locker at the end of my bed. Just some sweat clothes and towels.

Fuck.

I sat down on the bed hard, putting my face in my hands and rubbing. I needed to clear away whatever was going on in my head. I needed to be able to think. To be ready for whenever the other shoe was going to drop.

I needed a plan.

I looked out the window at the field outside of the...dorm? Barracks? Building. Building worked. People moved around, weeding a huge garden, with dark trees looming like a barricade in the distance.

Pretty words or not, I was trapped.

I was surprised when my eyes opened. Not surprised like '*what I'm seeing is really surprising*'. More like '*I thought I was a dead girl, and dead girls don't normally open their eyes and see stuff*'. That sorta threw me off for a second. I blinked. The ceiling was tall. A good fifteen or twenty feet up in the middle and maybe five feet less than that where it angled down toward the walls. I listened.

Nothing.

Taking stock of the situation, I realized my cramps and aches were gone. I wasn't sweating. Shit, how long was I out for? Riding the withdrawal train isn't a short process. I'd done it a time or two before, against my will, but this time felt different. Like I'd been flushed out. Cleaned? Cleansed?

I tried to stand up and found out that my legs had been replaced by rubber bands. Or so I assumed because they refused to listen to my brain or hold up my body, instead opting for wobbling a bit and tossing me unceremoniously onto the bed.

"Perfect," I muttered, rolling over onto my back and struggling upright again.

Looking around me, I became even more confused. I was wearing my clothes, but they were different. Wrong. They felt softer, and smelled like lavender.

Holy fuck, they'd been washed?

"Don't love the implications there," I said to absolutely no one. I was doing great.

I was sitting in what I guessed were barracks. It was very plain, and very long, with around a dozen beds running down either side of a central walkway. At the foot of each, there was a footlocker. I leaned over and saw one at the foot of the bed I'd been occupying.

I tried to gather my will and use the same trick I did to smooth over my withdrawal pangs, but my head felt fuzzy when I tried. Like it was stuffed with cotton. I put my hand back behind me for balance.

"You're awake!"

The voice flowed like honey, coating my brain and making me feel all sweet and numb, like chasing my high all over again. I looked over at the source, struggling to keep my eyelids from closing, and I saw my mystery man. He was resplendent in white linen pants and a matching jacket (no shirt, obviously), his silvery hair hung loose around his shoulders, and he was barefoot.

I tried to respond, but my tongue was too thick. Too awkward. I couldn't compare to someone like him. I blushed and looked at my Doc Martens.

"I–" I croaked in reply. He held up a finger toward my lips.

"Darlin' you don't need to say a word. I wouldn't be here if it wasn't for you chargin' in an' taking care of that mugger. Thought I was a goner."

That didn't sound quite right. I shook my head to try to clear the sugary haze that coated my brain. "No," I croaked. "I didn't–"

"Why, once those other two saw what you did to their friend, they just took off like you was gonna hit them next," he continued, ignoring my objections.

I frowned. "But I thought–" I said, trying to grab onto the memory that was sitting just beyond my fingertips.

"You thought they were gonna hurt me, an' you did somethin' about it. Least I could do is return the favor and do somethin' about what you were goin' through, right?"

I nodded vapidly, my eyes open wide like some sort of doll. "Least you could do," I mumbled.

Part of my brain was screaming that this isn't what happened, but the part that was in the driver's seat didn't care. I was willing to accept whatever story the man was spinning. I just couldn't force the thinky part of my brain back in control.

"Good girl," he said, cupping my chin. I shuddered in revulsion at his touch, flashing back to memories of that asshole Derek and a long line of assholes since. He frowned and cocked his head as he looked down at me.

"I'm–no one's–good–girl," I replied, forcing the words through gritted teeth.

"Oooh, you got spirit, kid. I like that. You'll do just fine," he drawled back, an easy smile settling on his lips.

Not his eyes though. They weren't smiling. The eyes that were boring into mine were off. Different.

He blinked and it was gone, replaced by normal, everyday baby blues.

"You see, you're not the only runaway staying with us. We've been pickin' up kids from all 'round Nerlins and helpin' 'em. Give 'em a place to get fed. Get safe. Get clean," he paused, looking at me meaningfully.

I looked back down at my boots.

"No judgment, darlin'. Whatever you went through out there is what you went through. What we offer here is a chance to get back to the way things were. Back to basics. Feel like you're part of the natural order again," he explained.

"How many?" I managed to ask.

"How many kids? Oh, I don't know…we got maybe a dozen here right now, but there's room for more an' we're always on the prowl for the right kinda someone. Someone with that spark and a need."

"Someone like me?" I asked.

"Someone like you," he agreed.

Look, living on the streets for as long as I had instilled a healthy paranoia in me and every alarm bell in my head was going off. The 'me' part of my mind was screaming to get out the door and put as much distance between me and this sex cultist as I could. Unfortunately, that part of my brain wasn't in charge. The part of my brain in the driver's seat was happy to be here. Happy at the very idea of someone…anyone looking for me without bad intentions was–

I wiped a tear from the corner of my eye.

He sat next to me and put an arm around me. I immediately stiffened.

"There, there, darlin'. You just let it on out," he said through a toothy smile.

I didn't want to cry in front of him. I hate crying in front of people. I pressed my lips together and fought back against it all: the haze in my brain, the sense of abandonment, the tears, all of it.

"I'm fine," I whispered, standing up and leaning on the headboard for support. "Just a bit tired and woozy is all."

A cloud passed in front of those baby blues, but was gone in an instant, replaced by that same friendly mask. "Not a worry, darlin'. You finish restin' up. You can meet the rest of the kids at supper in an hour."

"Supper?" I asked.

"Yeah, gotta feed ya'll. Plus what staff we got on site, of course. Can't have them goin' hungry, either."

"But where–what is this place?" I asked. The unease he triggered by putting his arm around me made it easier for me to control my brain to focus.

"A bit a' this, a bit a' that," he replied. "It's a farm and nature preserve about twenty minutes outside of the city. We find kids that are down on their luck. Special kids. An' we give 'em a place and a purpose.""Purpose?" I asked.

"A purpose," he repeated. "We get 'em fed up, cleaned up, and sobered up, like I said before. Then we teach 'em what they want to learn and send 'em on their way into the world with some clean clothes and a little money in their pocket."

"Why? I asked, frowning.

"Can't a body do somethin' 'cause they got a callin'? 'Cause it's the right thing to do?" he asked.

"They can, but they don't," I replied.

"Well, in this case, we do," he said. "My name's Donovan. Donovan Morgan, an this little operation's my doin'. The camp's been in my family for generations an' I gathered a few like-minded individuals together to help with the cause."

I nodded, waiting for more. He didn't provide any. He rose gracefully to his feet and brushed off some imagined dirt from his pristine linen pants. "You must be famished. I'll get food out a bit early so you can get a good head start. New kids always get swamped when they first show up an' you look like you've skipped some meals."

I nodded again.

He shot me a wink, then turned and headed out the door, leaving me alone once again.

I immediately checked in my left sleeve for my knife. Gone. I checked the foot locker at the end of my bed. Just some sweat clothes and towels.

Fuck.

I sat down on the bed hard, putting my face in my hands and rubbing. I needed to clear away whatever was going on in my head. I needed to be able to think. To be ready for whenever the other shoe was going to drop.

I needed a plan.

I looked out the window at the field outside of the...dorm? Barracks? Building. Building worked. People moved around, weeding a huge garden, with dark trees looming like a barricade in the distance.

Pretty words or not, I was trapped.

I fully intended not to go anywhere the cult leader said I should.

But sitting in a huge empty room with an even emptier stomach makes you reassess your stances, especially when the smell of beef stew starts wafting through the doors. I stood and followed it, mesmerized in a far more easily understood way by the enticing scent of dinner.

I paused at the double doors, going on tip-toe to peek in the small plastic windows with their black rubber rings. I'd waited long enough to see the people who'd weeded the garden sit down. Four people in their twenties or thirties and about a dozen kids around my age, each one wearing a white linen outfit.

"That's culty as shit," I whispered.

My mouth started watering, showing that my body didn't have an appreciation for maintaining dignity in the face of an attempted brainwashing. It wanted to be fed.

Against my better judgment, I threw the doors open and walked inside. Every set of eyes in the room turned and locked onto me. I fidgeted. I hated that I was fidgeting. My hands went into the pockets of my hoodie, then to the silver unicorn chain at my neck. My link to my dad.

I looked at them all, clean and fresh-faced in their little cult outfits while I stood there in my own ensemble: black Doc Martens, torn fishnets, black and white checkered skirt, a black Siouxsie and the Banshees t-shirt that was at least a couple sizes too big, and my black hoodie.

One of these things is not like the others. One of these things just doesn't belong.

One of these things never will.

My shoulders slumped as all of the clean, happy faces looked back at me, then Donovan was striding over, his arms open.

"Glad ya made it, darlin'," he drawled.

Then, without touching me, he gestured to the group. "Ladies 'n gentlemen, this is Nat. She saved me from a potential muggin' while I was down wanderin' the Quarter a couple days ago an' she seemed like she could use a place to unwind for a spell. She ain't decided whether she's stayin' or not, but she's welcome as long as she likes. Don't go crowdin' her, now."

The group of clean, happy cultists were suddenly all around me, their steps falling almost in unison, with the smallest lining up to give me long, warm hugs. I squirmed, initially trying to get away and distance myself. But as the second child stepped in, offering her arms, followed by a third, my vision started to blur as I blinked back tears.

I'd hated being touched ever since that night. Ever since Derek tried--and then the things I had to do to survive...old men with their grabbing hands and stinking breath.

Tears began to fall despite my best efforts.

Small child number four wrapped her arms around me and I was revisited by the first three children who joined in the group hug while I slumped to the ground, embracing them through deep, ugly sobs.

The dam had broken and there was no stopping three years worth of hurt, betrayal, and heartache as the tears came rushing out of me. I cried for my father, taken from me before I was ready. I cried for my mother, who she had been compared to what she became. I cried for my childhood, lost and shattered. For each and every compromise I made to survive. For every step I took through necessity rather than by choice.

I wept for who I was and who I could have been. I cried. I cried until I wasn't really aware of my surroundings, too wrapped up in my own grief and loss. It was my entire world, I lived in it. I wallowed in it. It was inescapable.

Until it finally wasn't.

I'm not sure how long I was lying on that floor with tears rolling down my face. I know it was long enough that by the time I stopped, I had a headache and my nose had joined in the leakage. I've always been amazed by men and women who can 'cry pretty'. They look up and to the side and gentle tears wind their way down their ridiculous high cheekbones and then drip elegantly off their stupid, perfect chins. Me? I look like I've been pepper sprayed and punched in the nose. Maybe kicked by a horse for good measure.

I wiped my sleeve across my nose and tried to blink the tears away. I felt empty, but a good empty. Like I had cried out everything that I'd been holding in for a really long time. I took a shuddering breath. Then another. Then another. Slowly, I became aware of my surroundings once again and realized that Donovan was holding me along with the rest.

Too tired to shrink back, I laid my head on the supportive blob around me and closed my eyes, feeling like I belonged somewhere since my father had been taken from me. I felt like I was wanted.

It's an intoxicating feeling.

People began to wordlessly move away, going back to their tables for dinner, peeling away one by one until I was left alone with Donovan on the floor.

"Ya gotta let go of what you were holdin' onto before you can start forward, darlin'. Why don't you go get somethin' ta eat?"

The stew tasted as good as it smelled, thick broth filled with beef, potatoes, and vegetables that filled your stomach and coated your insides like river mud. I ate like it was my job, leaning over the bowl to guard against any spillage.

"Donovan told us all about it! He was cornered by like, three guys! You just walked up really calmly and took 'em out all by yourself! You saved his life!"

I opened my mouth to reply, but the relentless verbal march spilling from the girl's mouth never gave me a chance. The source of endless commentary was a white girl who looked to be about my age, a bit taller and heavier than I was but pale to the point of feeling like she glowed, especially in the cotton clothing that everyone was wearing. Her dark hair was up in a pair of ponytails, and a light dusting of freckles surrounding her eyes showed she'd been out in the sun enough for it to matter.

"But I–" I tried once again.

"I don't know what we woulda done if you hadn't been there to step in! This place won't run without him, he's the boss! I think the owner too? It's all sorta vague and gets jumbled up in my head when I try to think about it too hard. That's why I don't try to think about it too hard anymore! See, easy answer!"

"But that doesn't–" I attempted.

"Exactly! I like you, you're so easy to talk to! I'm Jessica, what's your name?"

I narrowed my eyes, waiting for the next volley of dialogue. Jessica leaned forward slightly, her hands folded between her knees and her brown eyes wide in what I assumed was her 'I'm listening to you with every fiber of my being' pose.

"—I'm Natalie. Nat," I said, correcting myself. "I–"

"NAT! That's a great name!" she exclaimed, half-leaping forward to hug me. "Nat, we're gonna be best friends, I just know it!"

"Yaaaay," I replied in monotone.

She broke the hug and sat back, giggling. "That's funny. You're funny!" she declared before launching another hug. I was sensing a pattern.

"And you're squishing me," I groaned.

Jessica broke off the hug. "Sorry. Sorry, I get carried away sometimes. Too peppy," she said.

I offered a weak smile in return. "I don't have very much pep, so you can have my share," I reassured her, sending her into another giggle fit.

She beamed. "That sounds like a perfect deal. Can't have you operating at a pep deficit."

It was my turn to smile. I could feel it forming: a weak little thing, especially when compared to the high wattage version that my apparent new best friend deployed on the regular, but it was there for the first time in...weeks? Months? It had been a while, I was sure of that. How long of a while I wasn't sure.

God, that was depressing.

Chapter Five

The next couple of hours passed in a blur as Jessica took it upon herself to show me everything.

Everything.

The girl was boisterous and enthusiastic to the point of being exhausting, but in a good-natured and friendly way. In addition to the dorm, the cafeteria, and the kitchens, we took tours of the co-ed shower room, the lounge, a game room, and the staff housing, which was a separate area. They apparently got their own rooms.

"And Donovan gets a nice little suite," Jessica giggled. "With a hot tub, it's really nice in there."

"You were in his hot tub?" I asked. "Doing what, exactly?"

She frowned for a moment, then her eyes went dull.

"Me and some of the other girls asked to borrow it a couple of weeks ago, and he let us. Wait, you were afraid he tries to–no, not Donovan! He takes care of everyone, and I've never seen him so much as look at anyone creepy."

"Something about this whole setup is sus," I muttered.

"I thought so at first too, but it's not. I've been here for like four months, and everything's been above board the whole time. Some kids go after they've been here for a bit, and new kids come in, but that's the whole point of the program, isn't it? To help kids like us," Jessica said.

"What's that mean, exactly? 'Kids like us'? Kids like what? There are tons of kids on the streets that he could help. Why us?"

Jessica shrugged. "I dunno."

"How did you end up here?" I asked as we walked outside along the border of the vegetable garden.

"Well, like I said, I got here around four months ago, I think. I ran away from my foster family after another fight with one of their kids. I was on the street for about a month and a half when he found me. Hungry, running a fever, scraped up and...well...you know. He got me cleaned up, got me some antibiotics, and brought me here."

"Right, but why? No one does something for nothing. Why's he doing it?" I asked, looking at the ground. "Everyone's got an angle."

"I don't think he does," Jessica said with a shrug and a smile as her eyes cleared. "Maybe he's just a really good person?"

"Hrm," was all I could manage.

I'd been burned too many times to trust that this was on the level, especially when my brain got so cloudy whenever Donovan started talking to me. The fact that Jessica was willing to swallow it could mean a few things, and too many of them pointed to this place being a scam for me to be willing to let it go.

"You'll see. We're like a family here," she reassured me.

"That's what I'm afraid of," I muttered.

The rest of the day passed without incident. I followed Jessica around like an ugly duckling and tried to learn what I could. A lot of the things I learned were absolutely culty. There was no cell signal, no wifi, and no cable or internet. The lack of contact with the outside world was presented as a good thing. There were sign up sheets for the kids to do various jobs around the facility. No one was forced to work, but there really wasn't much to do aside from chores, and since that's where everyone else was, gravity or peer pressure or whatever sorta pulled everyone in that direction.

Then there were the staff. They seemed to know each other from someplace else. None of them were older than their late 30s, and all of them practically glowed with an aggressive sort of physical fitness. They seemed nice enough, but aside from Donovan, they kept the kids at arm's length while making sure we were well-fed and looked after.

As I laid in my bed that night and ran through the day's events, that same cloudy feeling fought to push in from the edges of my brain, and I had to fight to keep it at bay as I heard the steady breathing and snores from the other kids in the dorm.

It would have been so easy for me to give in and let that numb feeling wash over me. It would be like slipping into a warm bath. Comfortable. Relaxing. Easy. No one could blame me, really. No fifteen-year-old should have to deal with what I'd been through. Hell, no one of any age should have to deal with what I'd dealt with. There was something inside of me that wouldn't let me just go along with things. Wouldn't let me just accept anything as inevitable. Forced me to push back if something seemed off, or wrong, or unfair.

Something here seemed very off.

My eyes shot open.

Something was wrong. The clock on the wall ticked away in the shadows, its hands barely visible in the dim light creeping through the windows. Squinting, I read the time: 2:30 in the morning. I slid out of bed, the cold tile floor on my bare feet shocked me fully awake, and I had to suppress a scream. I stood for a moment, breathing before I quietly moved toward the window to peer out at the fields.

The camp staff were out there standing in a circle around...something. It was too far, too dark, and too small for me to be able to make it out. The group moved in unison, swaying in the moonlight with their hands rising and falling in time with a beat that was inaudible to me.

It was over an hour later and the ceremony was still going strong when I decided to slink back to bed. Whatever was happening out there was weird, and it was creepy, but it was also happening out there, and I was tired in here, so tired won.

The sun beat relentlessly against my eyelids to inform me that a new day was here. The other kids in the dorm/barracks moved quietly about their morning routines, getting dressed and organized for a trip to the cafeteria, then to whatever tasks they were engaged in that day. I followed the crowd in and ate breakfast alongside Jessica, who was just as talkative in the morning as she was in the afternoon.

"And by the time they're finished growing, we're gonna have strawberries and corn and potatoes and squash–" she said, the words spilling past her lips as if they were racing one another to see which could arrive to batter my eardrums first.

"Jess, are you really gonna list everything that they're growing here?" I asked.

"**We're** growing here," she corrected.

"Fine. We're growing here," I conceded.

She broke into a massive smile while making a high-pitched keening noise that I can only assume was a mixture of happiness and excitement. Or maybe a dog whistle. I guess that's also an option.

She collected herself. "I mean...yeah. How else are you going to know what fields you want to work on?" she asked.

"What if I'm more of the indoorsy type?" I asked.

"You'd rather be inside cleaning than outside enjoying the weather?"

"Oh, one hundred percent of the time, yeah," I quickly offered. "I've been on the streets for long enough that I'd much rather be inside where the climate is nice and controlled."

She didn't seem to know what to make of this, so she turned to a boy sitting nearby. "Francisco, you do indoor work, right? What sort of stuff do you do?" she asked him.

Francisco nodded. He was a Latino boy a little older than us. Lean, but not in the *'I've been starving'* way that I was, more the *'I'm a teenage boy and I can eat whatever I want, watch as my metabolism laughs at you'* kinda way. "Yup. Cleaning, fixing, stocking the storerooms, that sorta stuff," he said.

"I could totally do that," I said.

He gave me a vapid, hazy-eyed smile and nodded. "That's awesome, fam. Come on with me after breakfast and I'll show you the ropes," he said.

Soon I was following him with a belly full of breakfast and a head full of questions.

"Hey, Francisco? Last night I thought I saw something weird out in the fields," I began.

"We're not supposed to go out at night," he replied, as if by rote.

"Right, I get that, but I saw–"

He paused, then blinked hard and shook his head, before looking up at me with clear eyes. "You need to be careful not to go out there. You could get hurt." The haze drifted back across his eyes once again. " There are wild animals," he added.

"I mean, yeah, but not really, right? I mean there are probably some feral hogs or something. Maybe a coyote? But we're too far from the water to need to worry about gators," I replied, trying to get anything out of him. "But anyway, I saw the staff. The grownups out there in a circle around some sort of statue."

He frowned, looking at me for a moment, then shook his head like he was trying to get water out of his ear.

Or like he was trying to shake off a brain fog again. His eyes focused on me more intently, and he leaned in. "You need to be careful. You can't let them know you saw," he whispered.

"Let them know you saw what?" a voice asked from in front of us and around the corner.

Shit.

The question hung in the air like smoke as Francisco and I both froze.

One of the staff members rounded the corner. She was a tall black woman in her mid 20s, her hair braided tight against her head. She moved with a type of almost fluid grace that suggested she was gonna erupt into action at any moment. Probably violent action.

I swallowed as Francisco stammered.

"N-n-nothing, Sylvie," he said. "I was just joking around with the new girl, that's all."

Sylvie tutted at him. "Francisco, you know we don't accept hazing here. It's important to Donovan that everyone has the chance to settle in without any of that toxicity that you all left behind. You did leave it behind, didn't you, Francisco?" the question came out almost like a growl.

"Y-y-yes?" he pseudo-answered.

"Are you asking me or telling me?" Sylvie asked, leaning toward him.

"T-t-telling you?" he replied.

She stared at him intently. "How long have you been with us, Francisco?" she asked.

"A-a-around seven months?" he replied.

She took half a step back and her mouth split into a predatory smile. It was the first time I'd seen her smile since I'd gotten here. "Seven months? Hrm. Maybe. We'll have to see. Why don't you come along with me?"

"Maybe what?" Francisco asked.

"Don't you worry your pretty little head about it," she said, turning to leave.

"But I'm—I was gonna show Nat here where to find the cleaning stuff for working inside. Show her, like, the ropes," he protested.

"She seems like a clever, resourceful girl. I'm sure she'll be able to figure things out on her own. I need you to come with me. Now." Sylvie's tone didn't leave any room for argument or discussion despite her toothy smile, and Francisco didn't attempt either. Instead, the boy slumped his shoulders, hung his head, and followed at her heel as she moved further into the house.

I've gotta admit, I stood there for a good forty-five seconds arguing with myself about what to do. The smart, safe, and easy thing would have been to just go find the supply closet and start cleaning things randomly.

I've never been great at smart, safe, or easy so I did the stupid thing and followed them.

I could feel the brain fog try to settle in and push me toward that easy path, but I was focused, well-fed, and detoxed. My brain was sharper than it had been in months. Years, maybe. I was more than ready to force that fog back and keep it there. I silently willed myself to be quiet and uninteresting as I followed the pair down the hall toward the normally locked door to the staff area.

Sylvie produced a key and unlocked it before leading Francisco through and letting it swing shut behind her. Quick like a bunny, I darted forward and tried to block the door before it closed, the pneumatic arm slamming it into the back of my hand. I bit back a string of curses while admiring what a dumb idea that specific part of this overall dumb idea was.

Girl's gotta admit when she's got talent for something, and dumb ideas were apparently my sweet spot for today.

I slid inside the door and gently closed it behind me, then crept forward into the restricted area.

For a potentially sinister hideout, it wasn't living up to my expectations. It looked more like a shared apartment for a bunch of kids who just graduated from college or something. There were some abandoned bits of food, a TV with a couple of game systems, and some couches and chairs scattered around. Not exactly the sort of image that was being shown to the kids in the military-style barracks.

I held my breath and continued forward, pausing at every doorway to listen, despite knowing that most of the staff was outside with the kids in the fields. I got deeper in, passing closed doors for what I guessed were bedrooms. I was starting to hear talking, barely audible. One voice clearly belonged to Sylvie. I strained to hear the other voice, felt the brain fog come back with a fury and somehow I immediately knew it was Donovan. Despite my preparation, despite being clean, despite being clear-headed,

I could feel it forcing its way onto my brain like some sort of psychic pepto-bismol. I could feel myself starting to go. To give in.

So I clutched my unicorn and bit the shit out of my tongue.

I stifled a cry as my teeth pierced my own flesh. Tears welled up in my eyes and blood began to fill my mouth. I could feel my heartbeat in my tongue, but the pain gave me something else to focus on, and it drove the brain fog back. I inched closer, risking a peek into the room.

Donovan sat in an office chair in front of a desk, which Sylvie was sitting on. Just to the left of the doorway, Francisco stood, his eyes glassy and impassive.

"Sylvie darlin', I just don't know that the boy's ready. The Nkondi ain't interested in bein' fed someone. They like the hunt. He needs ta put up a bit of a challenge, otherwise we won't get all the juice we need," he said.

Sylvie made a rude noise. "He's as good as he's gonna get, Donovan. This kid isn't exactly gonna win any track and field medals, no matter what we feed him. This is as good as he gets."

I risked another glance to see if I could figure out what a Nkondi was. My eyes were drawn to a statue on the desk. It was around three feet tall, vaguely humanoid with glass eyes, carved out of a dark, worn wood, and had more than a dozen nails driven into its torso. When I wasn't looking directly at it, it seemed like it was moving in the corner of my vision, but when I looked back it was just a statue again: ugly and full of nails.

Donovan sat silently for way too long, then sighed. "Let's set him up for tonight."

I crouched in the doorway frozen as Sylvie took a nail off the desk and scratched it along the inside of Francisco's left palm, drawing a small line of blood. She handed it to Donovan, who took the hammer that had been sitting next to it, braced the statue, and drove the bloodied nail into the torso with a powerful blow.

She might as well have scratched the statue for all Francisco reacted. He stood there, eyes glazed, staring straight ahead while the statue seemed to swell, giving off a greenish-black glow as it stretched another few inches in each direction.

Nope. Growing statues were, are, and always will be a big nope from me. I was out.

I crept as quickly and quietly as I could, slid out the door to the common areas, and found the supply closet with the cleaning supplies. I had never been as motivated to mop a floor as I was at that moment. My hands shook as I poured something into the water and they continued to shake as I ran the mop along the floor.

What the fuck was that?

I could feel that brain fog trying to work its way back in. To smother my thoughts and concerns, but I was way past the point where that was gonna work on me. This whole thing started off as seriously sus, but this? This was fuckin' batshit crazy.

I felt a twinge of guilt, but I knew I needed to just watch Francisco for the rest of the day, then keep an eye out for what was gonna happen that night, and I needed to do it quietly. Whatever all of this meant, it wasn't good, and I'd be damned if I ended up with a bloodied nail in that statue.

Chapter
Seven

Dinner that night ended with Donovan and Sylvie standing in front of the assembled staff and kids with a smile.

"Francisco, will you join us, please?" he drawled.

Francisco came to his feet with a smile and approached with a clueless grin on his face. Like a lamb to the slaughter.

"We've been talkin' it over, an' we think you're ready, son. You feel like you can do it? Go back into the world and be strong? Spread goodness and charity?" he asked the boy.

Francisco silently nodded. He looked like he wanted to say something, but his brain wouldn't let the words come out. It could have been either brain fog or just good ol' fashioned awkwardness, but in the end, it didn't matter. There was a round of cheers and clapping, a cake came out of the kitchen that we all shared, and a bunch of happy congratulations for the soon-to-be graduated Francisco.

The walking dead boy.

I hung back, avoiding all of Jessica's attempts to bring me into the celebration.

"Sorry, Jess. Just got a bit of a headache," I explained.

"See, this is what happens when you work inside with all those cleaning chemicals instead of being out under the sun with the rest of us," she tutted.

"I know, I should probably try that out tomorrow to see if that makes me feel better," I agreed.

Jessica made that weird high-pitched keening noise again. If I really had a headache, that would have been it for me. My skull would shatter and leak brains all over both of us. Thankfully, I was lying, so I endured.

"That's amazing! I can show you all the things! I can't wait, we'll be farm buddies, Nat!"

"That's always been the dream, right?" I replied with a smile. I felt bad. Jess was sorta like an excited puppy who just loved everyone and everything in her general vicinity with reckless abandon, and I felt like my lack of buy-in on her joy was sorta like kicking her. Of course, one of us knew that there was something weird going on here, and the other was the human puppy, so I figured that if I could make sure she didn't end up as a nail, then I could forgive myself for whatever amount of lying to her this was gonna take.

Dinner and cake passed way too quickly. All the kids lined up and gave Francisco big hugs and headed to bed. I followed the flock, but stayed dressed as I ducked under the covers. One of the benefits of everyone being brain fogged is that they're not the most attentive bunch.

Then came the hard part.

I waited.

I'm sure there's a term that describes having to wait for something awful to happen. Soldiers have done it for thousands of years. I have no idea what that term is, but I've lived it.

I took deep, controlled breaths to try to show whoever might be looking that I was truly asleep. The sound of the second hand of the clock sounded off like thunderclaps as each moment ticked by. My body buzzed with electricity, like it could barely contain itself. Like it knew I was about to make it do something cataclysmically stupid.

Which made sense, because I was.

I risked opening my eyes and stole a glance at the clock. One thirty. Last night they'd been set up and in the middle of things by the time they hit three. Time to move.

Agonizingly slowly, I slid out of bed to the floor and stayed in a crouch, straining my ears for any sound that might betray that I was aware of what was going on. The only thing I could hear were the light snores coming from my roommates. Gritting my teeth, I crept out of the dorms and down the hall toward the exterior doors, then out into the fields.

The overcast sky masked a lot of the moonlight and I hoped that would give me a bit more leeway in my outing. With how they'd reacted to Francisco being slightly off task, I didn't guess that there was gonna be any forgiveness coming my way if I got caught out and about. Sticking to the shadows, I snuck along the edge of the house, careful to make as little noise as possible. As I rounded the corner near the fields, I saw them.

Donovan and the rest were all there in a circle around the statue from his office swaying slightly as Donovan's voice rang out in a language that might have been French. Live in New Orleans long enough and you develop an ear for recognizing it. It's sorta everywhere.

Kneeling in front of the statue was Fransicso. The boy had a bag over his head and wasn't wearing a shirt, but other than that, he seemed okay. Well, as okay as you can be in the middle of a circle of chanting people with a bag over your head. That limits the top end for 'okay-ness' in my book.

Donovan stepped forward, looking like a chiseled god in the dim moonlight. He shouted to the sky, then picked up the bowl next to the statue and began smearing patterns onto Francisco's skin. The boy shuddered as the glistening, dark liquid was drawn across his flesh.

Donovan stepped back and examined his handiwork, then pulled Sylvie in for a rough kiss.

I try not to judge, but apparently, **some**body had some **really** weird kinks.

The group re-started their chant, swaying and stomping in rhythm with the words. The pace increased, building as time passed, until reaching a crescendo and abruptly cutting off. Donovan slowly reached forward and yanked the hood from Francisco's head.

The boy blinked his eyes rapidly, then shook his head in a move that had become all-too familiar to me. The brain fog was lifting.

Whether Donovan allowed it to lapse, or Francisco managed to fight his way out of it, I'll never know. What I do know is that the boy looked around him in quickly building horror as he absorbed the scene he was a part of. He started to cry.

Donovan leaned forward, his silvery hair cascading down around his face and partially obscuring Francisco. The older man spoke softly to the boy, whose sobs echoed across the fields. After a brief moment, Donovan jerked back suddenly, arched his back, and threw his hands up to the sky, roaring.

The other five took up his roar.

Donovan turned to Francisco and said one word that cut through the night.

"Run."

I froze at Donovan's command to Francisco, watching in horror as the boy's eyes widened. Francisco backpedaled, seemingly afraid to take his eyes off the older man, whose features had split into a sinister grin. Donovan took a step forward. That was all the encouragement Francisco needed to turn his back and sprint for the treeline.

I watched him disappear into the black forest bordering the property, then turned my attention back to the six staff members, languidly strolling in a circle around the statue.

"My children!" Donovan's voice rang out in the night. "The hunt begins."

The six of them all howled into the sky in unison, but the sound changed in the middle. It went from something I assumed you might see at a rowdy frat party to something altogether different, and the staff changed along with it.

I watched Donovan, unable to take my eyes off him, but could see the others following the same path in my periphery. His face distended, the bone in his jaw and around his mouth pushed out, stretching the skin. His body gained bulk, splitting the clothes he was wearing and leaving them in tatters on the ground. His normally svelte, athletic body twisted. Muscles and bones slid under his skin, rearranging, the wet cracking noises audible, even at my distance. Donovan fell to all fours, howling in...pain? rage? excitement? a combination of all three?

Thick coarse hairs sprung up through his stretched, tortured skin, and his knees broke, bending backward in a rough mockery of a dog's back legs. After a torturous two minutes (give or take), the creature I vaguely remembered from my first encounter with Donovan stood in the middle of the field, silver-furred and resplendent. It looked over to the rest, my gaze following it and I saw brown, red, black, and tawny-furred reflections of him.

Werewolves.

Part of my brain was telling the rest that it was impossible. That everyone knew those were made up stories, but the more conscious part, the part that had been unwilling to accept the fog that had been trying to cocoon it since my arrival, rejected the argument out of hand. I knew what I saw. If I thought about it and pushed through that haze, I'd known since I got here.

The howling stopped. The contrast between the racket they were making a second ago to the eerie stillness made the night seem heavy. Oppressive. Like the darkness stood silently in anticipation of what would come next.

It didn't need to wait long. The...pack, I guess–burst into motion, plunging into the dark treeline on Francisco's trail. My stomach turned as I silently crouched, holding my breath. I had the feeling this wasn't going to take long.

I was right.

Within a minute, a high-pitched scream echoed through the night, followed quickly by howls. The scream cut off in an abrupt choking sound, followed by–nothing. I swallowed, shivering. I wiped my brow and realized I'd broken into a cold sweat.

I needed to go. I needed to get out. I couldn't end up like that. Hunted in the woods. I couldn't. I didn't want to die. I wasn't ready.

Panic had started to take hold of me, overwhelming any sort of rational thought. My eyes were wide, my breathing was rapid. I had to go, and I had to go now.

I took three steps and was roughly grabbed from behind and pulled against someone with their hand firmly over my mouth.

I bit the shit out of them.

"Motherfucker," the raspy, growly voice snarled. It was a guy. Looked old...like in his late 20's or early 30's. Even older than Donovan for sure. He had a scruffy, rumpled kinda vibe. Dirty blond hair, untucked white button-up shirt, blue jeans, and a black peacoat.

"What the fuck?" I hissed back, afraid to raise my voice even in my panicked state. "Who the fuck are you? What the fuck are you doing here? Just...what the fuck, man?"

The guy just looked at me for a minute and I didn't like it. I've been looked at by a lot of guys his age and older, and you can get a feel for where they were coming from. Some were creepers and wanted something very specific. Some were bleeding hearts and wanted to 'save' me. Almost everyone fell into one of those two categories.

Not him. His blue eyes took me in, analyzed me, and seemed to categorize me in a way I wasn't used to. He didn't want anything from me or to do anything to or for me. I was a potential complication. I didn't like thinking about how he'd deal with that.

"No time for that kid, your babysitters are gonna be back soon. Me and some friends are here for—well, something that's got nothing to do with you, but play your cards right and we might be able to help you get out of here. Make sure you don't end up like—" he gestured toward the woods. Toward Francisco. "Assuming you haven't developed a taste for blood."

His eyes felt like they were boring into my skull, so I broke eye contact.

As an aside, you can be one scary motherfucker, Bishop.

"I—yeah. I want—need to get outta here. I'm Nat," I said.

"Good. Nat. Here." He handed me a cell phone. "Hide it. You can contact us on it if you need. We're close, but not so close that we can do much if you get caught. There's one number in the contacts...that's us. Just text it if you've got anything. We'll text you to arrange a meetup. Questions?"

"Cell phones don't work here," I said.

"This one will," he replied. "Trust me. Any other questions?"

I numbly shook my head.

"Good. I'm gonna get the hell outta here before the pack comes back. Keep your head on your shoulders and keep pushing back against the numbness. That's them trying to keep you calm and subservient. The second it latches on is the second you're under their control. You do **not** want to be under their control."

"But why can't you take me with you now?" I asked, fighting back panic.

He shook his head. "You go missing and they go on alert. You'll get out. Soon. Just not quite yet. Remember, stay sharp, got it?" he said, making uncomfortably heavy eye contact.

I nodded, my head swimming. Trying to process everything this senior citizen was telling me. Trying to figure this out.

"I got it," I agreed.

Bishop nodded at me, then turned and moved along the wall, vanishing into the night when he turned the corner.

The moment he was gone, I started to shake. I don't know if it was coming down from the adrenaline high, the terror of seeing–well–everything I'd seen in the past hour or so, or the knowledge that my life was in very real danger.

Or all of them. Why pick, right?

Deciding that Bishop had the right idea, I snuck back inside, changed, and got into bed and under the covers.

I closed my eyes, but instead of sleep I just saw the grotesque, misshapen forms of Donovan, Sylvie, and the rest of the staff as they changed into those monsters, then chased poor Francisco into the woods.

Francisco. He hadn't even done anything that wrong. He just...attracted their attention.

Because of me.

I lay in my bed, eyes closed, and felt tears starting to form as the realization sunk in.

He attracted their attention because of me. If I hadn't pushed, he'd still be alive.

I got him killed.

I lived in that reality for the rest of the night.

Lying with your eyes closed and not being able to sleep is a special kind of hell. I got to live through hours of it that night. When the sunlight warmed my eyelids, I kept them closed, waiting until I heard other kids get up before I risked opening them.

Despite everything that had happened, the barracks looked the same. They should have looked different. When the world shifts under you the way it had last night, there should be some sort of mark. Different coloring. Some indication that things weren't okay.

But life doesn't work like that. It just grinds on, collateral damage be damned.

Sliding out of bed, I wandered past the window, casually glancing out to the fields beyond.

The statue was gone. The discarded clothing had been gathered. There was no sign at all of the ceremony last night. No sign of them hunting Francisco. It was like he'd been erased.

I felt sick to my stomach.

"How do you think Francisco's doing?" a small voice asked the room in general.

"Francisco? Donovan said he was setting him up with a job and a place at a halfway house. That guy's probably livin' the life. He's a wiz with computers, and everyone knows that's an easy job no matter what," another kid replied.

Felix. That was the smaller kid's name. Skinny little African American kid with his hair in tight braids. I had no idea who did them for him. The boy who answered was Mike. An older white kid. I wasn't sure how much older, but I got the feeling that he'd been here for a long time and was close to aging out.

I shuddered at the idea of what *aging out* must mean and sat back down on the bed to get changed, my left hand drifting near my pillow, where I'd hidden the cell phone that the old guy had given me last night. It was a lifeline. A security blanket. I didn't know the boomer from Adam, but I was at least mostly sure he wasn't gonna try to eat me, so that made him less of a threat than the literal monsters that ran the joint.

"But how do we know?" I asked.

The background murmur in the room died down.

"What do you mean?" Mike asked, his earnest blue eyes showing his lack of comprehension. Like he knew what each of the words I'd used meant, but had never considered them being arranged in that order before.

"Just what I said: how do we know that's what happened to Francisco?" I persisted. "All we have is their say so."

"Right. Their say so," Mike agreed, completely missing my point. "Why would they lie to us? The staff here has only ever helped us."

The rest of the kids murmured in agreement that had an ugly undertone. Even Jessica seemed irritated by my line of questioning.

"Sorry," I mumbled. "Just not used to–" I trailed off, looking at my shoes.

"No, I get it. You're still pretty new, and you were in bad shape when you got here. Trusting is hard when that happens. It takes a while for you to get your head right. You should have seen me when I first got here! I was ranting about all sorts of crazy stuff."

I frowned. "Like what?" I asked. The group was dispersing now that I was no longer sounding quite as much like an apostate.

"I can hardly even remember," he said with a shrug. "I was hallucinating all sortsa stuff. Monsters, cults, aliens. Stuff like that. I'm tellin' you, I was just this side of batty."

"Yeah, sounds pretty crazy," I replied in monotone. "What made it stop?"

"I talked to Donovan about it. We did lots of meditating and one-on-one work. Slowly, I stopped holding onto all of that negativity and let the healing in. It totally changed me. Made me a different person."

"I bet," I replied with a shudder.

"If you're still having trouble, you should ask Donovan. I'm sure he'd be happy to help," Mike suggested.

"Nah, I'm good. I think I just need a bit of time," I protested.

"Don't be like that, Nat," Jessica said, leaping into the last conversation I wanted her to be a part of. "You don't need to do everything on your own. That's why we're all here, to get help from a community."

"The help sounds great. Really. Top notch," I replied, backing up. "I'm just—I'm not ready, that's all. I've only been here a couple of days, and these things take time, right? Mikey, you said it took you a hot minute, right?"

Mike paused with his mouth open, then nodded. "Oh, yeah, totally. No one would want to push you into anything you're not ready for. You just take your time and work through stuff, Nat. I'm happy to lend a hand if you need it, or I can talk to the staff for you if you're nervous."

"Nah, I'm good," I said, forcing a smile.

"Right. Well, the important part is if you're not, know that we're here for you. Healing can't start without consent," he said the last part as if by rote. I had a feeling he'd heard it more often than anyone would like to count.

I backed away from the love and kindness being offered to me, for once confident that it was, in fact, a trap, even if no one else in the room realized it.

"Just because you're paranoid, it doesn't mean they're not out to get you," I muttered. Sitting on the bed, I reached into my pillowcase and put my hand around the cell phone. Making sure no one was watching, I pulled it out, shielding it with my body, and began thumbing the keys.

U there?

I asked.

Almost immediately the dots popped up on the screen, showing typing. It took for-fucking-ever. Fuckin' old people. They're gonna be the death of me.

As advertised

It said. He said? It was probably the guy from last night and he was a he. And why the fuck did it take that long to type two fucking words?

> Ok, what do u want, like what am I doing?

I typed back, then inwardly groaned. If two words took a long time, I'd be his age before he typed this shit out.

> Need to find the statue with a bunch of nails in it. You help me get it, I get you away from the wolves. Sounds good?

He replied.

> Rad, one change. gotta be all of us kids

I countered.

> No way. Too risky.

> That's the deal U get us all or u can find your own dolly.

There was a long pause with no dots, and for a minute I thought I might have blown it, but after a short forever the dots popped back up.

> Fine. All the kids. Do you know how much harder that's going to be?

> Dont care. Saw what happened 2 kid last night. Dont wanna see it happen again. If ur hot shit enough to sneak in and snag something ur hot shit enough to get em all outta here.

I flung back.

> This deal's getting worse and worse, kid. But fine. We'll get you all out. Let's start with where

the idol is. Probably carved of wood with a re-flective or crystal surface over the face

Yeah. Lots of nails in it. Around 2 feet tall looks a bit like a bad carving of a person

Good. Exactly. You know it

U walked past it last night on your way to grab me like a creeper. It was in the field

The dots took a really long time this time.

Are you fucking kidding me?

Hand to God

There were dots on the screen, but I figured he was just mashing his head against it. Maybe cursing. Speaking in tongues? I didn't expect another reply for a good long while.

Chapter Ten

Bishop's short-term plan for getting us all out of here was 'act natural.' That advice made me wanna bite him.

I get that my demand threw a wrench into his plans. A quick breaking and entering job is a lot different than a hostage extraction. Honestly, I wasn't sure why I demanded he spring everybody. I'd been on my own for long enough to know that caring about people is just an invitation for someone to use you, or for them to get hurt and for you to have to carry it around. Most of the kids here I couldn't give two shits about.

I mean, but Jessica was a sweetheart; I couldn't leave without her.

And Mike was an idiotic himbo, but his heart was in the right place. I couldn't just leave him to end up as dog chow.

Felix. I couldn't just leave Felix. He was basically just a baby. What kind of monster would I be if I just left him to fend for himself?

I paused and Francisco's face snuck into my brain, unwelcome and uninvited. I imagined that friendly, open face twisted in terror as he ran through the woods, the sound of massive wolf monsters closing on him. I imagined him backing away from them, too slow to get away, and too weak to fight off any of them, much less all of them.

My mind's eye spit out a whole smorgasbord of images, each worse than the one before. Fangs biting into his soft flesh, blood spraying from his wounds as he screamed. As he begged them not to do this. To let him go. Knowing that there was nothing he could do to stop them. The feeling of being trapped. Overpowered. Violated.

I wiped a tear from my eyes and tried to shove those images down. Tried to banish the memories of my own that it dredged up. Of my mom's boyfriend. Of my time on the streets when I wasn't quite fast enough. Of men who liked to scare little girls.

No. I wasn't going to let anyone else be another Francisco. I couldn't. Not if I was in a position to stop it.

Which, to be fair, I wasn't. But that guy seemed like he might, and that was sorta like having a big friend to protect you when the bullies were coming.

I followed the crowd out to breakfast, then shuffled over toward the cleaning closet that Francisco had shown me. I swallowed hard and filled the bucket with Fabuloso and hot water. The chore chart said today was mopping the kitchen, cafeteria, and dorm room.

Dorm room? Pfft. Barracks at best. Cellblock was probably more accurate. Or maybe a cattle pen.

I numbly wheeled the bucket into the kitchen and started listlessly moving the mop across the white linoleum tile, trying to figure out how I could help. That really wasn't much.

Moving over to the food prep area, I looked at the menu for the week. Today was gonna be Taco Tuesday for dinner, and tomorrow was pasta and meatballs with garlic bread. If only we were dealing with vampires. I started thinking harder as I mopped. Maybe there was a way to feed the staff something that was poisonous to dogs that wouldn't hurt us kids. That seemed like a neat solution. I remember that dogs can't have chocolate. And grapes were bad for them, I think?

I couldn't really think of anything else. We'd had a dog when I was much younger, but all I really remembered about him was that he liked to eat cat poop, which only eliminated cat poop as a potential option to use to poison them.

I "acted natural" all that day, waiting for Bishop to reach out to contact me. Being too afraid to reach out to him.

It was late afternoon on Wednesday and I was in the middle of mopping the cafeteria again. My mind was a million miles away, so it was a big surprise when I bumped into Sylvie.

Literally.

"Watch it, kid!" she growled.

"Oh. Oh! I'm sorry. I didn't see you there, I was—" I stammered.

"You were daydreaming. I saw," she said, with a hint of a smile curling her lip.

The smile confused me. Sylvie doesn't smile unless someone is suffering or she had some sort of advantage on them that they didn't realize.

And then realization hit me. She thought I was brain fogged. That's what the smile was for. I kept my eyes mostly unfocused when I looked at her.

"Daydreaming," I repeated.

"Whatever. That's fine, kid. You need to come with me."

"Come with you?" I repeated, my stomach dropping.

"Yeah. Donovan wants to talk to you. In private," she said, her smile widening.

"Oh. I'd love to talk to Donovan," I lied. I most definitely did not want to talk to Donovan, alone or otherwise.

Sylvie led me down the same set of turns that she'd taken Francisco on the day before. Any exhaustion that I'd felt creeping in from my lack of sleep was banished by a surge of fear-fueled adrenaline. My fight or flight reflex had engaged, and my body was asking me why I wasn't beating feet for the hills in a very pointed manner.

I wish I knew, body. I wish I knew.

The path didn't alter from the other day, and I soon found myself sitting in the office I'd spied on previously. The statue sat prominently on Donovan's desk while the man himself lounged in the chair. Sylvie waited by the door and Donovan gestured for me to sit.

"We've been good to you, haven't we?" he asked.

"Uh, yeah?"

"Treated you like family. Fed you? Housed you? Gave you clothes? Helped clean you up?" he continued. I didn't like where this was going.

"Yeah, you've been great," I agreed, frowning. "What is all this?"

"So, after all that we've done, why is it that we found this in your pillow when we were changing the bedding this morning?" he asked, holding up the cell phone Bishop had snuck to me.

My heart dropped into my stomach and my mouth went dry. I frantically ran through the text conversations we'd had in my head. Was there anything that I could say or do to get out of this?

He stood up, gesturing for me to follow. Sylvie remained just behind me every step of the way as Donovan led me further into the staff area, stopping at a thick metal door. He unlocked it and strode inside.

"Nat, we're here to help people like you. People who've been dealt a bad hand. People with the potential to be so much more. To do that, we need to maintain a certain level of–isolation. We can't have the pressures of the outside world fussin' with you all."

"I get that, Donovan–" My voice died in my throat as my eyes fell on the man from two nights ago tied to a chair. He looked like he'd been worked over. He was covered in sweat, his lip was split, and the redness around his left eye made me bet he was looking at a shiner if he lived long enough to grow it. "What's this?" I whispered.

"You tell us," Sylvie growled in my ear.

I jumped forward, moving away from her, and hugged myself. "I don't know," I said, trying to think of a way out of this.

"It's your phone?" Donovan asked.

I shrugged.

"But you had it?" he persisted.

I nodded.

"Why? What could you hope to gain? We asked him to open it for us, but–" he nearly spat at Bishop. "He's less than worthless. A liar. Said he was here to get his girl back, if you can believe that."

"There you are, kid," a raspy voice said. Bishop sounded nearly as bad as he looked. "Been lookin' everywhere for you. I think it's time to head home, don't you?"

I froze, but Bishop's voice pulled both of the werewolves' attention away from me.

"So our guest awakens," Donovan drawled as he turned to look down at Bishop. The contrast between the two was stark. Donovan stood over him resplendent and beautiful. His clothing was perfect, showing off his physique. His smile, broad and bright, and his hair falling perfectly around his shoulders.

Bishop started out a mess and took a beating to go on top of it. His hair was sweaty, his face puffy, and blood stained his shirt.

But somehow he sat up in the chair he was tied to like he was the one in charge.

"Love what you've done with the place. Got a real "boot camp cult" sorta feel to it," Bishop replied.

"We're here t' heal the land an' the people on it," Donovan drawled back in response. "The children we bring here need healin' too. We're performin' a service."

"Out of the goodness of your hearts?" Bishop asked.

"Something like that," Donovan replied. "Ain't no one out there in the world lookin' after these kids, so we step in an' help 'em. Nat here was an addict, livin' on the streets when we found her. Feral. Look at the difference in just a few days."

"Regular Mother Theresa over here," Bishop scoffed. "If you're so hot for bringing kids in, why do you only have the dozen or so that I've seen around the grounds? Food in the kitchen won't feed more than 20 from the look of it. You still feed these vast multitudes you helped?"

"When they complete the program, we send 'em out on their way with a bit of money and a room at a halfway house while they get themselves back on their feet," Donovan shrugged.

"Like you did with that kid the other night? Sounded like he was really enjoying his new opportunities," Bishop said.

"I don't know what you're talking about," Donovan said, breaking eye contact with the bound man.

"You're a worse liar than you are a babysitter," Bishop spat back. "Fucking cult leaders. You guys spend so much time with people telling you that your shit don't stink that you forget that not everyone's sippin' the Flavor Aid. You stink pretty, but that pheromone trick won't work on me."

Donovan looked surprised, then frustrated. "Who are you?" he hissed.

"Wallet says his name is Jason Bishop. Address is in town. French Quarter," Sylvie replied.

Donovan wheeled and glared at her.

"Jason Bishop? You knew he was an occultist and you brought him here?" he demanded.

"Who the fuck is Jason Bishop?" she asked.

"Darlin', ya gotta start paying attention to the world around you. This here asshole's a heap of trouble is what he is. Sticks his nose where it ain't wanted,"

"Never without an invitation," Bishop interjected.

"He's a con man," Donovan continued.

"Alleged," Bishop interrupted.

"An' failed priest and exorcist," Donovan added.

"Both true," Bishop said.

"And a freelance troublemaker," he finished.

"I prefer 'occult detective', or 'bartender'," Bishop corrected. "But now that we've all done the introduction thing, you realize you're in a ton of trouble."

Donovan stared at him for a long moment. "Word on the street is that you can see auras. Know the truth about folk."

Bishop shrugged.

"Which means you know what we are," Donovan concluded.

"Which means you know I run with a dangerous crowd, and if anything happens to me, they'll descend on this place like God's own wrath and burn it to the ground," Bishop corrected. "So why don't we all admit this is a hilarious mistake and just let me walk?"

"You're even stupider than I thought if you think you're walking out of here alive," Sylvie chimed in, drawing a sharp look from Donovan.

I swallowed as his gaze shifted back to me.

"Well, that's unfortunate. I was hoping we'd have more time with you." Donovan turned to look at Sylvie. "You gotta work on that mouth, girl. You can't just let things fly like that. Now the girl's gotta go too."

Now the girl's gotta go too.

The words blanketed the air, clinging to me. Suffocating me. I could feel panic rising up. My eyes darted around the room, trying to find any way out. Sylvie barred the door, the only exit.

I was trapped.

"Kid like this has more loyalty than sense. With all the help you said you gave her, she'll keep quiet. Hell, probably would help ditch my body if you asked nice and batted those eyes at her, Big Bad," Bishop teased.

Donovan's attention came back to him. I could feel something changing in his demeanor. The normally calm, droll demeanor he wore like a second skin was fraying. Bishop was pushing his buttons. Sylvie's slip of the tongue made it worse. He was like a hot and humid summer evening right before it broke into a thunderstorm.

And it looked like Bishop might be my only umbrella.

Yaaaaaay.

"I-I won't say anything," I promised, trying to keep my voice level and my eyes unfocused.

"She's lying," Sylvie barked.

Donovan held up a hand. "We'll see. I need to go into the city to see if I can find more kids. Sylvie, get the pack together. Once everyone here is settled, the hunt starts. Take her with you." he nodded toward me. "Let her watch. If she's good, we'll see about maybe having her sign up permanently."

"Sign up?" I asked.

Sylvie frowned, pursing her lips. "He's saying we'll make you a werewolf, darlin'. Like us."

Chapter
Eleven

Werewolves.

My brain tried to process it but kept trying to rewrite the word. I refused to allow it. I knew I'd seen Donovan turn into some sort of monster that first day. I knew it. I knew what they'd all turned into the other night with Francisco.

But then the doubt. Was it drugs? Was it exhaustion? Was I crazy? Donovan seemed so–

The fucker gaslit me.

I managed a nod. "Right. Join you guys. I'd like that. I'd like a—a family," I said in my most convincing voice.

Sylvie's hard eyes stayed locked on me, but Donovan nodded with a smile. "See, it'll be perfect. I told you, she's more gifted than any other child I've brought so far. Maybe that translates."

"Maybe," Sylvie replied, not taking her eyes off of me.

"You're getting a hunt together just for me? I didn't bring a housewarming gift," Bishop said, pulling their attention back to him once again.

"Your blood will be gift enough," Sylvie spat.

"Will it?" Bishop replied, his voice taking on a more sinister tone. "Because whether you know who I am or not, your boss dog here does. And he knows that you'll take me down, but this hunt's likely to end with at least a few of your little pack not coming home. Isn't that right, Donovan?"

Donovan barked a laugh but looked away, unable to meet Bishop or Sylvie's eyes.

Jesus. Bishop wasn't bluffing. Who the fuck was this guy?

"Call me if you need anything," Donovan instructed Sylvie, then turned to me, placing a warm hand on my shoulder. "You have to understand what an honor this is, Nat. We don't offer a place in our family lightly. We expect loyalty above all things."

I nodded. "Me too," I replied, thinking of Francisco.

He smiled, misunderstanding my response, and then walked out past Sylvie.

I looked at Bishop, who gave a slight shake of his head.

"You're gonna need to rein him in. Sylvie, was it? Last chance. Call this whole thing off and you and your buddies get to live. It's better than you deserve, honestly. Seems like you've had quite the little slaughterhouse going out here. How many kids have you sacrificed to get that Nkondi as bloated as it is? A dozen? More?" he asked her while she glared at him.

"It's not how he's making it sound, Nat," Sylvie began, turning to look at me as I backed away from both of them.

"No, it's exactly like it sounds," he corrected. "You just need to decide if that matters enough to you for you to do anything about it. You're a smart kid, you'll do the right thing."

"I–Sylvie, what do you need me to do?" I asked, my eyes remaining on Bishop.

I could see Sylvie's smile out of the corner of my eye as she took my shoulders in her hands. Bishop gave me the slightest of smiles and nods. He thought I was on his side.

Was I on his side?

I wasn't sure. I meant everything I said before about not wanting them to turn anyone else into another Francisco, especially since it was pretty clear that there had been quite a few Franciscos. Right now I wanted to make sure I wasn't going to end up as the next Francisco, and playing along with Sylvie put off the need for me to decide on anything.

I needed time. Time to think.

Sylvie put her arm around me and led me out of the room, closing and locking the door behind us.

"Look, he's just trying to confuse you. You know how guys like him are. If they're talking to a girl, they always want something, right?" she asked.

I nodded.

"Exactly. Here's the deal: we're werewolves. That part was true, but we're not monsters. We're the good guys. We're trying to heal this area. To use the magic in that statue him and Donovan were talking about to restore the land. To wash away all of the junk and all the pollution that gets dumped into Lake Pontchartrain from New Orleans. We're fixing that," she said. Her eyes were manic, bordering on feverish.

She didn't *want* me to believe. She *needed* me to believe.

I once again nodded.

"Exactly. You get it. It's the only way. Sometimes you've gotta do things you don't want to make things better for everyone," she said, almost to herself. "And for you - you'll get to join us. Just a little cut, then a little blood in there to carry the gift. We'll do it after the hun–after we take care of that guy in there," she said.

I swallowed, then nodded once again. So much for buying myself time. It was gonna happen tonight after the rest of the kids went to sleep.

Fuck.

I followed Sylvie back into the common areas where the other kids gathered like good little cultists, catching the door separating the two areas and easing it closed behind us as we walked and she prattled on about the natural order or some other bullshit.

I didn't wanna die.

I also didn't want to turn into a monster who was okay with eating little kids if it meant my lawn would grow greener.

Double fuck.

"I-I'm gonna finish cleaning up in here," I said. "Don't wanna let things get away from me."

Sylvie offered me a sincere smile. "See? Donovan was right. You're one of the good ones."

She turned and headed outside as I stared after her. "What the fuck is that supposed to mean?" I muttered. "Felt condescending, like you're talkin' to me like I'm a little kid, and at least a little bit racist all at the same time. Helluva trifecta, bitch."

I backed up, watching her walk, then turned on my heel and sprinted back the way we came. I wanted outta here, and I wanted outta here now.

Tearing through the doorway between the staff and common areas, I ran to the door where Bishop was being held and pulled.

Locked. Shit. I'd forgotten about that.

I stared at the hardware. It was a deadbolt, which meant there was no way in or out without a key.

"Bishop?" I called.

"Bad idea to be here, kid," he said through the door. "Get back out and do your worker bee shit. Everything's under control."

"Bullshit. This ain't the time to act macho. This is time to panic and get the fuck outta here," I demanded.

"What happened to getting all the other kids out?" he asked.

"We–we can come back for 'em," I lied.

"Look. Nat. Do you trust me," he asked.

"Fuck no," I immediately spat back. "Why the fuck would I trust you?"

I could hear him sigh through the closed door. "Do you trust that I don't want to die here?" he tried again.

"Yeah. You don't strike me as the suicidal or martyr type," I spat back.

"Then you need to trust that I have a plan when I tell you to get the fuck back out there. You don't wanna get caught back here."

My breath was coming in shallow gulps. Everything was moving around me so fast. I could hear my heart beating. I started shaking. "I can't do this," I whispered through the door. God, I hated that tremble in my voice. "I don't wanna–I don't wanna die, Bishop," I said, fighting back tears. "Please. You gotta get me outta here."

I turned around and put my back to the door and slid down to the floor, burying my face in my hands and waited, trying to breathe, but getting more scared by the second.

"Nat?" His voice sounded different. Less glib and more–I dunno, human? "Listen, when I first came here, I was only interested in one thing: that statue. I was ready to ignore whatever else was going on if it would help me get what I needed. You brought me up short and made me rethink what was going on and what I was willing to sacrifice to make it happen.

I've got a kid. Did you know that? Tiny little thing. Her name's Mary and she means the world to me. She's my baby."

"And?" I spat back. "No one here means a damned thing to you."

"You're right, but you making me promise to get them all out reminded me that they're all someone's babies too. Maybe their parents suck. Maybe not. Maybe the kid made a string of mistakes that landed them here and their folks are desperately looking for them. Maybe they've got something to go back to. Maybe they don't. Every one of those kids carries their own set of answers to all of those maybes and a million others, and even I'm not enough of a bastard to just let the book close on all of 'em. Just like I'm not going to let the book close on you."

All I could muster in response were a few sniffles.

"Now, for me to help you, I need to make sure nothing happens to you before they try to get rid of me tonight. That's all you've gotta do: get through to tonight. Do you think you can do that?"

I nodded, wiping the tears from my eyes, then realized he couldn't see me. "Y-y-yeah."

"Good girl. Now, head back out there, and don't worry about me. I've got it under control," he said.

"Your idea of *under control* is batshit crazy, Bishop," I replied, coming to my feet.

"Kid, you have no idea," he said through the door.

The rest of the day passed in a hazy blur. It wasn't the mind fog that seemed to sneak in whenever I hadn't paid close enough attention before, that seemed to have mostly left when Donovan went into the city on his recruiting trip. This was more of an *"I'm terrified of what's coming and can't really pay attention to what's going on around me."* It drew concerned looks from Jessica, a one-armed hug and encouragement from Mike, and long stares from Felix.

I hated every second of it.

Dinner was some bland spaghetti and meat sauce; the staff and kids seemed to lap up like it was some sort of contest. I felt like it needed more garlic, but beggars and choosers and all that.

As the rest of the kids headed to bed, Sylvie asked to talk to me.

"It's time to get ready. Come with me," she instructed.

Remembering Bishop's instructions, I nodded and did like I was told, like a good soon-to-be monster. We moved through the increasingly familiar corridor into the staff area, now fully occupied by the other–well, werewolves, I guess? They were in their individual bedrooms doing distressingly normal things. A couple were playing video games, one was reading a book. One was knitting for Christ's sake.

Sylvie led me through the pack and back to Donovan's office. Approaching the desk holding the Nkondi statue, she pulled open the drawer, took out a nail, and showed it to me.

"Now, this is important. We need to get his blood on this, then drive it into the statue. It has to be **just** his blood. If you so much as sweat on it, we need a different one. We really don't want to confuse the thing that lives inside this little guy into going after a different target," she said with a laugh.

I tried to match her, but my laugh bordered on hysterical as it escaped my lips.

She mistook my laugh for excitement and ruffled my hair, which I absolutely hated.

"That's the spirit, kiddo," she said. "C'mon. Let's get this started. Can't have the hunt without it."

"Is—is that what you're gonna do? Hunt him?" I asked.

Sylvie talked as she walked, not bothering to look back at me. "Yeah. We've done some hunts without Donovan before if that's what you're worried about. No one's ever escaped the pack on the hunt, especially when the statue's spirit is out for blood. It's miles and miles to the nearest house, so we're nice and isolated out here."

"Good thing," I replied without enthusiasm.

"Right? Besides, how's one guy gonna stand up to five half-ton killing machines?" she asked. "Any one of us is more than capable of taking his ass out. All five? No contest, baby. Wait till you experience your first change, it's like nothing I can describe."

She paused in front of the locked door, reaching into her pocket to pull out the key.

"What's—what's it like?" I asked, my voice coming out almost in a whisper.

She considered for a moment, a faraway look on her face. "Like a full body orgasm that ends with the most clarity you'll ever feel. You're stronger, faster, tougher. Your senses are sharper. You can smell and taste things much more clearly when you lean into the wolf inside you. It's—it's like being alive for the first time." she finished.

"That's—a lot," I replied.

She nodded with a smirk. "And that doesn't describe the half of it."

Then she unlocked the door.

Bishop was sitting with his eyes closed, muttering under his breath in a language I couldn't quite place.

"Hey, whatever you're doing, it's time to knock it off!" Sylvie shouted, kicking his leg.

He winced, opening his eyes and smiling. "Didn't know you were that desperate for attention."

She scoffed. "You wish, old man."

She strode forward, nail in her right hand, and drove it hard into his shoulder. He hissed in pain as she drew it back covered in his blood.

"Mmmmmmmmotherfucker. Most people use thinner needles," he commented. "Just a free medical tip to help your user reviews."

"That's right, keep up the jokes. We'll see how much you joke tonight," Sylvie spat back.

"Probably about the same," he predicted. "Maybe a little less. I might feel slightly guilty about what happens to you guys. You got taken in by a cult leader, and are gonna end up paying for his sins."

"You can't psych us out, Bishop. Every one of us knows what we're doing. We're all in on Donovan's plan for making New Orleans a better place," Sylvie replied.

"Forget about the *might feel guilty* part," Bishop replied. "Your flavor of Kool-aid drinking jackassery makes me sleepy. You deserve exactly what's coming for you. Now, last chance. You cut me and all these kids loose and I'll let you all go."

Sylvie laughed. Really laughed. Hands on her stomach and bent over sorta laughing.

"You're fuckin' delusional, man. I can't believe you had Donovan spooked," she said, wiping tears from her eyes.

Looking between the two of them, I frowned. Bishop seemed mildly disappointed, but not worried. Sure, he was in pain from having a nail stab him in the shoulder, and from getting knocked around when they brought him in, but not like a man who was about to die.

He knew something, had set something up, and Sylvie was too stupid or too cocky to see it, even though Donovan had made himself scarce.

What the hell was he up to?

"Do you believe this guy?" Sylvie asked me.

"Kinda, yeah," I admitted.

She blinked and looked at me more intently. "Ya can't let 'em get into your head, Nat," she implored. "That's how guys like him work. They get into your head and make you think they got something on you, then get you jumpin' at shadows so you make a mistake they can take advantage of. He's just like every con man out there: takin' credit for shit that happens around him like it's some sorta master fuckin' plan, like when a dealer hands out an ace and a jack and he smiles like that was the setup the entire time."

"Or he's a guy that doesn't like to gamble, so he stacks the deck in his favor before a hand of cards is ever dealt," Bishop said. "So when the blackjack shows up it's just the end of a series of events he set in motion days ago."

"Tough words from a guy that got nabbed in our kitchen," Sylvie spat back. "Did the big bad man need a snack?"

"Something like that," he replied with a shrug and a smile.

There. There it was again. With all the talk about cards and stacked decks, there was one thing I was certain of: Jason Bishop had an ace up his sleeve.

Sylvie scoffed. "We'll be back for you," she promised and took me and the bloody nail back out and down to the office.

"Hold the statue," she instructed, grabbing a hammer from the same drawer the nail had come from. "Bastard thinks he can mess with me with some vague threats? Acting like he's the one in control?"

I held the statue firmly in place while she drove the nail into its torso. One hit. Then another. Then another. She looked down and smiled.

"And that should seal that motherfucker's fate," she declared. "Bring it out to the field. It's time to get ready so we can shut this bastard up once and for all."

She tucked the hammer into her belt loop and we headed out of the office.

A good rule of thumb is that if you ever find yourself in the middle of a field in the dead of night standing just outside of a group of swaying and chanting soon-to-be monsters, you've made at least one poor decision to lead you there.

Looking at the five wolves in human clothing who formed a circle around the statue with all the nails in it and Bishop, who was lying on the ground with his ankles and wrists bound by some rough-looking rope, I was really feeling the weight of my choices.

The dark swaying forms chanted in a language I didn't understand, their low voices reaching through the night's stillness and prickling at the back of my brain. It triggered feelings of being hunted, alone, and afraid. Feelings of terror as the night waited to devour me, filled with bright eyes and sharp fangs. Feelings of helplessness. Primal feelings. Visceral feelings.

I wanted to be sick, but instead, I stood quietly just outside of the circle, watching. As I concentrated, I could see some sort of shimmery light around them. It was red. Angry and vibrant, with an aggressive vitality that seemed about to burst out of them at any second. It slithered under their skin, wrapping around muscle and bone while distorting their flesh, trying to change them, to reshape them. To force them into that giant wolf form I'd seen them take when they killed Francisco.

I shuddered and looked away, shifting my focus to Bishop.

The guy was just lying there, quietly watching. From time to time he glanced at the statue and mouthed some words like he was talking to it. The statue seemed like better company than the thirty-somethings. I was struggling with the idea of what to call them. "Pack" seemed a bit derivative with the whole "wolf" thing, but it felt accurate, and I didn't have a better word. After a moment I decided that my imminent death was more important than figuring out branding for the monsters.

The voices stopped chanting, and the pressure that had been building hung in the air, waiting like a circling vulture. I could feel something from inside the nail-filled statue. It felt hungry. Like it wanted something.

Not to be fed.

To hunt.

"Last chance," Bishop said as Sylvie stepped forward and cut his bonds.

She looked back to the rest of the group, and gestured to him over her shoulder "Do you believe this fuckin' guy? Time to run, old man," she said through a smile.

Bishop watched them, then calmly walked to the edge of the trees, turned around and put his hands in his pockets.

"You're a fucking idiot, but it's your funeral. The end is the same here as it would be in the woods. Now you're gonna die!"

Without another word, Sylvie threw her head back in a howl of rage and pain as those ripples moving under her skin tore their way out, reshaping her body. Her legs distended, her arms stretched, and her jaw malformed. Her friends did the same thing, slowly changing from a group of attractive adults into actual monsters.

Then their howls of rage turned to screams of pain.

Sylvie had been the first to transform, and the guttural shriek of agony she let loose chilled me to the bone. I startled and backed up, only to bump into Bishop as I was retreating.

"You may not wanna watch this part," he said, taking me by my shoulders and turning me around.

I could smell burning. Like meat being burned while the wolves all screamed behind me. I couldn't *not* look. I needed to know.

Flame had eaten Sylvie away starting in her stomach, leaving a horrible, gaping hole in her mid section that kept burning. She was on the ground, her back arched in agony as she screamed to the heavens. One of the other wolves had tried to change back to a regular guy, but seemed like he got stuck part of the way through the process. His bones had started to mold themselves back, but stopped halfway, leaving him a mishmash of human and wolf parts writhing in the neatly tilled soil.

"How?" I whispered. "How did you do this? What did you do?"

Bishop sighed. "I warned them," he said simply.

"Yeah, but warning people doesn't do this, Bishop. Warning people doesn't make their guts burn them alive. What the fuck is this, man?" I demanded.

Bishop was quiet as he watched the group die. Slowly. Painfully.

"Think," he said. "Where did they catch me?

I shrugged.

"Sylvie said it in front of you. They caught me in the kitchen," he said.

"So? How the fuck did you set their insides on fire?" I demanded again.

"I added silver powder to the spices they added to the pasta sauce you all had for dinner tonight," he said.

"You poisoned all of us?" I said, my eyes going wide and my hands coming to my mouth.

"Not unless you're all werewolves too," he said. "So, not impossible under the circumstances. Your liver and kidney's'll flush it outta you in the next couple of weeks, but for werewolves? Once they shed their human skin, silver does just what all the movies and stories say."

He nodded toward the dying monsters.

"That."

"You were serious when you were talking to them. When you threatened them," I said, frowning. "You kept trying to give them chances. Why?"

Now it was Bishop's turn to shrug.

"Same sorta deal on why I agreed to spring all the rugrats here when you decided to negotiate like a mobster. Because they were someone's babies too."

He looked at them and shook his head.

"But they were too far gone. Donovan got them in too deep."

He sighed.

"Look, CPS is gonna show up here in the morning to deal with the kids. You can wait for 'em, or you can head out. Your call. Me, I've got the statue now, so I'll just take it and meet up with my friends in the woods and—"

I never got to hear what the last part of his plan was, since the statue, the Nkondi's eyes opened and the massive panther-like spirit slithered out, its eyes locked on Bishop.

"Well, shit," he muttered.

The spirit oozed like tar, a blacker spot against the already dark night.

"Bishop?" I asked.

"Yeah?" he replied, his voice tense as he put himself between me and the predator.

"You accounted for this in your plan, right?" I asked. "The one where you had everything figured out?"

"Funny story," he started.

"Fuck."

"Yeah," he said. "When they were setting up for this ritual, what did they do? Wait. That nail. The one they stabbed me with. Fuck. They put it into the statue, didn't they?"

I nodded, then realized he probably wasn't looking at me.

"Yeah." I said

"Okay. Okay. We can work with this," he said, continuing to back up as the creature oozed slowly toward him. "I need you to get that nail outta that statue, okay? Don't sweat onto the wood, don't spit onto the wood, and definitely don't bleed onto the wood. Just get it out."

"How the fuck am I supposed to do that?" I demanded.

"You're a smart kid. Figure it out, otherwise, that thing's gonna run amok and start hunting anyone and everyone it comes across. That's what it does: it's a spirit of the hunt. There's gotta be some sort of ritual they used to put it back in its box," he said.

"But–" I started.

Then the thing lunged forward. Bishop shoved me to the side as he dove in the opposite direction. The spirit thing landed where we'd been standing a moment before and oozed, moving its feline head toward him. Bishop held out both hands like he was going to try to shield himself from the monster. It leapt forward, its jaws gaping only to run into a silvery burst of flame that shot out of Bishop's hands.

What the fuck?

I didn't wait to see what was going to happen next, I ran toward the statue hoping the thing would ignore me and just eat the old guy instead.

I ran past the dead werewolves, littered on the ground still smoldering from the silver they'd eaten, and slid on the ground toward the statue like my dad taught me during t-ball. I remembered the spot Sylvie had driven the nail and tried to pry it out with my fingers.

It didn't go great.

I put my feet on it and tried a variety of fingers, pushing and pulling. It was stuck fast. I braced against the statue and tried again, and all I managed to accomplish was to get a fucking splinter in my palm.

Fucker.

I glanced up and saw that Bishop had gone into the woods, leading the thing away to give me more time.

More time for what? I don't think he had a better idea than I did on how to put this thing back.

Wait. The hammer. Sylvie had it when we came out, so it should be with her clothes. I didn't even bother to stand and crawled over to her shredded pants. Seems like being a werewolf is hell on the wardrobe. Count another reason I'd rather pass, thanks.

I started rifling through, flinging pieces away when they didn't have a hammer. Just as my hand closed around the wooden haft, a large, clawed hand snatched my other arm. My eyes went wide as I saw Sylvie had rolled over and was clutching me with hatred in her eyes.

I screamed and tried to wrench myself free, but her grip was like a vice, and even with a quarter of her body burned away she still weighed at least twice what I did. Her claw sliced my left arm open as she gripped it, like a nightmarish game of tug of war.

"No no no no no!" I cried, trying to get loose. I failed. So I raised the hammer and slammed it into her skull.

The monster flinched, so I hit her again. And again, and again, screaming the whole time. I must have looked like some sort of lunatic and I couldn't have cared less. I wanted her off me and I wanted her off me now.

The issue is the one that Bishop brought up a few minutes before. "Beaten to death with a hammer" isn't how you kill a werewolf. You kill a werewolf with silver. Now, if I'd have had a silver hammer (get on that, DeWalt), I'd have been in great shape. As it was, whatever I did to her healed as soon as I did it.

It was fuckin' frustrating, fam.

Her grip on my left arm turned into her pulling me closer, going hand over hand. I could see that every movement sent jolts of agony through her, but it looked like she'd decided she was going to take me with her, the bitch.

I screamed louder, kicking her and hitting her with the hammer. I would have tried anything to get her off of me at that point.

Then a baseball bat with a bunch of nails driven through it smashed down onto the back of her skull, splattering chunky goo everywhere. Then it fell again, and again, and again.

Her claws let go and I looked up and saw the most beautiful man I'd ever seen in my life.

Now, Dave's tall, but when you're lying on the ground and he's standing over you, reaching a hand down to help you up, he seems like a giant out of a storybook. What I saw was this huge friggin' guy with gorgeous dark skin, a great big poof of hair, and the gnarliest eyes I'd ever seen.

"You good?" he asked. His voice rumbled like thunder on a steamy summer night, leaving me with goosebumps.

I nodded, letting him pull me upright.

"Bishop said to keep an ear out. In case you needed something," he explained.

I nodded again, then giggled.

"So, you were doin' something?" he prodded.

I nodded and giggled again, then shook my head. "Fuck! Yes!"

I ran back over and grabbed the statue.

"No!" Dave warned, but it was too late. My left, blood-covered hand made contact with the wood of the statue and there was a flash from the eyes.

"You're marked," Dave explained. "Now the spirit's got the taste of you. Get the nail out. Leave the rest to me," he said.

I laid the statue on the dirt and threaded the nail into the claw on the back of the hammer and started to pry.

"Dave, you have incoming!" a woman's voice shouted from the woods.

I yanked Bishop's nail out. Nothing. There was no flash. No shudder. Nothing.

Then I looked more closely. Each of the nails had a little bit of a white shimmer to them that ran out of the metal and into the wood.

"Uh, Big Sexy?" I asked.

"Dave," he corrected.

"That's what I said. What happens if I pull the rest of these nails out?"

"No clue. That's more of Bishop's thing," he said.

"Good or bad, do you think?"

I saw the creature emerge from the woods, an inky blob with a vaguely cat form. It had abandoned one set of jaws for seven or eight that were floating around in there, poised to hungrily snap up anything it came near.

All of them were oriented toward me.

"Don't think so," Dave announced, and I saw him swing his bat into the creature. It howled in pain and rage at having its prey denied it.

"Fuck it, it can't get worse," I said and started prying out the other nails.

"Yes, it can! It can always get worse!" the woman who belonged to the voice scolded me. She was another hottie. Red hair, tank top, itty bitty shorts, and combat boots. She had rings all over her fingers and was moving in and out as the monster tried to snap at her, precise in her movements, like a ballerina, only for ass-kicking.

I got the next nail out, and this time I wasn't disappointed. There was a bright white flash and a glowing ball streaked out of the statue straight into the sky.

"Fuck you," I whispered and started on the next.

The Nkondi spirit was getting desperate. It frantically tried to get past Dave and the new lady while they kept hounding it. I saw it try to flow back toward the woods to get around them, but Bishop was there with another one of those silvery fire bursts, which it didn't seem to like at all.

"This is for Francisco," I whispered and pried loose another nail. A bright pulse and another glowing orb flew up into the sky.

And another nail. And another. Each time an orb escaped, the creature shrunk. By the time I reached the last one, it was the size of a housecat. It was cornered between the three, hissing and looking to flee.

Looking at it, reduced like it was, I just got angry. Everything that had happened in my life came flooding back. Everything I'd had to do. Every compromise I'd made. Every time I'd been taken advantage of. These fuckers had been no different. They brought me here to feed me to this thing. This little demon.

"Would you just fucking die?" I demanded and stomped down on it, hard, focusing all of my anger and frustration into one motion. One intent.

The creature was crushed into the ground and vanished.

"What the hell?" asked the woman.

"That's...that's not possible," whispered Bishop.

"Sure it is," Dave corrected. "She just did it."

"But destroying a nature spirit that way would take a willworker of–" he trailed off, looking at me for a long moment, then over to the woman, who nodded.

"Right. Everyone, this is Nat. Nat, this is Dave and Ava. I think maybe you should come with us. We're gonna need to fill you in on some things."

I smiled.

"About fucking time someone did."

As Nat finished her story, Victor and Jackie stared for a moment, my ex's mouth partially agape until she caught herself.

"How in the hell are the rest of you so blase' about what she just said?" Victor asked.

"They were in the story, sweetie," Jackie reminded him. "They already knew. They were there."

I nodded.

"We were...and aside from a few...liberties she took—" I started.

"Not even one. Every syllable was the God's honest truth," Nat declared, holding up her left hand and crossing an "X" over her heart. "And everyone knows Bishop here is full of slander and lies."

She looked around the room, then shrugged.

"After the dust settled, Nat ended up couch-surfing around with the more reputable members of the New Orleans supernatural community," I said.

She nodded.

"I was worried for a bit, not gonna lie. Donovan was still out there, and I had no doubt he'd try to get his pound of flesh," Nat said.

I nodded. "He wasn't an issue. We handled him," I replied.

"How?" Victor asked.

"We taught him that when you play stupid games you win stupid prizes," Ava said with a light smile. "Nothing fatal, but me and Jason made his life very inconvenient for a little while.

"I had something to do with that, if I recall," Father Raimond added

Ava smiled. "Credit where it's due. Yes. Yes you did," she said.

"Right, but that doesn't answer—" Victor pressed.

"Victor, if we explain it to you, then Raimond here has to know everything that happened that wasn't directly related to him. Sometimes plausible deniability is the best approach. Let's just leave it at: Nat didn't have to face any werewolf-related revenge, and she moved on with her life and improved herself," I said.

"Yeah, and that big ass-face made me get my GED," she said, mocking me. "And whenever things started to get bad, or I felt like I was gonna backslide, all three of them always seemed to show up, sometimes with pizza."

"How did you all know when to do that?" Jackie asked.

"People like to tell me things," Ava replied with that infuriating dismissive shrug.

"The only real problem we ran into was that she refused to stay away whenever an issue came up," I said

"Call it 'a case', you know you want to," Ava teased.

"Fine, a case," I grumped

"What ever happened to Jessica and the rest of the kids?" Jackie asked.

"Jess is doin' great. We meet for coffee a couple times a week. She's helping to run the homeless program out of St. Louis Cathedral," Nat said.

"She has a great rapport with the younger people. The same offer is open to you if you'd ever like to join us, Nat," Father Raimond said.

"Nah, Jess is way better a public face for you guys than me. I'd do something to fuck it up for you," Nat said.

"Like tell church people you were fucking it up?" I asked.

"Exactly!" Nat laughed. "I'm still a bit rough around the edges."

"I'm just glad that Mary went to bed before...well..." Jackie commented after a sip from her apple cider.

"Yeah, some of our backstories aren't fit for human consumption." Dave agreed.

"Phrasing," Ava whispered from behind a smirk.

Dave sputtered for a moment, then shrugged, a big smile creasing his features.

"Wait. What's that supposed to mean?" Victor asked.

"You sure you wanna know, Osgood?" Dave asked, quirking an eyebrow.

"In for a penny," Victor shot back with a shrug. "It can't be worse than what poor Nat went through."

"Oh sugah," Nero groaned. "You do not know what you done just called down. Sweet Baby Jesus have mercy on y'all."

"Well—" I started.

"Sorry, Boss, but I don't think so," Dave said. "Like Nat said, you make yourself the center of things, an' this story goes back a lot farther than your part in it."

I opened my mouth to object, then nodded. "Fair enough. I know you don't love talking about this stuff."

Dave cleared his throat, then shrugged. "Sometimes ghosts from the past need exorcising. Now, I need y'all to remember: this one's not for the faint of heart," he said, his deep voice filling in the empty spots in the room and leaving a slight rumble in its wake.

"Are any of them?" Victor asked.

"Have you ever heard of the LeBlanc Family? Or Bayou LeBlanc?" he asked.

"No, should I?" Victor replied.

"Well, to really understand, you're gonna need to learn a bit about my family."

Book 2: Dave's Story

Chapter ONE

Have you ever been out in the Bayou after dark? Not on one of the tours, mind you. *Really* out in the swamp? In those places where the smell clings to the water, gators slide through the mud, and you can feel eyes on you that no human soul is meant to feel? People say it's like a different world out there. A different universe. Folks don't know how close to the truth they are. It's important for you to understand all of this goin' in.

There's parts of the swamp that haven't changed since before the first settlers came down here. Fleeing from the atrocities they committed back east or in the old country, these families held onto the old ways and were bound to 'em by tradition, by pact, and by blood.

The LeBlanc family, my family, was one of 'em. Probably the biggest and most successful. When they established the homestead there were only twenty, give or take. Shoulda been easy pickings for the local tribes, local critters, or the things moving in the shadows, but our shadows were darker. Our pacts ran deeper, and our family had less scruples than any sane group of people. We'd reached beyond the borders of reality itself and brought in...things. Not demons. Not spirits. Creatures that don't belong here. Eldritch powers.

My family traded scruples for powers generations ago.

The LeBlanc Plantation was settled on one of the few hills in the Atchafalaya Swamp. The house grew from the top of the crest like a cancer, spreadin' this way an' that without much in the way of plannin', with additions to the house haphazardly slapped on an' hooked up to the ancient boiler down under the kitchen. Everything was ramshackle and worn, and no one seemed to have planned any of it. Or so it seemed. The older members of the family had very particular dreams, though. Dreams where the things they trucked with would talk to 'em. Show 'em things. Things that almost always broke their minds. It was after them dreams that they'd get a fever for expansion, and another addition or another floor would go up.

Our "plantation" wasn't what you'd call a prime example of the antebellum south. More like a fever dream, but it did what it was 'sposed to. It held all of our kin, an' the reality-bending geomancy allowed them to build The Catacombs.

Louisiana in general, and Bayou folk in particular, don't have basements. That's just an invitation for water to come sneakin' in where it ain't wanted an' creatin' a foul-smelling swimming pool inside the house's foundation, so when I tell you that the LeBlanc Family not only had a basement complete with storage and a boiler room but also catacombs they had been workin' for over a hundred years, I need you to understand exactly how beyond the pale it was. The things went for miles, well beyond LeBlanc Hill and under the swamp itself. The hill sections were dry. Sandy almost. The tunnels runnin' under the bayou were darker. Damper. Even geomancy can only project and protect so much, an' a lot of those tunnels were waist-deep bogs or even completely submerged.

That suited the residents just fine.

My family wasn't the most supportive or loving, an' truth be told, I'm certain our family tree doesn't branch nearly as much as it should. "Keep the family's power close," was what my Mawmaw always said.

By the time of my birth, the LeBlancs had been on LeBlanc Hill for over two hundred years. Plenty of time for their plans to have progressed from a simmer to a boiling point.

The head of the family was Mawmaw. I don't rightly know her given name. I say given and not Christian 'cause ain't nothing Christian about that woman. She was a gnarled thing. Twisted and wrinkled. My first memories of her involved crying after she would pinch or bite me.

"Looks like this one's almost plump enough to eat," she'd say, then cackle in a wheezing, high-pitched way that cut straight to my spine.

Talk of eatin' the kids wasn't idle in our family, y'see. The family had kids aplenty, an' sometimes huntin' didn't go well, whether in the bayou or the towns around the borders, and meat needed to stay on the menu. Maw and Paw decided my best chance was to help feed the beast in the basement, so I stayed out from underfoot by shovelin' coal and mindin' the pressure with Paw.

Not that my parents were much better. My father's name was Willem, an' my mother was Anabelle. I think she mighta also been his cousin on one or both sides, but that ain't the sorta thing you talk about in the LeBlanc family. The older folk get together and decide who's gonna have kids with who. Sometimes they tell 'em to marry. Most of the time they don't. Every once in a great while they'll bring in someone from the outside to give the gene pool a quick refresh.

They normally don't last long after the first round of kids are born. Poor bastards.

I was probably eight or so when I got pulled away from the boiler room by my parents and taken to the kitchen to see Mawmaw. The air was thick with the sweet smell of cooking flesh. Might have been pork. Mighta been some campers out to experience the beauty of nature.

"Davey," she said in that high-pitched rasp that passed for a voice. "Come in, child. My, you've grown, haven't you?"

I swallowed and nodded, hoping this wasn't another 'big enough to eat' moment.

"Sit, sit," she sing-songed at me before looking to my parents and barking "Leave us."

The pair of them bowed and scuttled from the room.

"I dreamed of you, Davey. Dreamed that you'd been blessed by our *tataille*," she said, almost purring.

"You mean–" I began.

"We don't say His name," she spat, cutting me off. "Respect, Davey. He's blessed you and you must show him respect."

I blinked and nodded.

"What do you need me to do, Mawmaw?" I asked. I hated the tremor in my voice. I wanted to be brave. To be strong. To show Mawmaw that The Nameless had chosen well.

"Just what comes natural, Davey. But first, you must drink," she said, gesturing to a small pot bubbling over the steady flame of the range.

I looked at the liquid with not a small amount of concern and dredged up the courage to ask "Ain't it too hot, Mawmaw?"

"Not at all. Bubblin's just to show you it's good an' ready," she reassured me, her eyes shining with a feverish light.

I didn't like this. Didn't like any of it, but I was young, and when Mawmaw told somebody to do something, they did it so I picked up the warm black iron container in my hand and tipped it back. It was like trying to drink warmed swamp mud, which it might have been for all I knew. I fought the urge to vomit. To spit that foul-tasting ichor right into the fire, but seeing Mawmaw leaning forward, her eyes aglow, her mouth slightly agape, and her pale tongue running along her overly-pointed teeth chased that from my mind. Whatever this was was a far cry better than whatever was waiting for me if I didn't follow through.

I coughed as I swallowed. Mawmaw was there, sitting still. "That's it, boy. Drink it all up."

I did. I drank until I couldn't anymore. My stomach hurt. It felt stretched. Distended. I tried to put the small cauldron back down, but couldn't. My eyes went wide and I made a choking noise as the fluid continued to slide down my throat.

"That's right, Davey. There's a good boy," she croaked.

Something was wrong. I had no control over myself as I greedily slurped the vile-tasting muck into my gullet, then it got worse. I felt something slither from the cauldron and into my open mouth.

"Yes," she exhorted. "That's it!"

I could feel It wiggling Its way down my throat and into my stomach, then swimming around inside me. It was big. Too big for It to fit, but It was there. Coiled inside my guts. I fell to my hands and knees, retching and gagging. I tried to vomit It back out, but even as painfully full as my stomach was, nothing would come.

"There it is, Davey. You've been blessed. You're chosen. A sign of our ascension. Pack your things, boy. Tomorrow you're leaving the boiler behind you. You're starting your new life tending to The Nameless in The Catacombs."

Chapter Two

The Nameless need no light.

This was one of the first things that Mawmaw drilled into me as I assumed my duties in The Catacombs. The Nameless were creatures from beyond reality, from between dimensions. The original owners of reality who were cast out with those all-important first words: *Let there be light.* Ever since, bright lights have caused them discomfort, and the type of light that was shed on that first day, direct sunlight, could destroy their bodies and send their spirits screaming back into the void between worlds.

Which is to say she wanted me to make sure I didn't accidentally leave one of the hatches to the tunnels open. It wouldn't do to have gone through all the trouble and sacrifice to bring our guests, and possibly masters through, only to boil them alive on a clear day.

I started my duties in the tunnels nearest the house. These were occupied by the calmest and most pliable of The Nameless: each a void of inky blackness with teeth, eyes, claws, and just about any other unpleasant thing you'd care to imagine. Their bodies weren't just devoid of light or black though. That's not giving them enough credit. They felt like holes in reality you could fall through to where they were from and become trapped. Like they devoured the light even while it was hurting them.

I fed them the small critters we caught around the swamp: frogs, rats, birds, some younger gators, general vermin that no one would think twice 'bout missing. Every once in a while one of the family would get brave and bring in a feral hog. Those were dangerous days 'cuz The Nameless need their meals to be livin'. They didn't just consume their flesh, they ate the life energy, Mawmaw said. If we didn't nourish that need, they'd wither and die.

The hog's terrified screams filled the tunnels on the other side of the hatch. The beast recklessly threw its body against it, trying to force its way out and away from the hungry darkness that tore at it.

I was thirteen before I started asking questions. I'd already started to hit my growth spurts, standing taller and broader than most of my kin and Mawmaw had started bringing me into her room to help me with my Nameless. To let me understand It better. Commune with It, sort of.

Every one of those sessions would start the same, her burnin' some herbs, and us meditating. Every one of them would end the same, too. Me tired, dazed, and lightheaded, wrapped in a blanket and covered in sweat.

It was after one of these that I finally managed to work up the courage to ask her.

"Mawmaw?" I asked.

The gnarled old woman stared at the hatch with an erotic hunger, licking her lips at the sounds of the hog's struggle. Hearing her name snapped her out of her reverie and brought her gaze to me.

I didn't like it.

"What is it, child?" she asked. Child. Since I'd come to work in The Catacombs, I was never "boy" anymore. On rare occasions, I was David or Davey, but I was mostly *child* now.

"The Nameless. They eat life energy, you said," I started, my speech halting.

"Yes, child?" she prodded, her attention split between the horror occurring beyond the hatch and the beginnings of my question.

"Like a soul?" I continued.

"I suppose," she replied, still focused on the hog.

"And I'm carrying a Nameless in me. So It can be born into this world," I continued.

"Yes. A great honor for our family," she muttered.

"Is it eating me, Mawmaw? Will it eat my soul when it comes?"

Mawmaw's eyes focused on me then. Focused hard. "An' what if It did, child? After hundreds of years of sufferin'. Of sacrifice. All the LeBlancs that done come before you. What if It did? Is that you doin' any less than what they did to bring you this opportunity? This gift?"

I swallowed and shook my head. "No ma'am," I whispered.

Her lips split into a wide grin, revealing her sharp teeth, several of which had gone missing over the past few years. "There's a good child. Besides, nothing to worry about, you'll see. You'll learn to commune with the guest inside you. Learn to borrow Its strength. Merge with It. Make It feel all warm an' welcome."

She reached out and ruffled my hair. Her long fingernails looked sharp, and her bony fingers closed slightly around my scalp as she did. They felt inhuman, like she was iron on the inside.

I mutely nodded, fully aware that I was being lied to.

For near a month, I mostly avoided the rest of the family, spendin' most of my time in the dark with The Nameless. They were getting more accustomed to me as time went on, which didn't sit great with my worries about being eaten alive from the inside out.

Like any young teen at a total loss, I tried to ignore it till I couldn't take it anymore. That's when I approached my parents.

"Mom? Dad?" They were alone in their bedroom, whispering quietly to each other when I entered the doorway.

"David!" My mother looked up at me, her frequently-vacant eyes focusing on me. She was havin' one of her lucid moments. Lucky. More and more she ran away and hid inside her own thoughts, oblivious to the world outside. Made conversations challenging.

"I have—I'm scared," I admitted.

"What do you have to be scared of, David?" my father asked.

My mother looked at him, her eyes hard. "We both know, Willem," she hissed.

My father swallowed, then nodded.

"Mawmaw. She says—" I started.

"Shhhh. We know, Davey. We know," my mother said. Bringing me into an embrace. "We're here for you, child."

I stiffened.

"Child?" I asked, trying to pull away, only to find my mother's grip to be as immovable as the roots of an oak.

"There there, little one," she said, her voice growing rougher. Hoarser. Her arms felt longer and wrong as I pressed against them for space. Like they were sacks of muscle around bones of iron.

My father screamed and fled the room as the creature holding me completed its metamorphosis from Anabelle LeBlanc to Mawmaw. She cackled as I struggled against her impossibly strong grip.

"Now child, tell old Mawmaw what fears you," she rasped. "She'll make it all better."

"I don't wanna die," I cried. "I don't wanna get ate by one of the monsters!"

"Die? Child, you won't die. You'll live forever. Merged body and soul with The Nameless inside you. You have the chance to bring Them into the light. To anchor Them to this world. To open the door for Them for all time! You'll be more than human. More than a Nameless, even. You'll be perfect."

"I don't want that!" I cried.

"Don't want it?" Mawmaw held me at arm's length. She didn't look even remotely human now, standing over seven feet tall with a large humped back and arms that reached down nearly to the floor, covered in lean, corded muscle. Her gnarled face gave the impression of a diseased tree, with her left eye four times the size of her right.

"Want it or not, David, it's going to happen! Pacts have been signed and bargains made, so make peace with it, child. Willing or no, you've been blessed. Maybe we need to remind you what a blessing you've enjoyed."

I spent the next two months in the flooded sections of the tunnels. The Catacombs near the LeBlanc Plantation house are dark, but under the swamp with the muck dripping in from the ceiling and walls I found new levels of darkness. Of isolation.

Mawmaw barred my path back to the house with some sort of magic. What kind I don't know. Probably don't want to. What I did know was that I was on my own until she said I wasn't. I learned to hunt by sound and by feel, catching and eating frogs, swamp rats, and even more unpleasant things that happened down into my oubliette.

I don't know how long I cried when she first threw me in. Felt like forever, but time quickly lost all meaning to me. Time was reserved for places where things mattered, where there was light. Time didn't matter in the tunnels. In the dark forgotten places. It was a lie you told yourself to try to give meaning to the nothingness in which you were destined to remain.

During those two months, The Nameless inside me grew closer to the surface. I began to understand It. What It was. What It wanted.

None of it was good, but it didn't scare me. Not anymore. That David, the scared David was gone. Dead. Eaten by the darkness. The David that emerged from the oubliette after those sixty days was different. Changed.

You see, that David realized the only way that this could end well for him was to kill his entire family. Every last motherfucking one of them.

*Chapter
Three*

Being a child whose family had banished him to the lightless catacombs isn't something that lends you to having warm feelings about your blood relatives under the best of circumstances, and the LeBlanc family had no "best of" to offer. That being said, they wasn't a group you crossed lightly, especially not a family member who hadn't achieved their full growth.

I waited. I spent as much time away from the others as I could, aware of what had to come. I was surprised when my second cousin Babette took a shine to me. She was a few months younger than me and like most of my family, bore the physical marks of the years of incestuous breeding they'd taken part in. She had a club foot, meaning she got off light by LeBlanc standards. Other than that, she was a pretty little thing. Skin like midnight and high cheekbones.

I can see all o' you squirmin' in your seats a bit. I'll remind you of the family we're discussin'. I warned you, an' you all heard the stories before. To me, it seemed perfectly normal when the shine she took to me moved past anything innocent and straight into a physical relationship. Judge all you want, but it's possible that she's the only thing that kept me sane when I was there. I knew she clung to me like a liferaft. The kindness we showed each other was all either of us experienced in our lives to that point. We never saw Mawmaw watchin' us, but we knew who was in charge. We knew the rest of the family served as her eyes and ears, and if our partnership bothered her, she didn't do anything to discourage or dissolve it.

The years passed and I grew. Babette stayed a little slip of a thing. Her health was never the best, and especially with her leg, she wasn't able to walk very far or very fast. For myself, I had duties to attend to with The Nameless. Feedin' 'em, walkin' among 'em. Bein' Their high priest, basically.

I stood mutely by when Mawmaw and my relations would bring in a new sacrifice for 'em. Sometimes livestock. Sometimes not. The screams after the door closed when The Nameless showed up to feast is like nothing else. The inhuman wailing, even from the human throats.

Every time it happened, I swore it would be the last time. Every time after I'd prepare myself to confront Mawmaw and the rest. Every time after I'd think of Babette and what would happen to her if I tried and failed.

Every time I did nothing.

So time passed. Strangely, Mawmaw never ordered Babette or me to marry or lay with any of the other relations. She seemed content with the situation keepin' me in check and was willing to allow a bit of leeway to keep me quiet until The Nameless could rip its way outta me.

"You know it's only a matter of time, right?" Babette asked me.

It was the summer of my twenty-third year.

"What do you mean?" I asked. We were a spell away from the house, as alone as you can be in the bayou. Hopefully away from prying ears, sliding through the boggy water in a flat bottom boat.

"The thing inside you. It's just a matter of time till it comes out, David. It's like a tickin' time bomb. Just waitin'. Hangin' over everything."

I nodded. "I suppose you're right," I replied, not seeing much point in arguing over a true statement.

"There's gotta be somethin'? Someone you can talk to?"

I shook my head. "Who? Ain't no one in the family willing or able to put a stop to Mawmaw. Ain't anyone outside of the family that's got even half an idea of what we're up to out here. I've thought about this a lot, Babette. There's no escape hatch."

"Mawmaw talks about "enemies" all the time. Folk that would try to stop the family. Maybe one o' them?" she asked.

"I don't know where to begin findin' anyone like that. For all that she talks about 'em being legion, I don't think I ever seen an outsider here that wasn't intended for marriage or the tunnels."

Babette shuddered.

I carefully put a hand on her cheek to reassure her. Her face in my hand only served to remind me how small she was. How fragile. She'd be the one to bear the brunt when I failed. She looked worried. Sad. Defeated.

"I'll figure somethin' out," I promised.

She smiled at me, content that I was working on things. I really hated lying to her.

It was a few days later when things changed. I was moving through the tunnels when I saw a light coming from one of the peepholes scattered throughout. They'd been carved out, no more than four inches tall and six wide to help our family's allies to track prey without needin' to traverse the labyrinth. Even stranger, there were voices.

"Just admit you're lost," the voice said. It was male, a bit gravely. Not someone I'd ever heard before

"Sugah, we ain't lost. The issue is that the minds you're wantin' me ta track ain't exactly human, and they ain't exactly holdin' still," said a second voice. It sounded like another man, a bit more high-pitched and with a more familiar Creole accent.

"Nero, that sounds suspiciously like lost," commented a third voice. A woman this time.

"Babygirl, don't you start too," The voice (Nero I assumed) complained "I told the both of ya that I felt something breakin' down here. That the minds that were gatherin' were dark and inhuman.""You did," the man agreed.

"An' I told you that we should tell The Order an' let them handle it," Nero continued.

"Excellent advice," the woman's voice said.

"But here I am, wadin' through I don't even know what, tryin' to track down some sorta monster queen, ruinin' my cute shoes, and no doubt stainin' the hell out of these pants."

"Nero, don't!" the woman's voice yelled. There was a shifting noise and the sound of falling debris. After a long moment of not moving and holding my breath, I heard coughing.

"Who's not dead?" the first man's voice asked.

"Very funny, Bishop," the woman replied.

"Ava? Okay, good. Nero?" he (Bishop?) continued.

"Just kill me now, sugah. That damned doorway just went and caved in a bucketful o' slop right on top of me. It's as bad as can be."

"Shit. Okay Nero, hold still, what's hurt?" Bishop asked.

I heard a melodramatic sigh from Nero. "My shirt. This black gunk is absolutely gonna stain, Bishop."

I hear an immediate snort from Ava, then some very inventive cursing from Bishop. "Don't do that, Nero. I thought you were really hurt."

"I'm the victim of a fashion vivisection, but physically I'll survive," Nero replied.

"I wouldn't be so sure of that," Ava replied. "The cave-in blocked the tunnel ahead, and behind."

Things were quiet for a moment, then I heard Bishop speak. "Fuck. Yeah. There's some sort of blood magic woven into the walls and ceiling. Any non-LeBlanc sets it off. How did I not catch that when I was looking over the place?"

"Because you said that there were layers upon layers of magical effects placed on the hill, the house, and the tunnels. Unraveling them gave you a migraine," Ava replied.

"It's my job to find that shit," Bishop spat back.

"First, don't get bitchy with me. You're the one that wanted to keep working together after you broke things off. I said we should give each other space to make things less complicated for you, you're the one that said no, that you wanted to actually stay friends," Ava replied.

"I –" Bishop took a deep breath. "You're right. I'm sorry. I'm frustrated and took it out on you. I should have seen that fucking trap."

"You're not a superhero, Jason," Ava said.

"You two done? Good, Nero don't like it when Mom and Dad are fighting. Now get your gorgeous asses in gear and figure out how we get the fuck out."

They were quiet for a moment.

"I think you might have some trouble with that," I said.

Dead silence.

I waited. More silence. It was thick, the sort you began to question whether you could possibly hear over it.

"I said–"

"Aw shit, we heard you, Sugah. We're just in here trying to figure out what the hell to do about it," Nero replied testily.

"Nero..." Ava admonished.

"What? A voice deep as Darth Vader's out there in the dark sayin' we're in trouble? Oh bless your sweet heart, but we already knew that," he said. "Now if Mr. Dark and Mysterious Voice wants to come an' contribute, I'll be the happiest damned queen in these tunnels."

"I—what?" I asked. Like most people, I'd never met anyone quite like Nero and I was struggling to wrap my mind around what I'd heard so far.

"Nero's asking if you can help us," Ava said calmly.

"I—no. I came here to check the tunnels. It's my job," I said.

"How do you do that with all of the things roaming around in here? That's suicide," Bishop asked.

"The Nameless don't bother me," I explained

"The Nameless? Okay...but why? They're voracious hunters. It's all I've been able to manage to keep us off their radar," Bishop said.

"Ever since Mawmaw put one in me, they leave me be."

Dead silence again.

"You have one of those creatures inside you?" Bishop asked

"Yessir," I said. He felt older. Like an authority figure.

"Nope. None of that. No Sir. No Boss. No Mister. People call me Bishop," he corrected.

"I'm David LeBlanc," I said.

"LeBlanc? Honey, are you part o' the family that lives here?" Nero asked.

"Yes."

"Lord have mercy," Nero said with a sigh.

"I don't know if I can help get you out. Mawmaw will know the trap went off," I warned.

"Mawmaw?" Ava asked

"Yes'm. Mawmaw's the one in charge 'round here."

"Sweetie, please tell me she's just your grandmother," Nero asked.

"Sort of. She's been the Grandmother here for a long time. No one really knows how long."

"That's not how grandmothers are supposed to work, David," Ava said gently.

"I know...but that's Mawmaw. An' she's probably on the way now."

I left the three strangers trapped in the tunnels and hurried through toward the entrance nearest the house. Three quarters of the way there, I ran into Mawmaw in the tunnels.

"David? Where are you going in such a rush, child?" she asked.

I swallowed.

"Just coming to the house to tell you the latest offerings are in the tunnels. A hitchhiker and a couple," I lied.

The grizzled old woman regarded me with her rheumy eyes, her gnarled face unreadable. After too long, she nodded. "Well done, David. I'm happy to see that you've started taking your role more seriously. I expect great things from you before your Ascension."

I nodded, suppressing a shudder. She rarely passed up an opportunity to remind me of my impending doom. "Thanks, Mawmaw. I think I've come to an understanding with The Nameless. I know what I have to do," I said.

She nodded, placing a large, spindly hand on my shoulder, her distended fingers wrapping around it. She regarded me for a moment, then smiled. "Very good. I'll leave you to your charges."

She turned and headed back, and I breathed a sigh of relief. Mawmaw didn't know about the strangers, so that bought me time. Time to think. To plan. They represented something new. A new variable in a mostly unchanging landscape. This might be something I could use, but it might also be better to turn them over to buy myself more time for a more solid plan. I needed to think things through before I could act. I couldn't afford a misstep. Not now. I went back to see Babette. She was in the shack we shared a short distance from the main structure. It was a simple, one room thing, but no other family came there. It was ours.

She smiled as I walked in. "You're early."

I shrugged. "There's news,"

She frowned, cocking her head to the side. "There's never news. How is there news?"

"Something new happened. Three outsiders are in the catacombs. Got trapped by one of the cave-ins."

"But that means Mawmaw will know and–" Babette jumped in.

I shook my head. "Already talked to her. Said it was the sacrifices."

"You lied to her?" she asked, her eyes wide.

I nodded. "They've got some skills, Babette. For them to get into the tunnels in the first place means serious skills. Don't know what they can do in particular, but they know about The Nameless. Came here specifically because of 'em from what it sounds like."

"They want to take them from us?" she asked. "More power to 'em."

I shook my head. "Seems like they feel a certain kinda way about 'em and what they represent. Sounds like they're lookin' for a permanent type solution," I explained.

"Permanent? Can The Nameless even die?" she asked, concern writ large on her face.

I shrugged. "No idea. But folks like that don't show up without a plan, I don't think. Maybe they can help us?"

Babette sat very still for a long moment, worry playing across her features. "What if they fail? What if these outsiders got a plan that turns out to be nothin' but smoke and mirrors?" she asked.

"I don't know. But I know I'm running out of time. I can see it in Mawmaw's face every time she sees me. Like she's surprised I'm still me. The thing is growing. It's getting stronger. Soon It's gonna come," I said.

She touched my face. "Then we have to try, right? We have to do what we can."

I waited until nightfall before I returned to the tunnels. Night and day don't mean much once you're under, but I didn't need prying eyes to see me deviating from my regular schedule. I took the twists and turns with ease and arrived at the peephole to the chamber.

"You still there?" I asked.

"We considered heading to our other timeshare, but this one seemed so accommodating. We're trapped, of course we're still here," Bishop replied, then took a breath. "Sorry. It's been a frustrating kind of day. Let's start over. I'm Jason Bishop. These are my friends: Ava Dufrense and Antione Frye–"

"Nero," Nero's voice interjected. "Only my mama calls me Antione, sugah."

"Right. Sorry. He's Nero. And you're David LeBlanc. And this is still Ava," he said.

I heard a hiss from inside the chamber.

"What?" I asked.

"Sweetie, you in danger," Nero said before I heard Bishop and Ava trying to shush him. "What, he is? Poor baby deserves to know."

"You're talking about The Nameless inside me? I know." I said.

"He already does. He told us the first time he was here," Ava said. "You really need to pay attention."

"I'm not sure any of y'all do. That beastie has been strengthened. I can feel all sorts of strange energy workin' around it, binding' it and growin' it big an' strong."

"Yeah, that figures. It's like I've got a tickin' time-bomb inside my guts that's gonna burst out and kill everyone around it at any moment," I said flatly.

"Well, that's good. Mostly accurate from what I gathered," Nero said. "What? He deserves to know the truth! I was afraid it was gonna be all 'I've been blessed' and I was gonna have to be all 'Oh bless your sweet heart'. We all know how those talks play out. Way better for tall, dark, and handsome here to have his eyes open."

Bishop sighed. "So it's not some portion of the creature that was pulled through like the rest of them?" Bishop asked.

"Don't feel that way," Nero said. "More like somethin' that was born of a twisted mixture of the spiritual energies from the Outside an' good ol fashioned black magic here in the bayou."

"Can you feel it? Talk to it?" Bishop asked.

"Yeah," I said.

"What does it...say? What does it want?" he asked.

"It's hungry. All the time. It hates the light, but craves it too. Like It wants to eat it. Where It comes from It doesn't have any."

"Any light?" Ava asked.

"Yeah," I replied.

Bishop's face appeared at the peephole, looking out at me. He looked real hard, then cursed. "It's close to the surface. You can probably change one, maybe two more times before it takes over and you don't change back."

"Change?" I asked.

He sat still for a moment, weighing something in his mind, then nodded. "Yeah. Change. Take on the form of the Outsider. Of the...Nameless, you call them. That's something you do, isn't it?"

"No."

He frowned, then shook his head. "Your aura doesn't lie, David. You've done it. Multiple times," he said.

I thought back to all of those sessions with Mawmaw where I'd leave feeling lightheaded. Dizzy. My heart sank. "I think maybe I did, but not on purpose."

"Okay, that's worse. You see how that's worse, honey?" Nero said.

"When?" Bishop asked.

"Lots of times. Mawmaw said she was helping me grow my connection with it. To help me understand it."

"She was strengthening it. Acclimating it to our world," Bishop said.

"I've never even heard of one of the things beyond reality making it this far," Ava said. "The ones in these tunnels may be what brought us here, but they're nothing like this, are they?"

"No," Bishop said. "Those are just reflections from the other side of the border. Sort of a shadow cast that the things can puppet from the Outside. This? This is much different. I don't know what one of these things would do to reality if it were untethered from a human host."

"Not one," I corrected. "Mawmaw wants to bring over tons of 'em. Already has plans for the ones down here in the tunnels. I think she intends to bring 'em through once I hatch."

"You're taking this really well," Ava commented. "I think I'd have a bit of a panic."

"That won't help anything. I've known about a lot of this for better than ten years now. Lived with this thing inside me. Listened to It whisper in my mind–"

"Sweet baby Jesus. It talks to him," Nero lamented.

Bishop paused, then waggled his hand back and forth. "Kinda. I'd guess it's mostly impressions. Emotions. I don't think they talk or think in a way that we could really describe. And I don't think they're evil. I think they're just very alien."

"All due respect, but doesn't seem much different when the end result is gettin' torn apart," I observed

There was silence from the trio.

"I brought you some food. Mostly some bread, fruits, and veggies that I scrounged up after supper. I don't think you really want the stew," I said.

"Long pork?" Ava asked.

"We don't dress it up that fancy, ma'am. We just straight say we're eatin' people. I think cousin Beuford was on the menu tonight."

"I'm in hell," Nero whispered.

"Not quite," Ava replied "But this certainly feels like a suburb."

Chapter Five

I sat silently while the three outsiders ate their non-cannibalistic meal and drank all the water I brought for them. Folk don't tend to think about how thirsty a body gets, especially when they're under stress. Those three were plenty stressed, and with good reason.

This was the first time I'd gotten a good look at them and wasn't quite sure what to make other than they looked lost because they were **not** dressed for what they were doing.

I was surprised to see that Jason Bishop was a white guy. Probably in his 30s? Dark blond hair and light eyes that I couldn't quite make out in the dim light. He was wearing some sort of black coat that came down to his upper thighs, a button-up white shirt, and jeans, and had a backpack lying near him.

Ava Dufrense was a white lady, probably four or five inches shorter than Bishop. She was thin and wearing a loose fitting t-shirt and blue jeans.

Then there was Nero.

Nero looked to be about the same height as Bishop but somehow gave the impression he was shorter. He was a light skinned black man with a clean shaved head, and was wearing a long, unbuttoned red silk shirt with a white t-shirt underneath over a pair of blue linen pants.

Every item of clothing any of them was wearing had been thoroughly stained beyond hope of redemption.

Not one of them was the type we normally saw in the swamp.

"Okay. Okay," Bishop said. "This is a much different situation than we thought it was. We've got to eliminate the things in here, and do something about the one inside of Dave."

I'd spent my whole life as Davie, child, boy, or David. "Dave?" I said.

"Yeah?" he asked.

"Nothing. Nothing. Yeah. Dave," I said. It felt like a new name opened the door to the possibility of a new me. Like just that little change from David to Dave could help turn the page on the horrorshow that my life had been up to this point. "I'd–I'd appreciate that, Sir–I mean Bishop. But when we go, I got–we have to take Babette."

"We'll need to deal with that when we come to it, but the priority is dealing with these things, Dave."

"Hold up and pause just one second. Who in the blue hell is Babette? She one o' these cousin eatin' relations of yours?" Nero asked.

"She's...she's different," I said. "She's not like the others. Not like what Mawmaw wants us to be. She's nice to me."

I could hear Nero draw breath but Ava stepped in "Right. Babette. You lead us to her and we'll see that she makes it out safe."

"Then we have a deal. What do you need me to do?" I asked.

Bishop pushed a note through the peephole. "I need these supplies and I need you to be in here with us. We'll need about four hours for the binding ritual to take effect, so we need a time that other LeBlancs and the nightmares wandering this labyrinth won't bother us. It's going to be very delicate," he said.

I nodded, looking over the list. "I can get these, I think," I said.

"You can read that?" Nero asked.

"Yes."

"In this light?" he pressed.

I looked around at the dim light. "Side effect from the Nameless, I suspect," I said.

"How are you so calm about this?" Nero demanded

I paused, thinking for a moment. "Will panicking help the situation?" I asked.

"Well, no, but–" Nero replied.

"Not 'no but'. I didn't think it would help the situation. I'm not thinkin' about what's goin' on inside me or what that might mean. I know that to stop the terrible thing from happening, I need t' focus, and I need to take certain steps. Panicking just makes the bad thing happenin' more likely," I explained.

"Practical. I like him," Ava commented.

"I should be back in a couple of hours. I think I can get the cave-in cleared. Work on the south end of the tunnel and it'll go faster," I explained. "But be careful. Once the blockage is cleared, The Nameless will be drawn to you."

"Perfect," muttered Bishop.

I moved quickly and quietly through the tunnels with my list in hand. Most of what he needed was in the pantry or the supply closet: Salt, candles, some rope, a sharp knife, sage, and lavender. I paused with the bundle, glancing toward the shack where Babette was sleeping. I thought of taking her with me but decided against it. She would be safer there and we could collect her on the way out.

I blinked, realizing this was happening. One way or another, we'd be leaving here tonight. It wouldn't be possible for me to remain if Bishop did what he said he was going to do. Mawmaw would know. It was possible she'd know if they cleared the cave-in. I started to breathe faster. I could feel her eyes on me. She knew. She always knew.

I took a deep breath to calm myself. Mawmaw wasn't omniscient. She didn't know everything. She couldn't.

If she did, all of this was pointless. I just couldn't accept that.

An hour later I found myself lying in the middle of a salt circle on the muddy floor of the prison chamber that had contained Nero, Bishop, and Ava. They had managed to clear most of the cave-in before I got back, and I was able to lower a shoulder and barrel through the remainder.

Bishop was burning the sage above my head, and the lavender below my feet, and was speaking in another language. Latin, maybe? I'm not sure. He'd cut his hand and drawn symbols on my skin, which felt like they were getting warmer as he spoke.

Ava was standing in the doorway while Nero was seated between me and the door with his eyes closed. He was straining, his face screwed up with effort. "Sugah, they definitely know somethin's up. Keepin' them uninterested ain't easy," Nero said, his voice clearly strained. "They're pushin' back hard, Bishop!""He can't talk right now, Nero," Ava reminded him. She waited, patiently staring out into the dark tunnel, offering to serve as a slender dam against the onrushing flood of darkness that was going to find us.

The cadence of the Latin (?) changed, taking on a slower intonation. Bishop's voice dropped an octave or two and a strange resonance began to play about at the edges of it. Air swirled in a place that had never felt the touch of a breeze and from all throughout the tunnels, inhuman throats howled in hunger and fury.

"Aw, hell. Now you really pissed 'em off," Nero muttered.

"Leave it to Bishop," Ava said with a shake of her head.

The symbols Bishop had drawn on me flared to life, radiating a bright red light. The burning was horrific and I had to clench my jaw against the pain. It felt like a thousand hot daggers were being driven into each place a sigil had been drawn: my forehead, my heart, my hands, and my feet. I held back a strangled scream.

"Stay in the circle, Dave," Ava said, encouraging me.

I tried to reply but all I could do was make a low choking sound. The sigils served as ports of entry and that same burning feeling from them spread throughout my body. I watched in horror as lumps slid under my skin, pushing it and traveling like thousands of bubbles, rippling their way under its surface. There was no fighting this. No resisting it.

I threw my head back and screamed in primal agony.

"Fuuuuuuuuuuck," Nero replied.

Ava set her jaw and turned to fully face the tunnel. "Yup, that'll do it," she said..

I wanted to beg Bishop to stop. Tell him I couldn't take any more, but I couldn't make the words form in my mouth. My throat was outside of conscious control. My eyes bulged and tears flowed freely from them. With all the depravity and all the torments heaped upon me by my family, I thought there was nothing left that could surprise me.

I was wrong.

The Nameless inside me started bucking. The ritual was having an effect on It. One that It didn't appreciate. I could feel It surge toward the surface of my skin, trying to force Its way out, to emerge from my body like a hatchling from a shell so It could take Its place in the world. Six times It surged forward, stretching my skin, pressing Its hands against it, making their outlines clearly visible, pressing Its alien, insectoid face against it, distending Its jaw in Its need to gnaw Its way out. And six times the roiling fire beneath my flesh repelled It. The Thing was frantic in Its desperation. Its need. It vented Its fury in my mind, attempting to assail my psyche with Its pure malice and hatred, but there was no room for anything beyond the agony that was drowning me.

"Ava, behind us. The thing in Dave is trying to force its way out," Nero warned

"One catastrophe at a time, please," Ava replied in a singsong voice. "The other guests have found the chamber."

Through my haze of pain, I saw shadows roiling at the end of the tunnel. The wave of blackness surged like the tide, promising to sweep away anything in its path.

"Well," Nero said. "Fuck me."

Chapter Six

I could feel the fire inside me constricting. It started to sink deeper into my body, seeping into muscles, ligaments, organs, and bones as it made a slow and unstoppable journey to my center. I know I was screaming. No, that wasn't the right word. I know I howled like the wounded animal I was. The fire inside of me eclipsed every other thought. Every other consideration. At first, I was afraid I would die, but as the pain sank deeper I started to worry that I might not. That I might have to live like this forever.

But for each bit that the fire constricted inside of me, The Nameless was forced back. Driven away from my skin. Driven back into my depths.

"Ava?" I could hear Nero's voice, filled with worry.

"I've got this. Shift your focus, there's no point in trying to keep us hidden from them now. Either hit at them or help the boys," she said, then I heard her run from the room, charging down the tunnel.

"Ava, no!" Nero called after her.

Another surge of pain lanced through my nerves as The Nameless surged once again, focusing all Its strength, all of Its fury on one point, trying to cause a break in the slowly constricting perimeter of agony that was seeking to bind It. I raged against the barrier in desperation. Our connection grew thinner as It moved away from me metaphysically. I heard Bishop's voice echoing through the room, low and guttural, as if the words I heard weren't so much spoken as forced from his tongue against the will of his body. It sounded inhuman. Given everything I knew about my family, it very likely was.

And still, the perimeter constricted. I arched my back in pain, trying and failing to control my limbs as I writhed in agony in the mud. Sweat poured from me. I was short of breath. My throat was ragged and my voice hoarse. I think I begged Bishop to stop. I know I wanted to. Whether or not I did, and whether or not he heard me, he did not stop.

Tears flowed freely down my cheeks as I clenched my eyes against the never-ending and limitless pain that was now the totality of my existence.

And then it wasn't.

The pain stopped.

I could hear the sound of struggle down the hallway and forced my eyes open. I could dimly see Ava standing like a willow tree in the middle of the tunnel. A willow tree that bent, but never broke, and was somehow holding back the tide of darkness attempting to surge over her. She danced around the blows, this way and that moments before one of the surges of blackness made contact with her, at which point she countered, lashing out with one of her fists. Each time a fist struck, the rings on her fingers would flash with a reddish light, driving the creatures back and buying her precious space and time.

And then they surged forward and the dance continued.

"She needs help," I croaked.

Nero stood at the entrance to the tunnel, leaning hard against the wall I barreled through hours before. His eyes were open but glazed over, and he held a hand out in the direction of the conflict.

"Your six," I heard him mutter quietly. A split second later, Ava spun, holding out her hand and connecting with another surge of the darkness with the back of her hand.

"Go low," he whispered.

Ava crouched and shot her left arm up above her head, sending sparks flashing through the muddy tunnel as she drove her hand deep into the swell of darkness that had attempted to overwhelm her.

Unused to resistance, much less prey that could cause them pain, the Nameless in the tunnels retreated, moving back away from Ava and congregating near the curve in the hallway. Ava came to her feet and placed a hand on the tunnel wall for balance. The woman's breath was coming heavy and she had cuts and scratches all along her arms, legs, and face, souvenirs of instances where she hadn't quite managed to get completely clear.

I painfully came to my feet and looked down. The symbols Bishop had painted on me were gone, and for the first time in over a decade, I couldn't hear the Nameless inside of me.

"You killed it?" I asked, a smile creeping onto my face. "It's gone? Is it really gone?"

Bishop was on his hands and knees, slowly coming to his feet. He was pale, his eyes sunken. Like someone who hasn't eaten in too long. He smiled bitterly and shook his head.

"Gone? No, 'fraid not. You've got a hitchhiker for life, Dave. It's bound, so you won't have to worry about it getting loose unless someone does it on purpose."

"On purpose?" I asked.

He nodded. "Yeah. Someone with the right sort of know-how and the wrong sort of intentions could probably cut it loose again."

"And then?" I asked.

"Then it hatches out of you like a bird out of an egg shell," he replied flatly. "Hello Nameless and bye bye David. The thing inside you then goes on a tour and tries to eat all the energy in our reality, growing as it does. Fifty-fifty if anyone can stop it before it does the job. I'll be honest, I hate those odds."

I nodded. "Then why help me? Why not just finish me?" I asked. "I was helpless when you were performing that ritual. It would have been easy. Probably the smart thing to do."

Bishop's eyes locked with mine for a long moment and suddenly I knew.

"You almost did, didn't you? Right when the fire started moving inward. You could have burned me alive and burned both me and that thing out of reality," I said.

"Not exactly," Bishop said, "but honestly, yeah, that's not too far off."

"Bishop!" Nero said, his voice shocked. "You never said anything about that to us!"

"I wasn't in the mood for a moral or ethical debate. A call needed to be made, so I made it," Bishop snapped back.

"But you didn't," Ava pointed out. "The pragmatic thing would have been to kill him."

"Ava!" Nero gasped, holding his hand to his heart.

"What? Dave agrees with me, don't you?" she asked.

I nodded. "Yes ma'am. I had no idea the thing inside me was so danger-ous. If I had, I'd have done myself in years ago."

"But Bishop didn't do it. You decided to do the good guy thing and give Dave a chance. Do the whole 'hope and faith' thing," Ava said, talking to Bishop.

He nodded. "We don't need to get into–"

"Going soft?" Ava asked, pressing.

Bishop looked over and glared at her. "You tell me."

The air in the tunnel was thick and tense as the pair stared one another down.

"Here we go again," Nero sighed. "Might I remind you lovelies that we got a wall o' evil darkness waitin' to make a meal out o' the four of us right at the end of this tunnel? Ain't no kinda need for you two be helpin' 'em along now."

"No," Ava said. "But I–we need to know why. The Bishop I know doesn't take any bet but a sure thing and stacks the deck in his favor to make sure. Is that still who you are?"

Bishop looked at her for a long time and shrugged. "When I need to be."

"When you need to be? What sort of bullshit answer is that?" Ava demanded.

"The truth. I'll do what I have to do when I need to, but right now, we're dealing with God knows how many LeBlancs, a labyrinth full of shad-ow monsters, and whatever the fuck his Mawmaw is, which I'm positive doesn't qualify as human. So I thought it would be good to have a bit more help, and I made some adjustments," Bishop snapped back.

Everyone was quiet for a moment.

"What did you do to me?" I whispered, a sense of dread spreading in my gut.

Bishop pursed his lips. "I rearranged some of the terms of your pact. You're pulling energy out of the outsider now."

"The Nameless," I corrected.

"Sugah, if you *always* call it the Nameless, don't that make it its name?" Nero asked.

I opened my mouth, realized I didn't have an answer, and closed it again with a shrug.

"Bishop. What did you do to me?" I repeated, feeling my anger building.

"Gave you an advantage," he said.

"What did you do?" I demanded, forcing volume out of my raw throat. "Stop dancing around the question and answer straight."

"Sugah, you came to the wrong man for that ask," Nero muttered.

Bishop glared at him, then sighed. "Fine. Yes, I bound the Nameless inside of you, but I also Named it."

"What now?" Nero asked.

Ava shook her head "He used some really old rites to give it a True Name. That means it's something that this reality can accept since it belongs here and isn't just a bubble of wrongness. That's...a choice."

"Why, what's wrong with it?" I asked.

"True Names are used to control things. I used it to control the creature inside of you. You can too. If you think the Name and give it a command, you can make it do things," Bishop said.

"What kind of things?" I asked, frowning.

"It can make you stronger, faster, tougher, heal you. You can even assume its shape for short periods of time," he said.

I just stared at him.

"I don't know what being in that sort of alien physiology would do to you over the long term, but for short bursts, it should be fine. You'll just need to be careful. I'll write the Name down for you, but after I do, you should memorize it and destroy it. You don't want anyone to have that sort of power over you," Bishop explained.

"You've made me into a monster," I whispered.

Now it was Bishop's turn to just look at me.

"You made me into a monster! You were supposed to help me, not make it worse!" I roared, grabbing the smaller man by his shirt and slamming him up against the muddy wall. His head slid along the ceiling before I wedged him into the corner.

"Dave, think long and hard about the next thing you do," Ava warned. Her voice was eerily calm.

For his part, Bishop simply looked at me like I was a science experiment. Like he wanted to know what I'd do next, but only in a sort of academic sense.

"You were already a monster," he said, looking me in the eye. "I just set it up so it would be useful to you."

"Useful to *you*, you mean," I corrected. "You want to use me to get out of here, just like you said."

"Which is what you wanted anyway," Bishop replied. "I don't see this as anything but a win for you."

"You wouldn't," I muttered, then dropped him.

I stood there silently for a long time, closing my eyes and breathing. I could feel the sweat running down my flesh. The itch inside me where it felt like I'd been burned, and deep down, I could swear I could feel a small ball of dark anger holding a malevolent creature from outside our reality.

I sighed.

"Fine. Give me the Name and tell me what we have to do."

Chapter Seven

Bishop explained his plan.

I hated it. Ava hated it. Nero really hated it.

None of us had any better ideas on how to deal with all the problems that were laid out before us. With daylight fast approaching, all four of us were physically and mentally tired, and we had a long way to go before any of us were safe.

Nero went back to work hiding us from The Nameless as best he could. They'd vanished from the corner at some point after their attempted attack. I guess food that fought back wasn't really what they'd signed up for.

I took the lead as we wound our way through the tunnels, slowly coming up out of the muck and into the dryer ground under the house. My limbs were rubbery from the ordeal I'd gone through, so I had to concentrate, placing one foot in front of the other for every step. Willing myself to stay in motion.

We reached the trapdoor nearest the house and I paused, taking a breath.

"We don't have a lot of time to kill, Dave," Bishop prodded.

I nodded. "I need to get into position and get to work. It'll be up to you to get everyone into place," Bishop said.

I nodded again.

"If you're not up to this, tell us now. We can't be sitting around waiting for things to happen if you're not. We need you to tell us now," he prodded.

"I'm fine," I growled.

He stared at me again, holding me in place with that same calculating gaze, then nodded. "Be careful," he said before opening the door and moving overland back the way we came.

"It's a bit late for that, sugah," Nero observed.

The three of us crept out of the trapdoor and onto the hill that the LeBlanc plantation house stood on in the predawn hour. The torches the family kept to mark the path flickered lazily in the boggy, humid night air. Clouds had rolled in while we were underground, masking the light that the moon or stars might have offered through the tree canopy, making it feel like the dark from the swamp was reaching out to surround us. Like The Nameless in the tunnels had tried to do.

I swallowed, looking around me, certain that someone was watching. I could feel eyes on us. Knew this whole plan was doomed to end in disaster. I turned back to tell Ava and Nero we had to stop. To rethink things.

Then I didn't. I closed my eyes and took a breath, then willed myself to take the next step. Then the next. Each one was more terrifying than the one before. I knew in my bones that each step was one step closer to not just death, but to oblivion. My soul would be devoured by the Nameless and I would be cast into nothingness.

I smiled grimly. At least it couldn't possibly hurt more than the binding ritual from earlier.

We walked along the damp path to the house. The normal, ambient noises from the bayou were quiet tonight.

No, not quiet. They were missing.

I slowed my pace.

"Something's wrong," I whispered.

"Honey, I got a list," Nero hissed back.

"What?" Ava asked. "What's wrong, Dave?"

"It's never this quiet," I whispered. "There's something strange happening."

"So you're sayin' the front door is probably a bad idea?" Nero asked.

I nodded, then changed our path, moving to the door for the east wing of the plantation house.

"This area is rarely visited by the family, used mostly to house some of the more physically degenerate relations," I whispered as we approached.

"Why does that not sound better?" Nero asked.

"They're barely human. Their appetites are closer to The Nameless or other things from the outside than they are to regular folk," I explained.

"So very much not better," Nero amended.

"We move quickly and quietly, get to the boiler, then get out," Ava said.

We arrived at the entrance to the east wing. The white siding was lousy with moss and lichen, the awning drooped overhead, and the wooden support posts' paint was flaked and covered with a thin layer of green slime.

The door stood in front of me, its once-red paint as heavily flaked and pitted as the posts that stood silent vigil in front of it. I reached for the tarnished doorknob, turned it, then pushed the door open. The loud creek from the old, seldom-used hinges screeched through the still of the night like an angry bird, drawing flinches from me and the two people with me. Companions? Friends? I wasn't sure what any of us qualified as with each other.

We had a common enemy, and for now, that would have to be enough.

The gaslight wall sconces flickered as we entered the hallway. Covered with carpeting so moldy you could no longer determine its original color, the hallway stretched almost a hundred feet straight ahead before it ended at a "T" intersection. Immediately to our right, a set of stairs ascended to the second floor, and along the hallway in front of us, doors were spaced every ten feet on either side, breaking up the once beautiful wallpaper that had fallen to rot and decay decades ago.

I held my breath, straining to hear if the door's opening had alerted any of the residents to our presence.

There was a scratching sound coming from the second door to our right. Like someone gnawing at the ridges on the interior of the door.

"Termites?" Nero whispered.

I shook my head.

"Please lie and say they're termites?" Nero said.

"They're the Discarded. The things I told you about earlier," I said.

"You said they were physically degenerate," Ava said. "What exactly are we talking about here, Dave?"

I crept forward, freezing each time my foot came down on a creaky floorboard.

"Some of the Discarded are just severe birth defects. But there are others that are different. There have been times that the family tried to bond with things from the other side," I whispered as we moved.

"Like with you?" Ava asked.

I nodded. "I think so. Up till me the results always went wrong. Some just died. Others...changed. They warped until they no longer resemble anything human. It hurts your eyes and your head to even look at them."

"Note: Nero, you will keep your brain to yourself," Nero whispered.

"What do you mean?" Ava asked me.

"Something about those Discarded is just wrong. I don't have a better word for it. They don't belong here, and you know it when you see them. Your brain refuses to accept what you're seeing. It can't cope with the fact of the things in front of you. Mawmaw likes to use 'em as punishment when one of the family does something she really doesn't like. Just puts 'em in a room with the Discarded chained to the opposite wall. Some time during the punishment, their mind won't be able to take the strain any longer. It'll just break," I said.

"Sweet baby Jesus," Nero whispered.

"And they're in here? Loose?" Ava asked

I nodded. "Mostly on the upper floor," I said. "But they ain't restrained. There'll be a big door at the end of this hall and to the right. They can't go past it, but they've got the run of this wing."

"How many are there?" she asked.

"Can't say. Since no one can look at 'em, doing a headcount would be tricky, and they're not above tearin' into each other if they get hungry or mad enough," I replied. "I'd guess more than three, not more than six."

She nodded, her jaw tense and her eyes tight.

We crept forward, pausing every few steps to strain our ears against the silence. Straining our eyes to see if the flicker of gaslight was a prelude to something worse.

Halfway down the hall, the door three ahead of us and on the left slowly creaked open. A long, pale arm reached from the knob on the inside down to the floor, where it intersected with a knobbly jointed shoulder. A matching arm to the first reached out and clawed at the floor, dragging the rest of the body and head into view.

It was the stuff of nightmares. A fever dream made flesh.

The creature's head was misshapen, with lumps and divots in places no human head should have them. Long, greasy, stringy hair clung to the scalp and sides of its face, which had no eyes and a distended mouth filled with row upon row of needle-like teeth. It dragged itself forward, sniffing at the air, its mouth open and its tongue lapping at the air. As it came further into view, we saw that its torso ended in a trio of tentacles where a human would have their legs. They flailed behind it, leaving a damp trail in their wake.

Nero gasped, clamping both hands over his mouth as his eyes went wide.

Its head snapped toward the sound and it paused, propping itself up on both arms in the middle of the hall, sniffing the air.

We all froze, not daring to breathe.

It scented the air once more, then dragged itself further, moving in our general direction, sniffing as it went.

I swallowed, praying it would lose us in the general stink of the place.

Then it opened its nightmarish mouth and screamed, lurching toward us.

Chapter Eight

The scream was inhuman. Not a surprise considering the source. It had the feel of a bat with a high-pitched wail that went up beyond the human range of hearing, but you could feel in your gut. It sent shivers down all our spines and froze us to the spot.

The monstrosity came at us, its mouth wide, and hands reaching. It closed to within fifteen feet. Then ten. Then five.

I felt a small hand grab the back of my shirt and pull me hard, sending me toppling backward as Ava stepped between me and the Discarded, then danced to the side as it swiped at the place she was standing moments before. She moved back and stomped on one of the tentacles trailing behind it, drawing a different sort of scream from its throat as the tentacles flailed in agitation, flinging their slime everywhere.

I struggled to my feet and saw Nero, his face contorted in concentration once again.

"Nero?" I asked.

"Bzzzzzz!" he said, waving his hand at me. "Doin' what I can to make us as uninteresting as possible to anyone who might be otherwise inclined"

"But the Discarded," I started.

"Broadcasting, not receiving," Nero said. "Nero should be just peachy, sugah."

With a nod I took another deep breath, steeled myself, and willed myself forward. Ava had moved to the left side of the creature and was delivering a severe beating, slipping around its claw swipes and delivering punishing punches and kicks to its head and body. I slowed, as she showed she had things more than under control.

Or so I thought.

As she darted back from a claw swipe, one of the tentacles swung up and smacked her across her shoulder. With a hiss she took two steps away, then stumbled, falling to her knees, clutching the red welt that had already formed at the point of contact. A second later, she toppled onto her side.

"Ava!"

Someone shouted as I ran forward.

It was me. I shouted. And now I stood in front of the creature as it had begun to turn toward her prone form. I threw my shoulder into its face, barrelling us both over and carrying us away from her. I landed with my full weight on its pale, sickly body, driving the breath from its lungs. Its long, clawed hands dug deep into the flesh in my back, drawing a roar from me. I grabbed it by its throat with my left hand and started to squeeze as I raised my right fist and brought it down on the thing's face with bone-crushing force. Again. And again. And again. It was like hitting concrete.

It brought its left hand up and grabbed my right arm in a vice-like grip, then pulled. It was shockingly strong. It yanked me off-balance and more fully on top of it, then sank its needle teeth into my shoulder.

I hissed, taken by surprise by the pain. I squeezed harder, trying to choke the life out of it, but it was taking far too long. I felt the tentacles slap against my back over and over, and pushed off, trying to break the jaw's hold on my flesh before the paralysis that gripped Ava took hold of me as well. I felt flesh tear, then a shower of teeth as I yanked myself free with a growl. Dizzy from either the pain or whatever was on its tentacles, I surged forward, grabbed it by its chin and the back of its head, and savagely wrenched it to the side.

There was a sound like a thick branch breaking, then the creature slumped to the ground, one of the tentacles slowly twitching behind me. I gulped air, trying to will my heart rate back to normal.

"Dave, Ava?" Nero whispered. "Something's coming."

I could hear my heartbeat. My frantic breathing. I closed my eyes and focused.

Nothing.

Until I heard footsteps coming from upstairs, moving with no regular pattern.

"Fuck," I muttered. Ava still wasn't moving. I could see her chest rise and fall, but whatever toxin that coated the thing's tentacles seemed to have hit her hard. "Okay, Nero, you need to get Ava out of here. Go meet Bishop."

"Nero ain't a pack mule, sugah," he protested. "And you need me to keep people off you while you do the deed."

"All of that screaming sorta killed that idea. I'll get to the boiler room and do what needs to be done. You two are just going to slow me down now. You both need to go," I said.

The thumping continued, moving in short, skittering bursts, then pausing for a long moment, then skittering forward. Every time I heard the movement, my heart sped up again.

Nero looked up at the noises, his eyes wide. "Yeah. Yeah, I can do that, sugah," he said. "You be safe. Well. Safe as you can."

"Probably not," I said, offering a weak smile, as I turned and picked up Ava, carrying her to the door. "You close this and get clear."

Ava tried to protest, her voice coming out in a weak wheeze. She shook her head loosely.

"Yeah. We'll see you soon, right?" Nero asked.

I didn't answer, turning and re-entering the east wing. The arrhythmic footsteps from upstairs were getting closer to the stairs one short burst at a time. There was some sort of gibbering noise that was just now moving close enough to hear that did unpleasant things to my brain, scattering thoughts and robbing me of my ability to concentrate.

I focused on the job at hand. On the stakes. On Babette. On my new friends.

Yes, even Bishop.

I moved forward, ignoring my previous thoughts of stealth and running the length of the hallway. From upstairs, the Discarded howled, and skittered forward. I could hear it moving, its inhuman limbs sounded like they were on the ceiling or walls instead of the floor. I didn't turn to check. My long strides ate the distance to the intersection up ahead, the rubbery feeling chased away by my terror of the thing behind me.

The thing that was getting closer by the second. I reached the corpse of the creature that we'd fought moments before and heard the Discarded reach the bottom of the stairs, and knew from the sound it was on the ceiling. I risked a glance over my shoulder to gauge the distance.

Horrible mistake.

The thing closing on me was like nothing I'd ever seen and I pray I never see it again. Its horrific form seared its way into my brain and my mind refused to process what I was seeing. A mass of flesh with a long tongue or tube with multiple appendages jutting out in a variety of directions. But not really. I had the impression of barbs and claws, but again, not really. As my brain tried to process the paradox attempting to devour me, I promptly tripped over one of the tentacles of the dead Discarded.

I fell hard to the soggy, moldy carpet, skidding in the mucus trail it had left behind, and heard a cacophony of howls move without explanation from the ceiling to the floor. I scrambled, slipping on the carpet as I fought to regain my footing. The mind-numbing noise continued, getting closer by the instant until a surge of pure panic gave my limbs the coordination they'd been lacking. I regained my feet and sprinted for the door sequestering this wing from the rest of the house.

I ran with an eldritch piece of insanity in hot pursuit. I could feel its presence on my back as I ran, my very flesh recoiling from the unnatural wrongness of the creature. The part of my brain that wasn't in full-blown flight mode was very creatively cursing every ancestor in my family who thought these things were ever a good idea. I was steps ahead of the thing as I hit the wall at the T and bounced to the right a moment before it slammed into that same space. I reached the door and frantically pushed it open, falling through into the main house and kicking it closed behind me as I lay on the ground, eyes closed and panting.

Chapter Nine

I lay on the floor of the main house of the LeBlanc Plantation and breathed for a moment. I had expected the Discarded to try the door. To hit it, attack it. Maybe even just try to open it.

Nothing.

The door was eerily silent.

I slowly came to my feet, leaning heavily on the wall. Dragging my feet forward, I lurched toward the back of the house. Toward the stairs down to the cellar. Toward the storage. Toward my goal. The pre-dawn hours in the LeBlanc house saw most of the family under the same roof and asleep. I'd been worried about the noise from the east wing bringing someone to investigate, but it was a common enough occurrence that it wasn't a guarantee, and for the first time that night luck was on my side. The house had that feeling that only homes with multiple heavily sleeping people can project. A sort of quiet and fitful waiting. As if any noise will tear them all from their slumber and propel them into action to find the cause.

Or maybe that's just the sort of place I grew up. I don't really have a lot to compare it to.

I slid along the wall, leaving a trail of blood on the well-worn path toward the kitchen, staining the old, orangish-yellow wallpaper and obscuring some of their sunflowers. Just before I reached the heart of the house, I stopped, putting my back to the wall, and reached out a tired arm, twisting the knob and pulling the basement door open. The stairs down below were thin, old, and made of wood. The smell of mildew and wood rot had settled like a miasma. It seems that blood magic, sacrifices, and rites will only go so far in keeping the all-encroaching water of the bayou at bay.

I closed the door behind me and started down, shakily leaning on the railing as I descended. The basement and storage area was dark, dimly lit by the fire from the boiler in the far left corner.

My target.

I dragged myself forward, eyes locked on the massive boiler, its pilot light glowing under its squat, ugly form. It brought back memories from my childhood. From before Mawmaw had stuffed this thing down my gullet. Of times when my father showed me how to maintain the boiler. How to keep the pressure from building. To ease it off a little at a time so things never got too bad.

I looked at the valves, the lessons flooding back, and I wearily reached up and started twisting knobs, shutting off pressure releases, turning up the heat on the flame, disabling the safety mechanisms that would shut it down in case the worst happened.

Taking a step back, I looked at my handiwork and sobbed silently. It was almost over.

I searched around in the dim light and located what I needed. Picking up the wrench, I started hitting the knobs that would undo the reaction I'd set in motion. It didn't take long. It was old, tired, and rotten. Why wouldn't it be?

I peered at the pressure valve and saw it steadily climbing into the red. I nodded, satisfied.

"David, what have you done?" a voice behind me whispered.

I turned to see who it was, and my heart dropped. My father was at the bottom of the stairs, his eyes wide and a shotgun in his hands.

"It's over Paw. Done. This family's been a blight on the swamp since we got here. Time to wipe the slate clean."

The old man looked at me, and for the first time in a very long time, I looked at him. Really looked at him. He was shorter than me, and thinner. No, not thinner than me. Just thin. Like he'd been diminished. His once-thick hair was mostly gone, and that which remained clinging to the sides of his head was solidly grey.

"David, we're your family. After all we've done for you? How could you be so selfish?" he asked.

"Selfish? I've never gotten to live one moment of my life for myself! Not one! From the time I was born, right up to the point where you let Mawmaw put that thing inside me. That monster. The thing that was always intended to kill me–" I spat back, then stopped as he looked away. "You knew. You knew what she was going to do. To me. To your son. How could you?""Davie, you have to understand," he said.

"Did Ma know?" I asked, tears forming at the corners of my eyes.

"Davie, there are things you have to–" he said.

"Did. Ma. Know?" I asked. Enunciating each word.

He looked at his feet. "You have to understand the position we were in," he said.

I closed my eyes, then shook my head "I don't," I said, and started walking for the stairs. Every fiber of my body hurt from head to toe. I was bleeding, probably badly. I was exhausted from the binding from earlier. Everything hurt, and now I had confirmed my parents' long-suspected complicity in my eventual death.

I just wanted to lie down and close my eyes. To sleep it all away.

I opened my eyes again and willed myself forward one last time, heading to the stairs.

My father stared at me as I approached, then watched me walk past him. Seeing my back seems to have given him courage. I heard the unmistakable sound of a shotgun cocking. "I can't let you do this, Davie," he said.

I slowly turned around to face him, this little man standing so close to me.

"Enough," I said, reaching out and grabbing the barrel of the shotgun and lifting it up and away from me, yanking the weapon from his hands. "I don't think I'm going to let you stop me today, Paw. I'm leaving. Now. You're more than welcome to try to undo my work down here, but unless I'm wrong, it'll blow within the hour, and there's nothing you can do to stop it."

My dad stared at me, then backpedaled, turning to look over the boiler. "No no no no no," he said, looking it over closely for the first time. "Davie, this is...wait. All we need to do is....yes."

Wave of weariness washed over me as I looked at his sight line. The pilot. The flame was partially exposed. He could extinguish it and ruin everything.

"Sorry, Dad," I whispered.

I approached my father from behind as he laid on the ground on his hands and knees. I bent down and grabbed his chin and the back of his neck, and just like with the creature in the east wing, I wrenched hard.

The snapping noise was completely different. Whereas the creature sounded like a dry, thick branch breaking, my father's neck broke with a small, wet snap that was followed by a gurgling sound. He went limp in my arms, his eyes wide and staring. I watched his chest struggle to draw breath, then fall one last time.

I sat down on the dirt floor of the basement, cradling him in my arms, and wept.

Chapter
Ten

Get Up!

Nero's voice rang out in my head, snapping me out of my near-fugue state.

Sugah, I can feel somethin' truly awful happenin' in your head right now, but you don't got that kinda time. You gotta get clear and meet up with us to finish this up. Sun's gonna be up soon.

I nodded as if he could see me, then struggled to my feet and started back up the stairs. I stood at the bottom and looked up. It was a steep, thin ascent, and it was beyond me in my current state. I tried, but the muscles in my legs were exhausted and wouldn't respond, try as I might to will them to.

So I crawled.

I don't know how long I was crying over my father after I killed him. I don't know how long it took me to crawl up those stairs, moving hand over hand, but struggling to claim each inch of progress. I reached the top of the stairs and leveraged myself up with the door knob and the railing, then stumbled into the kitchen.

The window over the sink looked out over the bayou, and from our vantage point on the hill, the sky had gone from the black of deep night to the lightning purple that signaled the approaching dawn. I was running out of time. Subtlety wasn't an option, so I walked from the kitchen directly toward the front door.

My stumbling gait had me banging off the walls, which drew my relations from their rooms like moths to flame. Each one saw me, and each one backed away upon seeing the state I was in. I held my breath, waiting for Mawmaw's inevitable appearance.

It never came.

I reached the door, swung it open, and limped into the bayou without a backward glance.

Time had lost all meaning for me, so all I could say when I stumbled to the rendezvous with Bishop, Ava, and Nero is that the sun had not yet risen. Ava was mobile again, and looked worried at the sight of me. Nero, gasped. Bishop was focused on the next step, and simply locked eyes with me.

"You good?" he asked.

I nodded.

Bishop had laid out some sort of odd geometric pattern on the ground in the dirt and gestured for me to sit on one of the attached circles. I nearly collapsed, but did as he asked, bracing for another round of torment.

Bishop held out the knife to me, then paused.

"You might as well just use the blood you're already donating," he said, gesturing at my general state of distress. "No need to make even more holes."

Nodding, I reached up to my shoulder and scraped some blood off the skin, flicking it into the pattern as he'd instructed.

Then he started chanting. This time it was in Creole, that familiar patois of English and French that cropped up amongst the swamp folk of the lower Mississippi Delta in general, and around the bayous in particular.

"Aw hell," Nero said.

Ava quickly moved to stand behind me, and Bishop's eyes moved up and went wide. Sighing, I slowly turned, knowing what I'd see.

Sadly, I was correct. Mawmaw stood at the bend in the path in all her glory. Standing over seven feet tall with pallid green skin and stringy greenish black hair, her pupil-less eyes stared out at us, and her too-large mouth stretched into a ruthless smile.

"David, you have been a very naughty little boy," she said.

I wearily came to my feet once again and took a step toward her.

"Uh uh uh," she said, holding up a long, bony finger that ended in a cruel looking claw and waggled it. "I don't think she'd appreciate what happens if you get much closer."

With her other hand, Mawmaw pulled Babette from behind her.

"No!" I shouted.

"I'm so sorry, David," Babette said.

Ava slowly stalked to Mawmaw's left flank. Nero stood very still, his face grave. Bishop moved behind me, then to Mawmaw's right. He concentrated, then hissed, rubbing his eyes.

"That's right, and that's what ya get fer tryin' ta snoop where you've no business," Mawmaw spat at him, then turned her gaze back to me.

"Now, boy, here's what we're going to do: You're little friends here will gather back behind you and lay themselves down. You'll come to me, and I'll send Babette over to them. Then I can undo the damage that this hedge wizard has done," she said, spitting the words "hedge wizard" like the most vile of curses.

"Undo?" Babette asked.

"Aye. The boy's gone and allowed The Nameless to be hogtied within him. Poor creature can't hardly move at all," Mawmaw said.

"That was kinda the point," Bishop replied.

"I'll not have any more sass from you," she shot back at him. "You and yours have done plenty of damage already.

"You don't know the half of it," Bishop said.

Mawmaw looked at him. This time very closely. "What have you done, sneakthief?"

Bishop looked over his shoulder. To the East.

"Just timed things out," he said. Then the sun crested the horizon.

Immediately, red runes appeared all throughout the hill and swamp as soon as the sun's rays touched where they stood, glowing with a sickly light, then vanishing with a flash.

"What? What have you done?" Mawmaw demanded, her long clawed hand tightening around Babette's throat.

"You spent more years than I can count using blood rituals and blood sacrifices to maintain these catacombs, reinforced 'em really well...but you wanted to make sure that whatever you had in 'em wouldn't go after you and yours, so you had one link that held all of those things together," he said as bubbles started to erupt within the swamp.

"LeBlanc blood," Ava said.

"LeBlanc blood," Bishop agreed.

Mawmaw's eyes darted here and there as the horror of what was happening dawned on her.

"All someone would need was a sample of that blood and a little bit of know-how and they could pull that lynchpin out and set the whole thing to tumbling down," Bishop said.

"It won't matter a lick in the long run," Mawmaw said. "Once I've released The Nameless inside of that boy it will emerge and take Its rightful place. I'll be rewarded. It can bring back anything we've lost!"

"You just won't let him go, will you?" Babette asked.

"Never, foolish girl. You were only ever sent to placate him. To give the blessed creature inside him time to grow. To get strong," she said, tightening her grip on the girl's neck.

There was a loud rumble from behind Mawmaw as the LeBlanc Plantation House started to fall in on itself as the tunnels collapsed beneath it. A moment later a massive explosion ripped the house to pieces, sending debris scattering in all directions and launching a black smoke plume well into the sky.

"That'd be the boiler," I said. "Shame no one was around to bleed it, huh Mawmaw?"

Her eyes were wide and her mouth agape as she stared at the ruin of centuries of work. Her grip loosened ever so slightly on Babette's throat.

The girl looked at me, smiling sadly.

"Babette?" I asked.

"You won't use me to hold him!" Babette shouted, and rammed her neck sideways into Mawmaw's terrible claws. Mawmaw's jaw dropped from complete shock and she dropped the girl.

I was there, holding her. The cut in Babette's neck was deep, and blood flowed freely, pumping out of her with each beat of her heart. She looked into my eyes and tried to speak, but the damage done to her throat was far too severe for that.

There was a deep gurgling sound, and I could see the life leave her eyes as I held her in my arms.

"No. No no no no no no no," I whispered. "You were the only good thing in my life. The only good thing. Why? Why did you have to–?" I wiped the tears from my eyes and felt myself smear her blood on my face. It was warm and sticky. I looked at it on my hands.

Something inside me snapped.

The weariness melted away, forgotten as I rose fluidly to my feet.

"You're a monster. You turned me into a monster. You've surrounded yourself with monsters, and you destroyed the one innocent person this family has produced in generations. The one pure spot in our desecrated family tree," I said. My voice sounded strange, with an insectoid reverb echoing each of my words a split second later.

"Dave." Bishop said, his voice full of concern.

My arms felt longer, my skin felt different. Harder. Like armor.

"Aw, shit, sugah," Nero said, backing away.

I stalked toward Mawmaw, my eyes no longer seeing. I didn't need eyes right now. I could sense the things around me. Feel the life force.

It made me hungry.

Mawmaw looked upon me and her face went from shock to triumph.

"Yes! It has loosed its bonds! Come, my love! Come and claim all that has been promised!" she held her arms out wide, as if to embrace me.

"I think I'm gonna be sick," Nero said.

"Understandable," Ava said.

I now moved forward with a sinewy grace, the claws at the end of my hands and the chitinous armor covering my body were more than I needed to enact my vengeance, but since when was that enough for a LeBlanc and our Nameless benefactors? My barbed tail lanced forward, burying itself in her gut.

"GAHHHHHHHH!" she screamed.

Her fear tasted divine. An indescribable spice added to a delectable meal. I wanted more. I wanted her pain. Her sorrow. Her defeat. I wanted to taste all of that as I drained the life from her. Then I could move on. I would start with Ava and Nero. Bishop cared for them and he had failed to protect Babette. It was only fair for him to watch them die before it was his turn.

I extended my jaws and savaged Mawmaw's throat. Her eyes went wide, and she made the same gurgling noise Babette had.

Poetic.

I began to feed, drinking down her life essence and absorbing it greedily.

Then, Bishop was standing in front of me, looking at where he thought my eyes were.

Idiot.

"Dave. This isn't you, Dave," he said.

"Bishop, get the fuck outta there!" Nero called.

"Shut up and let the man work!" Ava shouted.

I snarled, raising a clawed hand to end him. He didn't flinch.

"You spent most of the day telling us you didn't want to be a monster, Dave. That you didn't want to let something like that loose on the world. I bound that thing inside you instead of killing out outright because I believed you. Were you lying when you said that?" he asked.

I shook my head. This didn't make sense. He deserved to die. They deserved to die. I was hungry. I would eat them. Devour their souls, then move on to the next group. I looked down at Babette's still form. Her staring eyes. At Mawmaw's claws covered in her blood.

I was the monster I feared.

"That's right. Follow it back, Dave," Bishop said. "Follow it back to yourself."

I could feel my body changing again, the bone-crushing weariness came washing over me like a tidal wave. I sank to my knees, naked and covered in some sort of viscera.

I felt a hand on my shoulder and looked up to see Bishop, who knelt down in the mud with me.

"Welcome back," he said.

I wrapped my arms around him and wept.

"Jesus," Victor whispered. "You're all lucky to be alive."

"Dave, I had no idea. I'm so sorry," Jackie said.

Dave shrugged. "The past is the past. Without that, I wouldn't be who I am, and wouldn't be doing what I need to be."

The table went silent for a moment.

"Not all of us are lucky to be alive," Nat observed. "I was **totally** not there. Probably would have saved everyone a lot of trouble if I had been."

"They'd have definitely eaten you first," I said.

Nat started to object until she saw Dave nodding, then decided to shrug. "Well, if they did, I woulda been delicious."

"Without a doubt," Ava agreed, raising her glass in a toast. "To Nat, the most delectable of us all!"

From across the table, Nero took a quick drink of his cider and said "I still don't believe you were gonna eat me," he said.

"Sweetie, I don't think he was exactly in his right mind. Dave had been through hell and back," Aaron said.

"And he was only gonna eat you because I wasn't there since I am famously delicious," Nat added. "And you know Ava woulda been tasty. She's a snack."

"No one encourage them," Aaron pleaded.

"Sugah, this lot don't need encouragin'," Nero protested. "'Specially those two," he said, gesturing to me and Ava.

"I didn't do it!" I objected. "Blame those two!" I said, gesturing at Ava and Nat.

Ava placed her right hand on her chest. "Nero, how could you?" she asked in mock offense.

"'Cause you know I speak the truth, gorgeous. Ya'll been that way since we first ran inta each other all that time ago."

Aaron smiled and looked at his love. "Why haven't you ever told me this before, Nero?"

"'Cause it don't necessarily paint any of us in the best o' lights, what with the thievin' and general anti-social shenanigans, " Nero told Aaron.

He took a big drink from his wine glass and shuddered.

"Let me preface this with a few reassurances: This story don't involve any sort of child prostitution, cannibalism, or incest. After you two I just wanted to put that up front."

"Fair," I said.

Nero quirked an eyebrow and pursed his lips.

"Uh huh. Well, sugah, when I met Bishop, he was a straight asshole,"

I opened my mouth to object, then closed it and nodded. "No, that's fair."

"Damned right it is. Anyway, my association with this bunch o' hoodlums all started with a key…"

Book 3: Nero's Story

Chapter ONE

More specifically, it started with a meetin' about a key. In addition to my fabulous readings and general tourist-trap business, I've been known to take consulting jobs. You know, with the police or for hire when someone offers me an amount o' cash that makes me choke a little.

What? I told you this story didn't put none of us in the best of lights.

I got a call from some assistant - always a good sign on the money side o' things. Rich folk don't tend ta make their own appointments. Little thing wanted to set up a meeting with me an' her boss, fella by the name of Charles Coates. Coates is one of those tech bros that hit it big in the 90's bubble, then rolled into some crypto cash an' was lucky enough for lighting to strike him twice.

If only, but I'm gettin' ahead of myself, sugah.

Now, Nero's nothing if not a cautious sort.

Stop laughing.

Ahem. As I was sayin', I was a bit worried about this Coates fella. You never could tell what these billionaire types would want, or if you could actually deliver for 'em. They're not used to being' told "no", and most of 'em won't take it for an answer.

So there I was, sittin' my pretty ass down in the outdoor cafe. This would be about twelve years ago, give or take. Early spring so the heat hadn't found its teeth yet. There I was, sippin' at my latte when Mr. Man himself strolled on up. Charles Coates. At that point, he'd have been in his late thirties or early forties and was just pretty enough to eat. Strong jawline, icy baby blues, that lean build that makes 'em look all hungry. If it weren't for his personality, background, behavior, attitude, and how he dressed, he'd have been an absolute dream.

Sadly for all of us, he is what he is.

Coates came striding' up wearing' a white fedora over a black silk shirt (unbuttoned, of course). He had on a wife beater and a pair of blue jeans. His facial hair was that sort of five o'clock shadow that you just knew he spent forever and a day on in front of the mirror. Sugah, it takes a lot of care to make it look like you don't.

I raised an eyebrow as he approached, then waved with my biggest, fakest smile.

"Over here, sugah!" I called out.

Coates jumped a little, then looked around like the fool thought someone was watching him.

"Nero?" he asked.

"The one and only," I said.

He slid into the chair across from me, doin' that hot boy squint where it looks like somebody threw dirt in his eyes. You know the one. All the actors do it.

"Good. I have something I need some help with, and I'm told you're the person I need to get the job done," he said. "It needs to be done quietly."

"Well, color me intrigued, sugah. What is it that little ol' Nero can do for you, Daddy Warbucks?"

He slid a piece of paper across the table, an act somewhat marred by the fact that we were sitting at an outdoor table with the little diamond grating. You know the kind? Well, not the smoothest of surfaces, and it sorta bunched and scrunched the sheet he was trying' to Spy vs Spy over to me.

Finally, I reached out and plucked it from the table to save us both the embarrassment.

"What have we here? A key?" I asked, looking at the drawing.

He nodded "Exactly. I want you to get it for me."

"And where is this key that you can't just have one of your many large, strapping' employees go and retrieve it for you, sugah?" I asked.

"The man who currently holds it is uninterested in selling it to me," he said.

"Is that right? What man would that be?" I asked.

"Renee Ivé. He runs a voodoo shop in the Ninth Ward, along with some street gangs," Coates replied.

I spit my latte out and stared at him in horror

"Ah, you've heard of him," he said.

"Renee Ivé. PAPA Ivé?" I asked. "That man is fell death on a stick, sugah. You do *not* wanna go crossin' him."

"I'm not going to. You are," he said.

I shook my head. "No. It don't matter what size check you're lookin' to write. I can't spend money if I'm dead."

"Two million," he said.

"No," I replied.

"Three.'

"Are you not hearin' me?" I asked

"Five."

I stopped. Five million dollars.

"Half up front," he promised. "The other half when you deliver the key."

"What if I fail?" I asked. "Ivé's one dangerous motherfucker. I've steered as far clear of him as I could and still be livin' in New Orleans."

"Don't fail," he said with a shrug. "Ivé has a scary rep, but he's just a man, same as any other. Wait till he's out, or sleeping, slip in, then grab the key and run. It's simple."

"Simple," I repeated, shaking my head. "Look, sugah, I'd love to help you. I would, but I don't think this can be done."

"You know what I learned about things that can't be done, Nero? I learned that it's bullshit. The only question is the will and the means to make that will happen. That's why I test myself against the toughest and most dangerous things I can. That's why I need that key," he said, his eyes taking on a far away kinda look.

"Come again?" I asked, wary of white boys and their delusions.

No offense, Bishop.

"The reason that Ivé won't part with that key is that it's a special key," he said.

"I gathered," I replied, pursing my lips.

"Yeah. It's supposed to be one of the seven keys to the Gates of Guinee," he whispered.

"The what now?" I asked.

"The Gates of Guinee," he said.

"Sugah, you can say it slower an' louder all you like, that don't make it so I know what you're talkin' about," I said.

"I thought you would—never mind. The Gates of Guinee are the entrance to the voodoo underworld," he said.

"So the underworld?" I asked.

"No, the voodoo underworld," he insisted.

I sighed.

"Sugah, that's the same—no, you know what, go ahead. What do you mean by that?" I asked with a shake of the head.

Coates didn't notice, so he dove right in on his explanation. All he was missin' was me being a lady an' him leading with 'well, actually' and he'd have been spot on. "According to voodoo tradition, there are seven Gates of Guinee scattered around the city of New Orleans, each with its own key. These lead to Guinee—"

"Well, that makes sense at least," I said.

"—the realm of the dead, where they wait until they pass through the deep waters to be reunited with their ancestors. There's one permanent resident in Guinee: Baron Samedi," he said with a smile.

"That name I know," I said.

"Right, so you know he's a powerful spirit who rules over the dead," he said.

"Everybody knows that," I said.

"Right. So I'm going to hunt and kill him," he said.

"You're what now?" I asked.

"I'm going to hunt and kill him. Think about it. The ultimate prey! I've already done all the big game hunting Africa has to offer. I bagged the big five: Lion, Leopard, Rhino, Elephant, and African Buffalo. It was sick, bro!"

"Ain't that super illegal?" I asked.

He shrugged. "That doesn't really matter. I've killed a tiger in India, big horn rams, moose, polar bears. You name it, and I've put it down. I need something. Something more. I reached out through some of my buds and they hooked me up with some guys that started talking about some Shadow Council and Liturgy of the Forgotten."

I swallowed and my eyes bulged. "Did they now? And who was that, sugah?" I asked, my voice trembling.

He waved a hand. "That's not important. What is important is that he told me about how there's this secret world with monsters and shit, and how it gets hidden by like the Church and stuff? So a couple years ago, me and my buds started doin' that."

"Doin' that?" I asked.

"Hunting monsters for funsos," he said, like the idiot he was.

"Hunting—" I trailed off.

"Monsters, right. Keep up. So anyway, We've bagged a few at this point. Old vampires are super disappointing. They just turn to ash, so there's no trophy you can really get out of 'em that you couldn't get out of a fireplace. Werewolves just turn into people when you bag 'em, and I've already done that whole 'people hunting thing'. It's not nearly as dangerous as you'd think. We did hunt for some sort of shapeshifter thing that just turned to a pile of goo, and some sort of ugly thing up in Pennsylvania that just cried and turned into salt water. Lame, am I right? But yeah, Samedi, he's a badass. When I take him down, that's major bragging rights," he said.

I felt sick. This was the sort of thing that the *Ordinis Templi Erinnys* would murder me for. As a real psychic, I'm close enough to a witch by their definition that I fall into the monster category. Or maybe it's a Catholic thing. It can be so hard to keep track of why people are hatin' on other people these days.

"But you–" I started, then shook my head. "Sugah, I don't think you understand what kinda danger you're in."

"Not just me. Both of us," he said with a smile.

"Come again?" I asked.

"Both of us. There's video footage of this conversation being filmed right now. If you don't do what I asked you to and bring that key to me, I'll release the footage to the internet. How long do you think it'll take for the Church to hunt you down at that point? You don't exactly keep a low profile, do you?" he asked, taking a sip of his tea. "Oh, delicious."

I swallowed again. "Well, shit."

"I couldn't have put it better myself," he said with a smirk.

"Well, ah guess I'm on the case, sugah." I said.

"Good man. I knew you would be. I'll have someone stop by tomorrow with your up front payment. In cash, of course. Don't want any records of this that we didn't intend, right, Nero?" he said.

"Can't have that," I said, closing my eyes and appreciating that I was well and truly fucked.

Three days later, I'd been given a bigger wad o' cash than I'd ever seen in my life, been to the Ninth Ward to look over Ivé's place, gone back to my place to have a good cry, went back to Ivé's place to look at the security again, then gotten drunk.

I needed somethin' else if this was gonna work, and when you're in New Orleans an' you really need to know somethin', there's really only one place to go: Ava Dufrense.

So I was plopped down at a table at the Bayou Review to wait for Miss Thing to put on her show. Zeke had waved me right through to a table, angel that he is. Now I would just have to get through Ava's act.

Here's the thing you need to understand when you're lookin' at a succubus or incubus: Yeah, the one you're lookin' at may not technically be the playin' field you're interested in, but somethin' about their magic makes you willin' to entertain thoughts that would never pop into your head in any other time. You remain fully aware that this ain't normal, but you just don't care. They kinda make you hate yourself.

Real dick move, overall. I think enough of us have that goin' on already, or already been down that road and got through it. We don't need the help, an' we don't need the reminder.

This show was no different from any other, although I could see Ava tryin' ta stay clear of my side of the room, there was only so much she could do. Still, her efforts were appreciated. After the show I was led back to her dressing room, where she sat in her robe, removing the makeup from her torch performance.

"Nero! I haven't seen you in a bit. I thought you might've gone legit and started just filching the tourists," Ava said, turning around to kiss each of my cheeks in turn.

"No, baby girl, I've just been busy with some business."

"Word has it you had a visitor a few days ago. Somebody with a lot of cash and very little sense," she said.

"You have no idea," I said, then closed my eyes and cast my senses out to make sure we were unobserved.

Clear.

"Ava, girl. I'm in trouble," I whispered.

"Trouble? What's going on, Nero?" she asked.

"That visitor yesterday? Charles Coates," I said.

"The tech bro?" she asked.

I nodded. "The same. One of his people reached out an' I got excited, thought I could get close to him and maybe work some of my magic on him to get some cash from someone who wouldn't miss it," I admitted.

"Seems straightforward. How'd he catch you?" she asked.

"He didn't. We met an' he started talkin' all sortsa crazy shit about keys and the Gates of Guinee, and Papa Ivé–" I rambled, staring at the floor with my eyes wide.

"He knows Ivé has one of the keys to the Gates?" she asked.

I stopped. "Yeah. But how'd you know?"

Ava gave me a withering look, as only Ava can. I held up my hands in surrender.

"So, he wants you to get it for him?" she asked.

I nodded. "I went over there to take a look at what I'm dealin' with, an he's got his place locked up tighter than Fort Knox. The place is lousy with bound spirits. They're everywhere."

"And worse than that. From what I hear he's got multiple layers of alarms and traps set up with magic on top of those spirit guards. You'd never even see the thing that killed you," she added.

"I'm royally fucked, Ava. What do I do? If I don't get him this key, he releases a video of us talkin' about the Liturgy of the Forgotten online. The Order won't stand for that. I'd be dead in days."

She nodded. "That's a tight spot, Nero. You need a team to pull off this sort of thing, and you don't really do the team-up thing."

I shook my head. "Aside from you, there's not a trustworthy soul in this city."

"He said to the demon," she said, laughing bitterly.

"I said what I said, girl."

She offered a weak smile, then looked at me for a moment. "I may have someone."

"Are they trustworthy?" I asked.

"Hell no," she replied. "But they're good. Really good. And he'd help if I asked him to."

"He? Who is it? What's he do?" I asked.

"Jason Bishop. He's an occultist, and more importantly, an apostate from The Order. His sister got sent to hell and he's been trying to find a way to get her back out," she said.

I nodded. "Great. How do you know him?" I asked.

She blushed slightly. "We're sort of seeing each other?"

I looked at her for what seemed like forever, then shook my head. "Fuck me."

"Nero, it's not like that," Ava said.

"Like what?" I asked. "Like you got a new boytoy and you're gonna hold him up like he's worth somethin'? Ava, I don't begrudge you your fun, sugah, but this is serious shit that I'm in. I need more than some guy that flunked outta priest school.

"Jason has been active in the community for years now," Ava objected.

I raised an eyebrow.

"Okay, it's closer to eighteen months," she said.

"Bzzzz," I said, waving my hands at her. "What are you tryin' to do to me, girl? I thought we were friends."

"We are friends, Nero. You asked who I thought could help, and I'm telling you, Jason Bishop is the only guy that can do it," she said.

"I can't do it," Bishop said.

I gave Ava a long look. She held up her hands.

After she finished getting changed, Ava had brought us to a little bar on Rue Toulouse called Bishop's Crossing and got all smoochy with the guy behind the bar. I could see the appeal. He had that bad boy look goin' on. Hair tousled just so. Black tank top. Black jeans. Combat boots. He took us into the back room off the bar and we sat down for me to lay out my predicament.

That's when he gave me that assessment.

"Well. Fuck me," I said.

"Look, what you're describing is an item of incredible power. The Ivé person is gonna have it locked up tight," he said.

"I'm aware," I said. "But I've got no choice, Mr. Bishop."

"Just Bishop is fine," he muttered, waving his hand absently. "Okay, so this isn't a problem."

"It's not?" my heart soared.

'No, it's a bunch of problems. Plural," he said.

"I hate you a little bit, sugah," I said.

'I get that a lot," he said.

"He does," Ava added.

"First problem: Everything I've seen about the Ninth Ward tells me that if any of us roll in there, the residents are going to see us coming a mile away. You said Ivé had guards?"

"Lots of 'em. With guns," I said.

"The residents put up with them for a reason," he said. "And they'll probably tip 'em off before we ever get close."

"Which gets us shot," Ava said.

"Yeah. Second problem: Once you get close, there'll be the spirits that are bound to the place. Ava tells me that Ivé is some sorta voodoo king, so he'll have all sorts of loa at his beck and call. You'll need a way to get past them that won't set anyone on alert."

I nodded.

"Third problem: The physical wards. From what Ava tells me you're looking at a multi-layered death trap with alarms and lethal protections piled on top of each other like a razor-covered Jenga tower," he said.

"Love the image," I said, shaking my head.

"And don't forget about Ivé himself," Ava said. "The man is an incredibly powerful willworker. He can kill any one of us with a stray thought if he wants to. We need to either avoid him or give him a reason that he doesn't want to kill us."

"And what's that?" I asked.

"No idea," Bishop said. "Like I said, I can't do it."

Ava stood and slinked over to him. "Jason, Nero is a really old friend. It would mean a lot to me if you could help."

Bishop closed his eyes and sighed. "Fine. For you," he said, pulling Ava down into a lingering kiss.

And I mean *lingering*.

I cleared my throat and they removed themselves from each other's tonsils.

Breeders.

"Great. You'll help. What's next?" I asked.

"Next we're gonna come up with a plan to save your ass. Meet me back here tomorrow. We've got some work to do," he said.

I was at the bar the next morning in the vague approximation of bright and early. Bishop was standing outside of his bar smoking a cigarette. A clove, because he needed to be from as deep in the nineties as he could.

I strolled up looking as fabulous as ever, wearing a sun hat, and a tasty ensemble that reminded me of a tropical drink.

He looked me up and down and shook his head.

"Don't you start, fashion victim. I know I look good."

We spent the rest of the next two days going through the Ninth Ward. We drove past Ivé's store front. Past the corners where his people were set up. Past a few random buildings that Bishop 'had a good feeling about'. And so on.

It felt like we were wasting time, but he assured me, it was all for the plan.

Chapter Three

On the third day, we were ready, or so I was told.

The plan was simple: Starting late at night, we'd begin with a good ol' fashioned fire at a warehouse that Ivé owned nearby. Bishop was convinced that once the thing went up the goon squad would go runnin'. Once they were clear, we'd start with some stinky sage burnin' to shoo off the ghosts, then use some sorta toy Bishop had to take care of the rest that lingered.

Once we cleared the ghosts, it was into Ivé's place, where Ava and Bishop said they could deal with the magical traps an' wards. My job was to find Ivé an keep him sleepin'. Then it should be easy enough to find the key and run our pretty little asses outta there.

Two fifteen in the morning had us in a car watching a warehouse.

"I didn't know you had a car, Bishop. Where do you keep this thing?" I asked

"I don't," he said.

"Not sure I'd want my name on a rental associated with tonight, sugah," I said.

"Neither would I," he said, staring at the warehouse.

"Not a rental?" I asked.

"Nope," he said.

I sighed. "Stolen?"

He nodded. "Don't want it linked back to us. We'll dump it after we're finished tonight." he looked at his watch, then nodded. "It should start in three minutes. I did some digging since we chatted about Ivé. You picked a real interesting guy to irritate."

"Thanks. Why do things halfway? How'd you time this out?" I asked, hoping to stop talking about Ivé and other scary things that were going to kill me.

"Pretty easy, honestly. I donated to their non-profit and stashed a small incendiary inside one of the smaller boxes inside. It's set to go off in three minutes. Correction, two minutes," he said.

I frowned. "Donated? What did you donate?"

"Food," he said with a shrug, taking a drag from one of his damned cloves.

I stared at him. "This warehouse stores food?"

He nodded.

"But it's run by Ivé's gang," I said.

He nodded again.

"Yeah, he's got his fingers in a lot of pies, but one consistent thing that comes up is that he wants to take care of 'his people'. With how things are around here, part of that's keepin' 'em fed. I figure that as important as it is, once the fire starts, it'll pull every one of his guys that's anywhere near here," he said.

"But you're burnin' food for poor folks," I objected.

He turned and leveled a look at me as I sat in the back seat. "Yup. And that's the sort of thing that happens sometimes when you have to make plans. Sometimes innocent people lose things. Sometimes innocent people get hurt. Now you need to decide right now if that's something you can live with or not, because either fucking way, that warehouse will be–"

FWOOSH!

Smoke started to pour out of the windows lining the top of the warehouse, obscuring about a fifth of the building in a thick, black cloud..

"How big was that bomb?" I asked.

"Big enough. Let's move," he said.

We took a meandering path back to Ivé's store, Swinging well wide of the main streets. We could see cars full of people rushing toward the warehouse, I assumed to try to salvage as much as possible.

Ava rested a hand on my arm. "I know. None of us like it, but it was the best way," she said.

I wasn't sure I believed her, but it was too late now.

Bishop parked a couple o' blocks from Ivé's and we all walked all sneaky-like up. I closed my eyes and could feel the spirits swirlin' around the house. All stirred up by the strong emotions of the people who had gone to the warehouse.

Bishop took out several large bundles of sage and lit them with a strange-looking candle. He looked at me and shook it.

"Blessed beeswax from Jerusalem. Gives the sage a little extra kick," he said. Then he started lobbing the burning sage in a path between us and the house. That man brought more than a dozen bundles of the stuff. I could feel the spirits move away from the smoke, deflected from their purpose by the strong smell.

I coughed. "Sugah, I don't know about the ghosties, but this shit's gonna be the end of me if we don't move," I said.

Bishop was holding something small and shiny in his hand as we moved. "What in the world is that?" I asked.

"Ancient mirror. It was dipped in the Pool of Narcissus. Anything that looks into it is shown its deepest desire and can't look away. Ghosts have it worse since their entire purpose is around their deepest desire. For them it can get a bit messy," he whispered as we moved forward.

At first, I thought he was messin' with me, but as we walked, Bishop pivoted and held his little mirror out. I couldn't see anything, but the sound heard from the other side was immediate. Screams. Wails. The sounds of pure, unadulterated longing rang out across the psychic landscape, making me pray that Ivé' either couldn't hear or was a heavy sleeper.

I reached out, trying to find any human minds awake or asleep in the house. I found one sleeping in an upstairs room. I encouraged it to sleep, but as I touched it, there was something off. I pushed a bit further, feeling the thoughts flow.

My eyes went wide.

"Fuck. Ava. Bishop? Ivé ain't in there," I said.

"What do you mean he's not in there?" Bishop asked. "The intel said he almost never leaves."

"Almost isn't the same as never, Jason," Ava said. "Who's in there, Nero?"

"A little girl," I said. "I think it's his daughter."

All three of us went silent and still for a moment.

"Did you know he had a kid?" Bishop asked Ava.

She shook her head. "No one does or I'd know."

"This is bad," I said.

Bishop looked undecided for a moment, then he set his jaw. "Yup. It's bad, but it doesn't change anything. We need to move fast and get out before he gets back. Chances are our distraction was a little more effective than we'd hoped and he's at the fire."

"But he's a wizard type. Don't that mean–" I said.

"Yeah. We're short on time. Let's move," Bishop said, hurrying forward.

As we moved, he pointed to certain spots, saying to avoid stepping there. To not touch that. To move around this other thing. From time to time he touched other things, and there would be a faint flash. Or the smell of ozone. Or something else unobtrusive.

And before we knew it, we were through the outer layer of wards and up to the house proper. Ava had the door open in seconds. Seems that bein' the voodoo king of New Orleans means you don't gotta invest in a decent door lock.

The inside of the house slash store wasn't what I'd have expected. There were voodoo knick knacks all over the walls, a bunch o' stuff in a glass case at the counter, and some downright silly paraphernalia.

The place was a tourist trap.

"Huh," I commented. "Not what I was–"

"No time," Bishop cut me off, moving back through the shop and into the house behind. His eyes were constantly on the move, looking left, right, up, and down as we moved through room after room seeking out the key.

As we rounded the corner to the third room, I paused. I could feel something echoing from the other side. My eyes darted left at the same time as Bishop's. In a locked roll top desk drawer, something was calling.

"Ava?" I asked, pointing.

With a quick nod, she went to work, and the desk was open even more quickly than the front door. I reached my hand in and wrapped it around something cold, cylindrical, and metallic.

I pulled it out and saw one of the keys to the Gates of Guinee.

Chapter
Four

For bein' such an important thing, the key looked as ordinary as can be. It was a silvery color with a big empty ring on the top with a picture of gates on it. It had some old-timey teeth spaced out irregularly, and just sorta sat there. The pressure it exerted on my mind was something else entirely. LIke someone had taken an air compressor to my sinuses.

"I was expectin' something a bit more grand," I whispered, then put it into my pocket. "And a bit less solvable with aspirin."

"We need to go," Ava hissed. "If Ivé's in the wind and his kid is upstairs, the last place any of us want to be is where he can find us."

When a girl's right, a girl's right. We all got the hell outta there. I was up front on the way out for about ten steps when Bishop grabbed my shoulder and yanked me back, hard. I fell into him. I didn't scream.

Okay, I didn't scream all that loud.

"What the hell?" I whispered. He helped me regain my balance and held a finger to his lips.

"You almost stepped right on one of the traps. They're all still active," he said.

I opened my mouth with a reply but bit it back then gestured for him to take the lead. I consoled myself with the view as we exited. Out on the lawn, we collected the sage bundles, then ran to the car as quick as our feet would carry us.

"I do love it when a plan goes smooth," I said.

Bishop was frowning, looking around. "Yeah. Very smooth," he agreed.

Ava stood still, looking at the smoke billowing from the warehouse in the distance. "You had to burn down a food bank?" she said.

"It was the best way to get it done, besides, they'll have it under control before it does any real damage. The smoke makes it look worse than it is. Look, you're always saying there's no halfway in this world, right? That if you're going to walk in the Gloaming, you'd better be prepared to do what it takes, right?"

Ava looked at him and nodded.

He shrugged. "That's what it took."

Ava looked down at her feet, then nodded. "I did and it is," she agreed.

"Sugah, I think you might have learned that lesson a little too well," I said.

He looked from Ava to me and back again, and shook his head, opening the car door and climbing inside. A moment later, Ava and I both followed.

It was a quiet drive back to the Quarter.

The weird otherworldly headache from the key went away as soon as I was out of the car. It was so late that even Bourbon Street was at a low ebb. The sun would be up in the next couple of hours. My feet took me meandering to Jackson Square Park, where I took some time to look at the big ol' cathedral squattin' at the end. The St. Louis Cathedral is always a sight to behold, and in the small hours of the morning, I've always found it a welcome sight, 'specially when things are itchin' in my head.

I squeezed the key in my pocket and kept repeating that I didn't have a choice. That Coates had forced me into this. Try as I might, I just kept seein' a smoke-filled warehouse full of food for poor folk bein' burned up, and knew that was on me. I'd brought him in on it, so what he did was my responsibility.

"Fuck," I spat, shaking my head. "How do I get myself into these messes?"

"How do you get yourself into these messes, bro?" a familiar voice asked. I turned on the bench and saw Charles Coates sauntering across the park toward me, a different fedora perched atop his head. "I was afraid you weren't gonna get the job done, but bringin' in the hottie and her boytoy, then burning down a warehouse? I was geekin' out, dude!"

"You had me followed?" I asked.

"No, bro. I had you watched. That's totally different. I invested two and a half mil into you. I don't like taking risks on my investment, so I took out some insurance, and bought a couple of these sick toys called 'drones'. Gonna be all the rage in a few years. You can fly 'em up high and have 'em film shit. Keep an eye without havin' to be anywhere near 'em. Awesome, right?"

"No, not awesome, sugah," I said. "That damned drone coulda tipped off Ivé or fucked up in a million other ways."

"Yeah, but it didn't. Stop bein' such a whiny bitch. Jesus." Coates shook his head. "You know what? Whatever. You can be pissed, but you can also get the other half of your Benjamins. Now gimme the key and I'll give you the cash."

I took the key out of my pocket and shoved it at him. "Take the damn thing," I said.

"Don't mind if I do," he replied, grinning ear to ear. He snapped his fingers and a large man walked up with a briefcase, then handed it to me.

"Do you just have these guys stashed in some cubby?" I asked, looking around.

But Coates was already walking away, talking on his phone. "Babe? I fuckin' got it, just like I said I would!"

I shook my head and sighed, then started home.

Something was itching at my mind. Just a little thought that kept worrying at my calm. Something felt off.

I mean, aside from the obvious.

First Bishop said it couldn't be done, then he agreed without much prompting. Then the whole thing went off smooth as silk. The plan wasn't that good, but it was incredibly successful. He didn't seem the kind to depend on luck.

So he knew something. What did he know?

Ivé.

He had to know Ivé wouldn't be there, so he'd just need to deal with whatever–

Ava had said he wanted to get into Hell to save his sister. The key to the Gates of Guinee would get him to Baron Samedi in the underworld. Samedi could probably get him to Hell.

But I had the key.

Didn't I?

I played it over in my head again. The pressure that the key caused. That sense of the otherworldly.

That pressure went away when I got out of the car and Bishop drove off. Bishop had the key. How?

I ran things over again and shook my head. "The trap on the way out. He must have grabbed it when he pulled me back. Motherfucker."

I'd just given a fake key to Charles fucking Coates because of Jason fucking Bishop.

"I'm gonna fuckin' kill that boy," I muttered.

*Chapter
Five*

When you're lookin' to murder a white boy in New Orleans, it's always a good idea to do your due diligence. I hurried back to my place and sat on the floor in my bedroom. I took a deep breath to center myself, closed my eyes, and pushed my mind out.

I've never really had to describe what that feels like to someone, but the closest I can get is to imagine your brain is wearing a shirt that's a size too small. It's constricting and uncomfortable. Then you take it off and you can feel it expand to the way it's supposed to be. The size it wants to be.

That's what it feels like.

My brain desperately wants to reach out and touch someone, messy bitch that it is. I have to bring it back inside my pretty little head to make sure I don't get drowned in the volume of thoughts that are floatin' around out there. People carry some ugliness in them, and no one wants to experience that on the daily. Not if they wanna try to stay sane.

Well, sane-ish, I guess. Don't wanna false advertise.

I sent my thoughts out, focusing on the flavor of Jason fucking Bishop I'd picked up when I was with him earlier. Not the clove cigarettes, Old Spice, and Irish Spring sorta physical flavor. More the feel of his mind and spirit.

So honestly, clove cigarettes, Old Spice, and Irish Spring isn't far off.

I scoured the city, spending nearly an hour zipping here and there like some sorta sugar plum fairy on meth. There was no sign of him.

It was frustratin', but not unexpected. Guys like Jason Bishop were good and going to ground to wait for the heat to die down, so I tried Ava instead.

I focused on a sweet floral scent over cinnamon and vanilla, with a hint of sulfur. Miss Thing was much easier to find. She was back at Bayou Review in her changing room.

I pushed my way into her mind.

"Bitch, I have known you for five years and you just set my ass up to get robbed by your boytoy," I shouted.

"The fuck? Nero? We've talked about this," Ava said, her voice echoing in my head, "Boundaries."

"Fuck your boundaries and fuck you. Your man's little switcheroo probably just got my ass killed," I said.

"What are you talking about?" she asked.

"Bishop," my brain spat his name like a curse. "He switched keys on me."

"No. He wouldn't," she said.

"Would and did, sugah," I said.

"I had no idea, Nero. You have to believe me," she said.

I paused for a moment. I did, in fact, believe her. I could feel the sincerity dripping from her mind.

Or I was talking to a succubus who knew exactly how to tell people what they wanted to hear.

"Sugah, it's only a matter of time before either Papa Ivé or Charles Coates kills me for this. I need that key back to fix this. Why would he do it? Is it for the money? I'd have given him however much he asked for out of what Coates was giving me."

"No, I don't think it's money," she said after a pause. "I think it's worse than that. That key opens a gate to the underworld?"

"It does," I said.

"It's his fucking sister," Ava said. "The one stuck in hell. He's fucking obsessed with getting her out. If he thought he could use that key to do it, he'd try it in a heartbeat."

"But he couldn't do that unless he got past Baron Samedi," I said. "Your white boy ain't crazy enough to try that."

Silence.

"Ava, tell me your white boy ain't crazy enough to try that."

"I wish I could. This could be bad. Meet me at his bar, I'm heading over now," she said.

Fifteen minutes later I was standing in front of the bar at Bishop's Crossing demanding to speak with the owner. The kid behind the bar just kept repeating that he was out and didn't know when he'd be back.

Then Ava arrived.

Dressed in a red shirt and black jeans with combat boots, Ava's face was a thundercloud ready to burst. She descended on the boy like the wrath of God.

"Edward, I swear to you, whatever your boss told you to say is not what you want to tell me right now. Where the fuck is Jason Bishop?" she demanded.

The bartender (Edward I now knew) stared at her for a moment, then pointed a shaky hand at the storage room near the stairs. "He went in there, then left, but he said not to go in. That there was an alarm?" he said.

Ava started striding back. "I've got a key," she said, pausing at the door and muttering a phrase in a language I think was Latin. Shapes on the doorframe glowed, then she grabbed the door and turned the handle.

Locked.

"Fuck you, Jason," she growled, then savagely twisted the knob, shattering the locking mechanism inside and pushing the door open, revealing a room lined with floor-to-ceiling bookshelves with some random brick-a-brak on them.

"What the hell?" I said, looking around.

"He's a bit of a hoarder. If he finds something magical that he thinks might be useful he holds onto it. This is where he keeps them," Ava said, looking at a table in the middle of the room with a map laid out on it.

"The Quarter. What are these dots?" I asked, pointing to a series of ink droplets on the paper.

"Blood," Ava said, her face twisted into a frown. "He did some sort of ritual, quick and dirty."

"What did he do?" I asked.

She shook her head. "I can't tell from this, but he was probably looking for the gate location. He's got a key, so he'll need a lock."

"Come again?" I asked.

"There are seven Gates of Guinee. Each gate corresponds to a key, just like any other door," she said.

"So he needs to match the key to the gate," I said.

"This was probably him looking for a resonance," she said.

"So why don't we just follow that?" I asked.

"Because the little shit dropped extra spots on the map, probably in case anyone was trying to track him down. He's muddied the waters," she sighed.

I stared at the map. There were dozens of little droplets.

"We can't search all of them. It would be next week before we found the right one," I sighed.

Ava paused. "Okay. We need to find Jason Bishop when he doesn't want to be found. Let's try to think like him."

"No thank you, sugah."

"No, we can do this. He wants something. What does he want?" she said. "To find his sister."

"Right, that's why he wants to go through the gates," I said.

Ava's head snapped up. "No, he doesn't."

"He most certainly does. He took the key to do it," I objected.

"No, he took the key to get to what he wanted," she corrected.

"The underworld?" I asked.

"Close. He wants to get to Baron Samedi. Bishop will want to either make a deal with him or trick him to get him into Hell," she said, a smile creeping onto her face.

"That's great for him, but how's it help us find him," I asked.

"It's better than that," she said. "We'll do what he'd do. We'll make him come find us."

"How in the pretty blue hell are we gonna manage that, sugah? The boy's made himself pretty scarce," I said.

"Simple. He wants to find Baron Samedi, we'll steal him. We're going to summon Baron Samedi," She said.

"We're gonna what?" I asked.

"Summon The Baron. Well, you are," she corrected.

"I don't even know how to begin to do that," I said.

"I've seen it done. It's not that hard. Honestly, it's much easier than it has any right to be," she said.

"So why me? You seem healthy enough an' I know that there's plenty 'round these parts that are interested in takin' your skin for a ride. I ain't about gettin' possessed by a jumbo sized spirit," I said.

"He won't take my offering. I'm part demon. There's no soul. If you want to find him, this is our best bet," she said.

"What has my life come to? Fine. Let's invite Baron Samedi over."

Chapter Six

So.

There I was, lying on my back in a dingy back room of a bar with a white girl torch singer who happened to be a succubus standin' over me smokin' a cigar and holdin' a big bottle o' rum. The smell from the cigar quickly filled the room, tickling at the back of my nose.

Fuck my life, right?

Ava started chantin' in creole, takin' puffs of the cigar an' pourin' out a glass of rum an' sittin' it on the table with the map.

The smoke from the cigar started to thicken, swirling above the glass, then thickening more, taking the hazy shape of a skeleton of a man. Or possibly a man of a skeleton.

Baron Samedi was a tall thin black man, and also a skeleton. He definitely was wearing a top hat, formal tails, and slacks, and holding a cane with a shiny silver knob at the top.

He lifted the glass of rum to his lips, which were both there and not, and drank, simultaneously goosing Ava's ass. She instinctively swatted away his hand.

"Baron Samedi, thank you for heeding our call," she started, still fencing with his persistently grabby hand. "Nero here is offering himself as a vessel so you can eat, drink, and make merry. And maybe stop grabbing at my ass."

"What's the fun in that, demon-girl? Ya'll called the Baron just when things were gettin' interesting with your little priest friend."

"Bishop?" Ava asked.

"Fuckin' A. Of course Bishop. Little asshole opens up the gate and comes through tryin' to project some big dick energy on the ol' Baron. My sister this, and storm the gates of hell that. But then I get a call from a demon-adjacent hotty offerin' up a psychic to ride? Whoooo. This I had to see."

"Do I get any say in any of this?" I asked.

"'Course, psychic! Baron don't go where the Baron ain't wanted. You tell me no, an I'll toddle on back to chat with your little priest. He's probably pissin' his pants. Some of the dead get grabby when the Baron ain't around to corral 'em."

"Will they kill him?" Ava asked. "'Because I'm still considering it."

"Nah. Yes? Nah. Maybe," Baron Samedi said, running through literally every possibility with a smile. "It'll be a good surprise for all of us, yeah?"

Ava gritted her teeth. "Baron, we need that key that Bishop used to get to you."

"Ask him yourself. The Baron is the arbiter of life and death, not a delivery service," he said, plucking the cigar out of her mouth and taking three deep puffs. "That's the stuff. Say the word, psychic. The Baron will take you for a ride and leave broken hearts up and down the streets of the Quarter. And some drained motherfuckers in the process. The Baron loves himself a party, the shape of the participants don't really enter into it, ya feel?"

"And why does it have to be me again?" I asked.

"Hot stuff over there? She's part demon. Not as much soul. We loa, we really need somethin' to hang onto, if you know what I mean," he said, making lewd pelvic thrusting motions.

I stared, open-mouthed at this ancient, powerful, otherworldly pervert.

"Can't argue with that," Ava said with a chuckle.

"Look, sugah," I said to Samedi, "What we really need is to get her boything to get his lily white ass back here with that key so I can either return it to Ivé or give it to Coates. Either way one of 'em is like to kill me over this."

"Nah, you do the Baron this favor an' he'll refuse to dig your grave, just this one time," Baron Samedi replied.

"Come again?" I asked.

"Uh, Nero? What Baron Samedi is generously offering is that if you let him skin ride of your own free will, he'll give you a 'get out of jail free card' on dying one time."

I blinked "He can do that?" I asked.

"He can," Samedi replied with a laugh. "When he's properly motivated. You don't worry your pretty little head 'bout nothin'. Everything's gonna be alright."

My head spun, but I didn't see any other options, so I nodded.

Samedi smiled wide, which is a peculiar look on a skeleton who's not a skeleton. He spit in his hand and held it out to me. I very gingerly dribbled some spit into my hand and held it out, scrunching up my eyes.

Then I felt him grab me and kiss me full on the mouth. Skeletons are *not* supposed to have tongues, and they're certainly not supposed to grind on a body the way the Baron did on me.

Not gonna lie and say it was unpleasant. It was just a bit unexpected is all. I'm ready for a good time as much as anybody, especially when I was unattached like I was back then. The kiss went on and on, the heat and passion building as it did. I could feel his strong hands roaming and warmth flowing from him into me. The room was spinning, my breath coming in shorter gasps as I lost myself in the moment. I could feel his need mirroring my own as I fell into his kiss with all my heart and soul.

Then I found myself as a passenger in my own body.

It's karma, really. There have been times where I've had to be stern with someone and step into the drivers' seat in their brain. Times I haven't been concerned about what my mental intrusions were doing to folks. This was years of karmic debt paid back in one lump sum. I could feel my body moving, hear me speaking words, feel the sensations as the Baron piloted me through the Quarter. But I had no ability to act on my own. I couldn't so much as redirect a pinky-twitch.

The night is a blur. Baron Samedi drank what felt like gallons of rum. Smoked enough cigars that my lungs have to look like shriveled raisins, and ran roughshod through men and women. I lost track of how many and what he did to each.

It's better not to remember some things, sugah. Much better.

The next morning I woke up in my bed. Someone had superglued sandpaper to the back of my eyeballs and my mouth had been used as an ashtray during a Tom Waits concert. I felt around my head to find the seven or eight icepicks that it felt like I'd have shoved in there, but shockingly found none.

The smell of coffee drifted in from the kitchen, tantalizing and nauseating simultaneously.

With a loud groan, I hauled myself to my feet, noting that I'd been changed into pajamas, at least.

I dragged myself into the kitchen, blinking back against the harsh white light assaulting me from every window, and regretting my obsession with natural light as I slumped against the kitchen counter and fumbled with the cabinets to retrieve a mug.

With shaky hands I started to fill it with lifesaving coffee, then paused.

The hangover made thinking hard, but something wasn't right.

"Nero, we need to talk," the voice sitting at my kitchen table informed me.

With a scream, I wheeled and saw Jason Bishop, his hands steepled in front of him.

And that's when I remembered I don't have an automatic coffee pot.

*Chapter
Seven*

As soon as my brain caught up to what my sandpapered eyes were reporting, I did the only reasonable thing I could think of and threw my coffee mug at him.

"Jesus! Nero, wait!" he objected.

I was having none of it, I stumbled into the living room, pausing to fling books over my shoulder, toss pillows blindly, and use my general decor as the ineffectual weapon that it was turning out to be.

"Look...hey! I'm trying—stop that—look—Did you just throw a shoe?" he said as he walked after my slow retreat, weathering the barrage of not-at-all dangerous objects.

"Bitch, you already took the key from me, what more do you want? Don't wanna wait for Ivé or Coates to do the job themselves? Lookin' ta make a name finishing me off?" I asked, still trying to retreat, but hampered by my hangover and the current bout of light-headedness I was experiencing.

"Nero, I'm trying to return the key," he said with a sigh.

I paused, a DVD of Casablanca held poised to fling. "Come again?"

"I—I shouldn't have taken it. Stolen from you," he said, holding his hands up in surrender in the face of my terrifying weapon. "I came to bring it back. Return it."

He held out the key.

The real key. I could feel the psychic pressure pulsing off it. Feel the power emanating from it. Under the circumstances, it made me wanna vomit. I took the key from him, fully expecting another trick or ruse. Strangely, there was none.

I eyed him warily. "Go on," I said slowly.

"I was in the underworld, standing face to face with Baron Samedi," he began.

I shuddered, half-remembered images of debauchery running roughshod through my mind.

"When you did whatever you did. He vanished straight away. Absolutely brilliant, by the way. What did you do?"

"Called Ava. The two of us tracked you down to your bar," I began.

He nodded. "I found the door."

"Yeah. Well, we found your little trick with the map and realized we couldn't find you, and Ava suggested that if we couldn't find you by going to Samedi, we should bring Samedi to us."

"You summoned the Baron? What was the offering?" he asked.

"Cigars, rum, and a body for the night," I said with a shudder.

"Yours?" he asked.

I nodded, the motion of which almost made me puke.

"That explains why you look so rough. Baron Samedi has some serious appetites," he said. "You're lucky to be alive."

"I don't feel very lucky or very alive, so I reject the premise of your statement, sugah," I replied. "If your ass hadn't taken the key, none of this woulda been necessary."

"Yeah. I'm–I'm sorry. I saw it as a chance to save my sister and I grabbed it. I told myself that I'd return it before you had any idea I'd made the switch and that it would be in your hands before you would ever meet with that Coates moron," he said.

"Then why'd you work so hard to cover your tracks?" I asked.

"In case I was wrong and you figured it out. The plan at that point was that it's better to ask forgiveness than permission."

"That's the shittiest fucking thing anyone can say, Bishop. Ain't a damned thing that feels worse than someone you depended on stabbing you in the back. And if you think I'm mad, you wait till Ava gets her claws on you," I said.

"How bad are we talking?' he asked.

"You should look into tradin' places with your sister," I suggested.

"Fuck," he muttered. "There's no excuse, but I wasn't in my right mind. It was like, I don't know. Like something I needed to do. Like I couldn't resist it," he said.

Alarm bells started going off in my head. "What do you mean?"

"Just what I said," he said.

"Bishop, did you check this thing for enchantments when we were at Ivé's?" I asked.

He shook his head. "Can't. There's so much magic wrapped around it it's like trying to find a match while you're holding it up to the sun. Wait. You think that–" he said, his face growing grave.

"I think it's possible that we're very, very fucked," I said.

"You have a truly astounding gift for understatement," a voice said from my doorway.

Both of us snapped our heads toward the sound to see a figure leaning against my open door frame. Standing six and a half feet tall, he was an absurdly thin, dark-skinned black man with a shaved head and an obsidian-black, neat little trimmed beard. He wore a similar top hat to Baron Samedi, and he wore skull face paint underneath.

"Papa Ivé, I presume?" Bishop said.

"Boy, you will give me what is mine. Fail to do so and you will have seconds to live," he said. His voice carried a soft patois that suggested either Creole or Haitian roots, but as someone who grew up here, there was something just a little off about it. Like it was older. From a different place and a different time.

I'm not ashamed to say that the man terrified me.

"Look, Mr. Ivé? Papa? Sugah?" I tried. He didn't seem to appreciate any of them. "This has all just been a huge understanding."

"Is it?" he asked. "I misunderstand that you set fire to a food bank for my people so you could break into my home, where my daughter slept, and rob me?"

"That actually sounds pretty spot on," Bishop commented.

I waved at him and tried to shush the idiot.

Ivé's eyes went wide. "You dare mock me? I can see you, charlatan. You have little to no power of your own, instead acting like a magpie collecting shiny objects and stealing what items of power you can con from people. Like you tried to do with my key."

"Successfully did with your key," Bishop corrected. "And I'm not mocking you, Ivé. I'm just not lying to you. That feels more like respect than mockery."

"You have an odd definition of respect, charlatan," Ivé snorted.

"Not the first time I've heard that," Bishop said.

"It could get you killed."

"Not the first time I've heard that either," Bishop said. "Back when I was in the seminary they said it all the time."

"The seminary? Here in New Orleans?" Ivé asked, his eyes narrowing. "You're associated with The Church?"

"Loosely," Bishop said. "I've been known to do the odd job for them, off the books."

He sat very quiet and very still for a long moment, then snorted. "There is enough truth to your words to warrant further examination, but be aware: there is a marker owed, charlatan. From you to me for this insult done to me and mine."

Bishop nodded. "Agreed."

Then the two shook hands after Bishop handed over the key, and some sort of weird spark thing flared when their hands touched. Like the power of friendship or some shit. Sugah, I couldn't even.

Ivé glared at the both of us for a minute, then vanished in a swirl of shadows, like some sorta damned diva.

"What the holy fuck just happened, Bishop?" I demanded. "What was that with you takin' the blame, an' the marker, and...all of it?"

"Ivé's part of the Shadow Accords. My affiliation with the church makes pretty much anyone in that world at least a little nervous about just killing me. They're not sure how much heat that'll bring down on them. Ivé is bad news but not even he wants a fight with The Order if he can avoid it."

"So that's it? I'm free and clear?" I asked, breathing a sigh of relief.

"I don't know about free and clear, but Ivé has his face-saving marker. I'm sure whatever he has me do will be awful,"

"Serves your ass right," I said. "But I forgive you for the key fiasco, sugah. I'll even put in a good word with Miss Thang to get you outta the doghouse."

"I'd appreciate that," he said, smiling.

I went back to the kitchen, and threw open the shutters, looking out into the beautiful French Quarter morning, hangover chased away by adrenaline. "Thank you, New Orleans!" I shouted.

And was promptly shot in the chest.

Chapter Eight

First: Rude. Who shoots a body when they're just standin' in their kitchen window sayin' hello to the day and mindin' their own business? Outside of New Yorkers, I mean?

Second, being shot is a weird sensation. From what I'm told, everyone feels it a bit different. For me the first thing I noticed was that someone had hit me in the chest with a hammer, followed quickly by a burning feeling and me falling backward onto my floor.

So there I was, layin' in a rapidly spreading pool of my own blood when there was a light rap on my door, which then opened, allowing Charles Coates to enter. The tech billionaire strutted in wearin' what looked like some version of a safari outfit of all things.

"Damn, bro. That's a sick-lookin' chest wound. Props to Marcos!" he declared. Then he noticed Bishop kneeling beside me. "Shit. Didn't get the memo that there was other company in here." He took out a walkie-talkie and spoke into it, "Haynesworth, make a note to fire Marcos for not telling me there was another loser in this fuckin' dump?"

"Very good sir," the device squawked back.

I was terribly confused as I lay there. I was in pain, but it seemed like the big ol' hole in my chest shoulda been much more of a problem than it felt like it was. I was losing blood, and it hurt enough that I was fightin' back tears, but I wasn't getting light-headed, or feelin' cold, or any of that other stuff I've heard people talk about when they're bleedin' out.

I felt irritated, but fine, otherwise.

Bishop also seemed to pick up on my current 'not dying from a fatal gunshot' issue and promptly blocked Coates's view of me.

"Who the fuck are you?" he asked.

"You don't know me? Me? You ever read Wired? Scientific Fuckin' Weekly? Maxim?" Coates demanded

"Not really. I'm generally too busy for that sort of trash," Bishop replied.

"Trash? Motherfucker, you're lookin' at Charles fuckin' Coates. Hold your applause," Coates said.

"Charles who? Are you one of those reality TV stars? I don't bother with that sort of thing," Bishop said, displaying his true superpower of 'being a dick.'

Coates seemed to be at a loss for how to deal with someone who didn't care about his money, influence, or status. "I'm a fuckin' billionaire, man. It's sick!"

"Oh," Bishop replied.

"Oh? Oh? Is that all you've got to say when you meet one of the richest motherfuckers in the world? I'm fuckin' famous just because I'm so god-damned rich!"

"I mean, should I be impressed by you? You just shot my friend," Bishop said, his voice calm and level

"Now, legally speaking, I didn't shoot Mr. Frye," he said seriously, "I had Mr. Frye shot!" he added with a chortle, bending over and slapping his knee. "Oh, c'mon, man! That was fuckin' hysterical! Laugh!"

Bishop just looked at him, hands in his pockets.

"I'm good," he said.

Coates sputtered, then brought the walkie-talkie to his lips. "Haynesworth, laugh!"

A forced staticky chuckle came through the speaker.

"See? I'm a goddamned riot," Coates said with a smirk.

"So you're the one that hired Nero to steal from Papa Ivé?" Bishop asked.

"You're goddamned right I did. Ghoulish motherfucker wouldn't sell me the key, no matter how much I offered," Coates said.

"Some things aren't for sale at any price," Bishop replied, his voice still calm.

"Bullshit. Everything's for sale if you know who to talk to and are willing to pay. You want drugs? Name it and I can get it in less than a day. Newest tech? Newest toys? Girls? Kids? I've bought it all. I've hunted endangered species! Got their fuckin' heads hangin' in my library!"

"Right, because books just get so dull," Bishop replied.

"Are you mocking me, motherfucker?" Coates asked

"You know, this time I can answer yes. Yes, I am mocking you, you fucking manbaby., Bishop said with a chuckle. As Coates's mouth opened and closed like a fish, Bishop continued. "Nero told me all about your asinine plan to try to hunt a being who's basically a god. How stupid are you? Or are you just that spoiled?"

"Stupid? Spoiled? Would a stupid or spoiled person bag himself Africa's Big Five, bitch?" Coates demanded.

"Yes!" Bishop shouted. "That's exactly what an idiotic, spoiled little man baby would do. Then they'd get bored and look for something even more dangerous and somehow stumble onto some things they can't possibly begin to understand and set themselves up to die a horrible death. If they're lucky."

"What the fuck do you know, anyway. You're just here cryin' over your dead friend. That's what you fuckin' get when you double cross Charles fuckin' Coates," he said.

"No, I'm the guy that's here to tell you to get the fuck out of New Orleans," Bishop said.

Coates laughed. "Man, you're almost as funny as me."

"Did I stutter? Get. Out. Of. My. City!" Bishop said, poking Coates in the chest after each word.

"Back the fuck off man, I know Brazilian Jujitsu! Got trained by Renzo fuckin' Gracie!" Coates said, wildly gesticulating and making noises like he was in a Bruce Lee movie.

Bishop watched him for a minute, then took out a cell phone from his pocket and pushed "play". Coates stopped waving his arms around, his eyes going wide as he heard the conversation they just had played back to him.

"That won't be admissible in court!" he shouted.

"I didn't send it to court," Bishop replied.

"You sent it out?" Coates asked, going pale.

Bishop nodded.

"Where? Who did you send it to?" Coates demanded.

"I told you to get out of New Orleans. It's not because of anything I'm going to do to you, but Papa Ivé's probably gonna be pretty pissed off about you robbing him and calling out a hit in his city. He's also got some very specific feelings about human trafficking and the slave trade? I'd guess you have ten to fifteen minutes before him and a bunch of his guys show up to have a chat with you," Bishop said with a smile.

Coates coughed. "No. You're bluffing."

"Maybe. Let's wait here together to find out."

Coates backed up and stumbled, falling on his ass before scrambling down the stairs, running as fast as his toned legs could carry him.

As soon as Coates was gone, I sat up and looked down at what should be a fatal wound. "What the fuck, Bishop?"

He shrugged. "I've got no clue, but you should definitely be dead."

"Aw shit. The Baron said I'd get a freebie. One death he wouldn't dig my grave for!" I said, with a smile. "But what do I do about this hole in me? Won't it cause problems ?"

"I'm not a doctor," Bishop said with a shrug. "But I think so? Probably want to get it taken care of. I know somebody that can probably take care of it."

"It's Ava isn't it?" I said.

"I know more people than just Ava!" Bishop objected.

"But it's Ava, isn't it?" I said.

He paused, then nodded. "Yeah. It's her."

Interlude
Three

Aaron hit me.

"Ouch!"

"How dare you put my baby in danger like that?" he demanded.

He hit me a second time.

"Ow! What the fuck, Aaron?" I asked.

"That's for burning down a food bank!" he said.

"I didn't burn it—ouch!" I said.

"Stop making excuses!" Aaron demanded

He hit me a third time.

"That's for stealing from him!" Aaron said.

I looked at Ava, who shrugged. "I told you what I thought about what you did at the time, Jason. I haven't changed my mind about it now. It was a dick move. You made a lot of dick moves."

I paused, then nodded. "You're not wrong. Would it help if I would find a different way to handle it if I had it to do over?" I asked.

"A bit," Aaron said, mollified. "It means there's hope for you yet. Slim though it is."

"Holding out hope for me to change for the better is a losing hand. Ask Jackie," I said.

Jackie quickly took a drink and motioned that her mouth was full.

"I don't believe you guys called Papa Ivé on Charles Coates and the man lived. I guess even The Voodoo King of New Orleans isn't willing to take on that much heat," Victor said.

"Oh, I never sent him anything," I said.

"Come again?" Jackie said.

"Ivé. I never sent him anything about that conversation. He was pissed at me and Nero and had just left. I figured it would be better not to make him even angrier," I said.

"You bluffed your way out of trouble with Charles Coates? That guy's been on that Shark show. With the businesses?" Jackie said.

"He's a fucking moron," I said.

"He is," Nero agreed.

"So, the only one left to hear about how you met is Ava," Victor said.

"I'm not sure this is that sort of party," Ava said.

"I know you and Jason knew each other before I met him," Jackie said.

"Bishop met Ava around the same time he met me," Father Raimond offered. "It wasn't long after he left the seminary. After the—incident with his father."

"Me and Bishop had our thing. We were on again, off again for a bit, we messed around with some big players and stopped a bad person. End of story," Ava said with a shrug, taking a drink.

"Is this when you found out about dragons?" Nat asked.

"*Dragons?*" Jackie exclaimed, spitting out her drink.

Ava sighed. "I don't think we need to get into all this."

"Please?" Victor asked.

Jackie nodded, eyes wide. "I want to hear what you guys were like at the very beginning of all this craziness."

"Are you sure you want to hear this, Jackie? All of it?" Ava asked.

Jackie paused, took a drink, then shrugged. "I mean, you don't need to be super explicit," she said.

"This is a bad idea," Ava said, shaking her head.

Book 4: Ava's Story

Chapter ONE

Okay, I guess we're doing this.

Fine.

I met Jason, we hooked up, we broke up, and we got back together a bunch while meeting everyone else, and then you know what happened next.

The End.

No? We're *really* doing this?

I was the first member of the supernatural community who met Jason if you discount the Church. Which I do.

Before him, my life was great. Easy. Uncomplicated. I was a succubus and making my living and fulfilling my needs was effortless. I'm still in the same spot at Bayou Review and the act has changed over the years, but the gist is the same. Sing a little tune, get the crowd riled, and suck in the ambiance. At the time there were no worries about larger struggles. No concerns about deeper meanings.

Like I said: simple.

I first laid eyes on him when he wandered into my club. He was a wet-behind-the-ears occult practitioner, convinced he was the smartest, sneakiest, and dirtiest player in any game he was in. It's a miracle he hadn't gotten himself killed before we met, but I guess he was either too stupid to die or just lucky enough to survive until he'd caught wind that I was someone who knew things and he came to me looking for information.

"Ava Dufrense?" My name was used as a question, and somehow the voice that carried it managed to cut through the background noise in the club and reach me. I quirked an eyebrow to look at its owner.

He was a good-looking guy in a scruffy kinda way. He wore too much black and had too many silver rings on his fingers. I almost dismissed him as an older scene kid. Some refugee poseur from Hot Topic who was trying too hard, but there was something in the air around him. The faintest taste of sulfur. A bit of copper. It intrigued me.

"You found me, champ," I said.

His right hand stayed in his pants pocket. Maybe gripping a crucifix or some sort of charm to protect against me ensnaring him with my infernal wiles. There are tons of those things out there. Some of them even work a bit. Most don't.

"I'm Jason Bishop. I've been told that people tell you things. That you *know* things. Know people," he said a bit stiffly. Like he'd rehearsed it.

Adorable.

"That's me, and maybe. It all depends on who's asking for what and what they're willing to pay to get it. Do you have something you want to give me?" I purred, leaning in and tracing a finger from the collar of his black tank top up to his throat.

He stammered a bit, swallowed, then tried to rally. "I've got—ahem—I've got something to trade for your help in finding someone."

"You're looking for a private detective, slugger. That's not really what I do," I said, turning away.

"I think you'll find that it is," he said. "I was contacted by The Order. Do you know what that is?"

I froze. Those were the last words I expected or wanted to hear. I slowly turned back to look at him, guarding my expression. "And if I do?"

"Then you'll know it's important. Can we speak somewhere? Privately?" he asked.

I motioned him to follow me and called out to the bouncer. "Zeke! I'm taking an hour. Don't send anyone back for anything."

Zeke smiled and gave me a thumbs-up. As an aside, I've never really understood why you think he's so scary, Jason. Zeke's a pussycat.

I led Jason back to my dressing room and locked the door behind us, then perched on the edge of my makeup table, crossing my legs to maximize the distraction they would cause. Because boys are dumb and I'm a succubus.

It worked, his eyes were nowhere near looking at mine.

"So, you said you have a job from The Order and you need my help?" I prompted with a slight smile.

"Yeah," he said, coughing and shaking his head. "Yeah. I—I was." He stopped, closed his eyes, and took a deep breath. When he reopened them he was very deliberately looking me in the eye. "Sorry, I was—it doesn't matter. Like I said, my name's Jason Bishop. I'm an occultist and former seminary student from Notre Dame Seminary before I—well, I left. Let's just leave it at that," he said.

Something he said itched at the back of my head. Something about a seminary student and a house explosion. I nodded. "I've heard of you," I said.

"I figured. So, after the seminary, I talked to a lot of people in the church. Tried to call in any shred of a favor I had. Most of them thought I was crazy, but a few believed me. Said that all the things I was saying sounded plausible, but that I needed to be more careful about what I said and who I said it to," he said. "I heard there was a secret society inside of The Church that kept a lid on things like that. Made sure they didn't hurt people?"

"That's how they explained the Order to you?" I laughed.

He nodded, smiling bitterly. "Yeah. Talk about a hard spin. I sorta freaked out on the guy. Father Raimond over at St. Louis's Cathedral. I asked how they could have let something like this happen to my family if they were supposed to protect regular people from the supernatural. Accused them of being shit at their jobs. Of not having any care for the little guy. All sorts of shit."

"Takes either no brains or giant balls to dress down a member of the Order. They like to kill first and question later," I said.

"I wish I could claim it was me being brave, but the truth is I didn't know how dangerous they were and I just lost my temper with him," Jason said. "The guy just stood there and took it. I'd have gotten just as much mileage screaming at one of the stained glass windows. Finally, when I'd ranted myself out, he said that he appreciated my frustration and that the Order would be in touch if they had any further information for me."

"You got an in-person form letter?" I asked.

"I sure did," he replied. "Might as well have told me 'Do not reply, this mailbox is unattended.'"

I leaned forward. "So how did you get from 'don't call us, we'll call you' to 'we have a job for you'?" I asked.

"That's just the thing, I don't know. That was around a year ago. Since then I've been looking into stuff and reading as much as I can about everything. I've been watching some of the movers and shakers out on the streets and getting a feel for this world I'm trying to move into," he said.

Jason paused once again, closing his eyes and shaking his head to try to clear the cobwebs. I smiled. It appeared whatever he'd been using wasn't particularly effective in safeguarding him from my influence.

He looked up at me, forcing his eyes to meet mine. There was something there. Something more.

But, that wasn't the truth, or not all of it. You could see the self-destructiveness hovering over him like a cloud. This man spent most of his nights at the bottom of a bottle. The other nights he found even more destructive pastimes.

"This isn't a place for tourists, Jason. Doing this half-way's a good way to get yourself killed. Especially if you show up with baggage filled with demons," I told him.

"Kind of an ironic phrase coming from you, but I know. That's why I've been so careful."

I looked at him and raised an eyebrow.

"You know what I mean. Or I had been so careful with the supernatural stuff. Yesterday when I opened up my bar, I found a note sitting on the floor near the mail slot. No return address. No stamp. My name on the front, and that's it. I opened it thinking it was some sort of neighborhood watch thing. It was from the Order."

He handed me a folded note from his back pocket. *Mr. Bishop,*

> *I trust this message finds you well. I am reaching out to you because of your past experiences and your intended dedication to Our Lord and our cause. The Order has need of your talents, Mr. Bishop.*
>
> *There is an itinerant preacher calling himself Brother Avery who is operating in the New Orleans area. The man is dangerously delusional. He sees the servants of Lucifer everywhere and doesn't hesitate to denounce them from the pulpit. This behavior isn't uncommon amongst our Protestant brethren, but in the case of Brother Avery, the targets of his denunciations have been dying unexpectedly within hours of drawing his wrath.*
>
> *The Order feels that your unique talents would make you an ideal individual to take up this investigation, and would be in your debt if you were able to address this for us in a suitable manner.*
>
> *Yours,*
>
> *A*

I folded the paper and handed it back to him. "Unique talents?" I asked.

He nodded. "I can see auras. Around people. Objects. It helps me recognize supernatural creatures and power. The thing is? I never told anyone in The Order about that. I never told *anyone* about that."

"Why not?" I asked, frowning.

"Because when you spend most of your life thinking you're crazy, the last thing you want to do is to invite other people in to confirm it for you," he said bitterly. "I've got enough baggage kicking around in my head. I don't need to go looking for more."

"It's a neat mystery and all but I still don't see where I fit in," I said.

"Research," he said. "I need someone who knows how things work on the ground if I"m going to look into this shit. I need to find this Avery guy and get the goods on him so I can meet whoever this "A" is and find out how he knew about my hidden skill."

"That sounds like a great deal for you, but what about me?" I asked. "I don't work for free, tiger."

"Of course not. You would be the one that gets the favor from The Order," he said.

I blinked. "Excuse me?"

"What?" he said.

"I thought you said you would transfer The Order's favor to me," I said.

"That's exactly what I said," he replied.

"I appreciate the offer, Jason, but I'm a demon," I said.

"Half demon," he corrected. "And yeah, I noticed."

"How did you know that?" I asked.

"Your aura. It's not quite right for full infernal," he said with a self-satisfied smirk.

"And you get that just by looking at people?" I asked.

"Not quite. I have to concentrate a bit. If I do it for too long or to too many people, I get a killer headache. But yeah. It'll tell me what sort of supernatural creature a person is, if they're under the effects of magic. Their general emotional state. If they're lying. Things like that," he said.

What sort of supernatural creature a person is.

I let that roll around in my mind. This former priest looked at individuals who were in the supernatural world, walking in the twilight as people. He looked at me like I was people.

I was honestly moved.

"And what's mine saying now?" I asked, a sly smile pulling at my lips.

He stood up and walked over, getting closer, and staring at me closely. "You're a bit amused, but you've looked like that most of the time I've been watching you. You're curious. Intrigued, even. You're part infernal," he paused, smiled, then added. "And you want me to kiss you right now."

I smiled languidly at him. "You see all that, do you?"

He nodded. "Except for the kissing part. That was me hoping."

"Seems accurate to me," I said, putting my hands on his shoulders.

He leaned in and brushed his lips against mine, sending little butterflies fluttering through my stomach as they touched. Soon, I felt myself pressing up against him as he traced kisses along my neck and allowed his hands to roam freely, leaving a trail of goosebumps on my skin wherever they traveled while I grabbed two handfuls of his hair to guide the path.

"You're—yup. You're gonna be no good for business at all. A girl has a feel for these things," I said.

After my show wrapped, Jason and I stepped out into the muggy New Orleans streets. Few places, if any, have that same feel on your skin. There's something about the heavy air, the way it mixes with the booze on Bourbon Street, the stink of human sweat, and the Spanish Moss that makes it feel like every time you look down an alley, every time you round a street corner, there might just be a little magic hiding there. To the city's credit, there often is.

I don't know if other cities are quite as active on the spooky side of the street as New Orleans is. I was born here, raised here, and haven't traveled very far, but I can tell you that even if they have similar amounts in New York, Chicago, or Los Angeles, it'll never have that same flavor.

We strolled down Canal Street at a leisurely pace, the streetlights casting their halos into the thick air.

I walked next to Jason as he attempted to glower around the silliest grin I've ever seen. He was happy and energetic. Jittery, almost. Probably because I didn't take a piece of him when we were together.

Why? I still don't know. I just – it never occurred to me in the moment. It's strange.

I was turning that over in my head when he finally broke the silence.

"Do you have a plan on where we can get information?" Jason finally asked me after we had quietly walked for ten minutes.

"I do," I said. "We're going to have to consult an expert."

"You're an expert," Jason reminded me.

"I am. I'm an expert on what's happening in the city, but this is an expert on all things ephemeral. Of those fleeting little wisps of nothing floating around, carrying their knowledge with them."

"What are they?" he asked.

"I—I'm not sure. I think she's probably a hag," I said.

"A hag? They're fae, right? That's not a very reliable source, they're famous for being the definition of fickle," he mansplained.

I stopped, put my hands on my hips, and gave him a flat look. He had the good grace to look ashamed of himself.

"Which you already know, because that's why I came to you," he admitted.

I patted him on the cheek. "Good boy. He can be taught. Since you're such a well-read proto-priest, hags aren't like that. They're believers in making deals, just as much as the infernal are. The difference is their payment terms are a bit more eclectic."

"This doesn't sound promising," he said.

"There's no telling what they'll ask for or what they'll accept. It could be anything, and I mean that literally," I said. "It could be something tangible, it could be a favor, or it could be something highly personal."

Jason shook his head. "Sounds dangerous."

"Rita's not so bad. The Church knows she's here and hasn't moved against her, so that's almost like having their seal of approval, right?" I asked.

"I'm positive that's not how that works," Jason replied. "But you think she'll know about this guy who sent me the letter? Or at least the guy who the letter wants me to check on?"

"With a hag, they can literally find or do anything, if the price is high enough," I said. "And ta-da. We're here."

I gestured to a dingy little shop that looked like a homeless lean-to. The wooden door was barely three feet wide, had mismatched planks that left large gaps, and a big green doorknob sat loose in its moorings on the left side.

"That?" Jason asked, his disbelief clear from his tone.

"Uh-huh. She's fae, what did you expect?" I asked him. "That's Mad Rita's. No sane person would run a shop like this."

Jason huffed, then turned the knob and walked in, with me on his heel.

I would have warned him what to expect when he went inside. I really would have, but with Mad Rita, you could honestly never tell. Sometimes it looked like a tent sitting in the crumpled alleyway. Other times you might find yourself in a bubble at the bottom of the ocean. One time I came to her and she met me in a massive castle, complete with guards in shining plate mail and little dragons flitting about. Or large dragons that were far away.

The point is, whatever you think it's going to be, it never is.

This time Mad Rita's looked like a shop out of the Ren Faire. There were rickety wooden shelves with a variety of random objects on them running from waist level to absurdly high up into the rafters. Colored bottles filled with mysterious liquids sat next to shiny miniatures, which were next to buttons that looked like they'd been messily removed from a coat, and a box labeled "The Color Fivrese".

It's things like that last one that make me pause from time to time when I'm here. Like an unscratchable itch to know what in all the worlds that could be, but I know better. The cost is unlikely to be something I'd be willing to pay.

The shelves lined both walls and down the middle of the twenty by thirty foot space. And at the back of the store sat Rita.

I assume.

Much like the store, Rita changes depending on–something. No one knows what. Today Rita was an old woman in her early one hundred and tens, hunch-backed with large arthritic joints on her hands with one eye rheumy and one eye clear. Her grey tinted skin pulled against her bones like it was too tight. Her too-long arms hung down past her knees and she smiled as we entered, an unpleasant sight given this version of Rita only had five teeth.

"Hello, my little duckies, what can Rita do for ya today?" she asked, her voice thin and wheezy.

Jason looked at me and frowned. Apparently, I was in charge of this conversation.

"Rita?" I called.

Her good eye locked onto me. "Ava Dufrense. How's your mother?"

I gritted my teeth. "The same. We're not here about her. My friend here–"

"Friend?" she interrupted. "Demons don't have friends, Ava Dufrense."

"My friend," I repeated.

"Well. Okay, *Friend*, come here," she said, holding out one long, bony arm that stretched halfway across the store.

"Fuck," Jason muttered, then took two steps forward. The old woman's hand reached up and grabbed him by his chin and yanked him forward the remaining forty feet to the back of the store.

Yes, I'm aware it was only thirty feet long. I said what I said.

Rita held Jason up to her good eye, her face only inches away from his as she moved him this way and that, his feet dangling off the ground.

"Why this one?" Rita asked.

"Uh, lady? I'm right here," Bishop objected.

"Hush when your betters are talking, boy. Ava: Why this one? You've come here before, that's true, but always with a 'colleague' or 'client.' Even that handsome devil. What was his name?" Rita asked.

"He's a demon, and his name is Ivan," I said.

"Right. ee-VAHn. Pretentious. Even he was just a 'colleague'. What's different about this sad little broken man?" she asked.

"Still right here," Jason objected.

"I-I don't know," I admitted.

"Oh, okay then!" she said, her voice chipper and happy. She dropped Jason, who fell to the floor. I hurried forward, but he was already dragging himself to his feet.

"That sucked," he said.

"Wait for it, duckie. I haven't given you my price yet," Rita chortled.

"How do you—right. Never mind," Jason said, showing he's not a complete idiot. "So, what's the price?"

"What's the question?" Rita asked.

Jason blinked. "You just said you knew—"

"Well, yes, but it's still nice to be asked, you see. I get so few visitors. Let's me savor the moment," she said.

"Not many visitors? I can't imagine why," Jason muttered.

Both of Rita's eyes snapped over toward Jason. "Muttering at the hostess in her own domain is rude, little duckie. Do it again and Rita'll have your tongue in her pot."

"I–I apologize, Rita. I shouldn't have said that," he said.

"Forgiven! No need for me to enact a blood price over something so trivial. This time," she said, her voice dropping at the last two words.

"Uhh, t-thank you?" Jason said.

Rita waved her hand. "But you have a question."

Jason nodded. "Where is the man who sent me this letter?" he asked, holding up the missive from The Order.

"No, that's not the right question," Rita said.

"But that's what I want to know," Jason objected.

"But not what you need to know," Rita replied.

"Fine, what do I need to know?" he asked.

"You tell me," Rita said, drawing a growl of frustration from Jason.

He took a long, deep breath, closed his eyes, then opened them and nodded to himself.

"Rita?"

"Yes, duckie?"

"Can you tell me where to find the man who I've been tasked with locating in this letter?" Jason asked, overly enunciating each word.

"Are you sure you want to know that?" Rita asked.

"Positive," Jason said.

"Really sure?" she asked, causing a vein in Jason's forehead to start to throb.

Swallowing a string of curses, Jason nodded. "Yep," he said, his voice coming out strangled.

"Then I agree to sell you that information and not how to get your sister out of her torment in Hell," Rita replied, opening a massive tome that appeared next to her, taking a quill pen that appeared out of midair, and beginning to scratch a new record in.

"You, Jason Bishop, son of Edward Bishop and Joan Bishop nee Whitman, do hereby agree to exchange the memory of sunshine from the twenty-third of October when you were seven for information on the location of the man you've been tasked with locating in the letter you bear. Is that correct?"

Jason looked at me confused. I gave him a nod. It sounded like a good deal, but with Rita you could never tell.

He nodded, at which point Rita spat in her hand and held it out toward him. Jason paused, then steeled himself and spat in his hand and shook hers. Despite seeming to be the same size, her hand dwarfed his, swallowing it up and eclipsing it like a whale swallowing a minnow. Purplish smoke poured out where their hands met, smelling of daisies and warmth, settling onto the counter next to Rita and coalescing into an old-fashioned radio, scaled down to a foot tall.

The antique flared to life, the dial emitting the same purple glow and the voice coming from the speaker was deep and powerful, possessed of an underlying feel of authority.

"Thank you for joining once again, my brothers and sisters, for our Communion in The Lord. I am your humble servant, Brother Avery James, and this is the Church of the Divine Promulgation, spreading the Law of The Lord.

We are but two days away from our great tent revival in the den of iniquity itself, New Orleans. The Crescent City has fallen far from the Light of The Lord, opening its doors up to sinners of the worst kind. Purveyors and purchasers of flesh, drug dealers that peddle their poison and cause children to become a blight upon the world.

But we all know there's more than just the seven deadly sins at work within this once great city, my brothers and sisters. We do indeed. For the hand of the Great Enemy, himself, rests heavily upon the city. And as Lucifer's grip tightens, more and more of God's Children fall under his sway. Are coaxed into paths of evil by his words.

No longer.

No longer will we stand idly by while the wealthy and depraved slake their thirst on the flesh of the young and the innocent!

No longer will we stand idly by while monsters in the guise of men poison their brothers for profit!

No longer will we watch as child after child is fed into the heartless cogs of the machine of the public education system, ruthlessly and relentlessly ground down until their love of the Lord and their spark of creativity are excised from their soul in their entirety!

Oh, no. Not any longer, my brothers and sisters! For we bring with us a Reckoning!

In two days' time, we shall raise our revival tent in the middle of the city, and we will raise up our voices, calling down the wrath of God upon those who would seek to injure His flock. We will see this den of iniquity raised to nothingness, purged from the face of His Creation like Sodom and Gomorrah in years gone by.

Together!

Together we will bring His love back to His flock!"

"Jesus," Jason whispered.

"I think he's looking a bit more Old Testament than that," I said.

Chapter Three

"Well, thank you," Jason said as we left Mad Rita's Curiosity Shoppe. "I wouldn't have known where to start looking without your help."

I stopped, and put my hands on my hips. "So, that's it?" I asked.

Jason turned and looked at me. "Yeah. I asked for your help finding the guy, and you did. Now I know what I'm looking for," he said.

"Do you actually think you can do this without me?" I asked him. "You're a babe in the woods when it comes to The Gloaming, Jason. You'll be dead within the week. Make that two days."

"Do you think I don't know that?" he snapped. "Do you think I don't realize that ninety percent of the people who go bump in the night will see me like a naive poseur? Like I'm someone to use or manipulate? Like I'm a target, or even worse, a snack? They'll underestimate me just like you're doing right now."

"I'm not," I said.

"Then why? Why do you care? Why do you want to help? You've got your deal. The favor from The Order will transfer to you once I get it, or do you think I'd screw you out of that?" he asked.

I shook my head. "It's not that."

"Then what is it, Ava? What's the angle? No one helps for nothing. You've already got the only thing I'm willing to barter away. The well's dry," he said.

I looked at him for a moment, biting back a bunch of well-deserved comments. "I'm not looking for anything from you, Jason. I'm not looking for a payment or a deal. I'm not trying to steal your soul. I—look, this has been interesting. Fun, even. You're unexpected," I slowly replied, trying to vocalize a vague concept. A feeling I didn't quite understand myself.

"This ain't a field trip, Ava. This shit sounds dangerous, just like you said," he said.

I snorted. "No offense, but you don't need to worry about me on that front."

He looked me up and down, a far more calculating look than the lust-filled prior experience.

"You weigh what, a buck ten? Buck twenty? A strong breeze will blow you over," he said.

"You know, for someone that's done a lot of studying about the world you asked me to introduce you to, you get really stupid when you think it'll be convenient for you. I'm not going to dignify your implied question with a response, Jason. We both know you already know," I said, glaring.

He watched me for a moment, then nodded. "Fine. Guilty. You're really in just because you think it's interesting?"

"Don't sell interesting short," I said.

"So, we're what? Partners?" he asked.

"Partners sounds awfully permanent. Let's say we're currently co-workers with benefits," I said.

Heat rose on his face as a blush spread. Yes, you heard me correctly. I made Jason Bishop blush.

It was adorable watching him try to act gruff and professional while his complexion betrayed him that way. I could've watched for hours.

"I–yeah. That–that'd be good, I think," he stammered.

I sauntered over, putting a bit of extra swish in my hips just for fun, then put my hand on the side of his face and trailed my fingers down the side of his neck before leaning up and placing a gentle kiss on his cheek. "Me too. So, you–no–*we've* got a lead on him. What would you do next?"

"Next we check the internet," he said with a shrug.

"We what?" I asked.

"We consult the world wide web. The fire and brimstone types love to post their manifestos online. I'm willing to bet if we search for the Church of the Divine Promulgation or Brother Avery James we'll get some hits," he said with a smug grin.

He's always recovered quickly from being flustered.

"Guys like the one we heard on that radio thrive on attention and human misery," I said. "They can't work without it. You should check homeless shelters and camps. Drug dens. Places like that. I know a believer when I hear one, and he's that in spades. He'll want to do work that'll get him attention and that the big churches don't do enough of. Your choices are homeless or LGBTQ, and his flavor of fire and brimstone is too judgy for the latter."

"I–" he opened his mouth and closed his mouth like a fish a few times. I reached up and closed it.

"Shhh. Don't worry, looking online sounds great, but it's gone past 'very late' and straight into 'you're kidding me', Jason. Girl needs her beauty sleep so let's skip some of the flailing around."

"Right. I can meet you at your place first thing tomorrow," he began, then paused as he saw my amused, skeptical look.

"Look, I like you. Honestly. But I'm not an idiot. I've got fans, stalkers, and a bunch of creepy crawlies that would really like to know where I lay my head at night. How 'bout we meet at your place?" I said.

"That's fine. It's a bar on Toulouse. Bishops Crossing? Between Bourbon and Royal," he said.

"You live in a bar?" I asked. The name suggested he might.

"Nah, I live upstairs. I own the building," he said. "Ask the kid at the bar if I'm not down there already."

"So you live a couple blocks from here?" I asked.

He nodded.

"I...don't. If we're getting an early start tomorrow, it's silly for me to go all the way home and come all the way back," I said pointedly.

Jason Bishop likes to play dumb when it suits him. This time he was downright astute.

"Yeah, just plain silly," he agreed.

And that's the first time I saw Bishop's Crossing. No matter how many times I've been here, the first time will always stick with me. It was dream-like. The flickering light from the gaslights on the exterior sent shadows dancing around the entrance. The interior was dark, with the ambient light offering the vague outline of tables with chairs turned up on top, and a long bar with mirrored glass and bottles dominating the wall behind. It looked like a pipe organ, ready to play a funeral dirge to a long-lost love.

I was smitten.

I paused, taking it all in. I'll never forget the next part. Jason took my hand to guide me through the dining room area toward the stairs at the back. I know, it's a stupid thing. I know he didn't think anything of it at the time or probably since, but he guided me through the unfamiliar room, making sure I didn't bump into anything and going around that weird dip in the floor that's to the left of the center row of tables. He guided me just like I was a normal girl on a date he was bringing home. Not like I was a succubus he couldn't wait to get into bed. Not like I was a monster who could take whatever he could throw at me

Just me.

It might be the sweetest thing anyone had done for me up to that point.

He led us up the stairs to the apartment. The big windows let in the light from outside, continuing the ambiance from the bar. He directed me to the restroom, then disappeared for a moment, returning with a pair of sweatpants and a t-shirt.

I took the t-shirt and held it open from the bottom, peering inside

"What are you looking at?" he asked

"The Ringling Brothers," I said. "I think they might be inside this tent. Why do you have something this big? We could both fit in here," I said.

"Needed it for research," he replied vaguely. "I figured you could use it as a nightshirt if you wanted, or go with it and the sweatpants," he said.

I laughed. "That's sweet, but I generally just sleep in my underwear, Jason," I said as I padded my way back toward the bedroom.

"Or that," he agreed, following after me.

I stopped in the doorway and turned to look into his eyes. "It's late I'm going to sleep in your bed with you. What's the verb in that sentence?" I asked.

"Sleep," he said, looking down at the floor.

"Good boy," I said, patting his cheek again. "We've got work to do tomorrow."

The next morning I was awakened by the morning sun and yawned. I stretched before sitting up and looking around. Jason was still asleep next to me, his hair a tousled mess and his mouth slightly open. I slid out of bed and got dressed.

Even after a quick trip to the Review to pick up another change of clothes, I was still back with beignets in hand before Jason woke up.

He came stumbling out of his room while I sipped tea on his couch and looked out the window while nibbling on one of the pastries.

"Ready to face the day?" I asked.

He mumbled something and vaguely waved toward the window. I reached over and picked up a cup of coffee I'd grabbed on my way back.

"You're an angel," he said, putting the cup to his lips.

I froze, looking down at the table. "I–don't joke about that," I whispered.

"No joke, Ava. You're a godsend," he said.

"I said don't joke about that," I repeated more firmly.

"What're you–oh, shit. I'm sorry, I didn't mean–I forgot," he said.

I stared at him for a couple of beats, frowning. "You forgot?"

He nodded.

"You forgot I'm a demon?" I asked, incredulously.

'Half," he said. "But yeah. You're not–you don't feel like a demon," he said.

"Motherfucker, if you follow that up with 'you're one of the good ones', I swear to you, I will toss your ass right out that window," I said.

He held up his hands in surrender. "No offense intended! I swear!"

I grumbled and crankily drank my tea.

"I'm sorry?" he offered.

"Damned right you are," I muttered into the cup.

"Seems like someone forgetting you're a demon would be a good thing, a compliment, even," he said.

I sighed and put down the cup. "Look Jason, I appreciate what you're trying to do right now. I really do. You're fun, what you're doing is interesting, and you—you're easy to be around. But I am what I am," I said.

"Popeye?" he asked.

"It's not funny. I'm a monster. Something from The Pit. Doomed to torture humans in eternal damnation after I shuffle off this mortal coil. I'm a good time, but you need to discard any sort of notions about this being anything past just some fun to pass the time, okay?"

"Are you breaking up with me before we even go on a real date?" he asked.

"Let's not complicate things, okay? We've known each other for like five minutes, and you're getting that puppy-dog 'I'm gonna marry that girl' look on your face. Stop it. This girl isn't for marrying. Thinking about it is just foolish," I said.

"I'm sorry," he said.

I shrugged. "It is what it is," I said, once again half hiding behind my teacup

"I think you're wrong–" he began.

"Okay, let's get to work," I said, cutting him off. "We've got some revivalist lunatics to watch. I can't wait to go to their tent party tomorrow. They'll love me," I said with a disingenuous smile.

He gave me one of those looks. You know the ones. Those Bishop looks. The ones where he's trying to see inside your head and he's weighing a bunch of options on how to best get what he wants out of you. He got up and turned on his laptop without saying another word.

Later, I hovered over his left shoulder, staring at the horror that unfolded in front of us. Half an hour in, we'd seen a variety of older men screaming at a variety of cameras about the horrors of sin and the horrors that should be inflicted upon the sinners.

"Cheerful bunch," I said.

"This is nothing," Jason replied. "The bad ones can't keep their content up on reputable websites. They're the ones who explicitly call on their followers to hurt people. If the radio blurb we heard yesterday is any indication, Brother Avery skirts that line."

Twenty minutes later, we found him.

Brother Avery stood behind the pulpit on the screen. He was a tall man, his Einstein-like brown hair shooting away from his head in all directions, and his blue eyes burning with a fervent devotion you only see in true believers and the clinically insane. He ranted from the pulpit and finally called out a lustful man named Eric Marshall, a Congressman who was purported to traffic in young girls. Multiple investigations had found insufficient evidence to charge him, but his tastes had become an open secret. Congressman Marshall died five weeks ago, on the day the video was recorded.

Later in that same video, he cured a blind girl. Her parents' car had been struck by a drunk driver on the way home from a Girl Scout meeting, robbing her of both her sight and her father.

We found another one with Brother Avery standing in front of the stage, Bible in hand as he thundered to the assembled faithful about the injustice that allowed a greedy man like televangelist Oscar Jacobson to live in opulent luxury off the backs of donations he extorts from his followers, while he locks his doors against those in need in moments of crisis. Jacobson died four weeks ago, on the day of the recording.

This time he cured a man's late-stage lung cancer.

The third video was Henry Walters, who was an extreme diet success story. The man at one point weighed over five hundred pounds, which appeared to outrage Brother Avery, who declared him the very face of Gluttony, and felt that his transformation was too little, too late after taking food from the mouths of the hungry and devouring far more than he needed. The video was recorded three weeks ago. Henry Walters was found dead in his home on the day of the recording

At the end of this video, he cured a 40-year-old father of three of his Parkinson's.

I stared in a combination of awe and revulsion as we located all five of Brother Avery's sermons that ended in the death of the target of his wrath and a miraculous healing.

"It can't be a coincidence," I said. "Somehow Avery is taking the life or the energy from one person and giving to the other."

Bishop shook his head. "I don't think he can do that. None of the trappings are there for him to be performing ritual magic."

"You know this because–?" I asked.

"I know how to perform ritual magic," he said absently, clearly still thinking out loud. "No, there's gotta be something else at play here."

"How did the people he targeted die?" I asked.

He looked at me, frowned, cocked his head to the side, then smiled. "I don't know. But that's exactly what we need to find out?"

"Some of that ritual magic you've got tucked up your sleeve?" I asked.

"I thought I'd just make a few phone calls and lie to a bunch of people," he replied.

Chapter
Four

Three hours and dozens of phone calls later had seen Jason Bishop pretend to be a reporter, a medical student, a police detective, a priest, an insurance adjuster, and a funeral home director. And he'd gotten our answers.

"All five died of heart attacks," he said. "The youngest of the bunch was Martin Lewis, age twenty-seven. Only one of them had a prior history of heart disease, and the last guy I talked to–the one in Houston said that the man's heart seemed like it had been squeezed. Almost crushed."

"I don't know about rituals, but a willworker could do that," I said.

He shrugged. "No ritual that I know of or heard of, but if it's a willworker?" he shrugged.

"What now?" I asked. "This has all just offered up new questions instead of any answers."

"I think we go pay Brother Avery a visit," he said.

"At the revival tent?" I asked. "Yeah, that was the plan."

"No. At the homeless encampment. Right now," he said.

"To learn what?" I asked.

"I'm–I'm not sure," he admitted. "Just a gut feeling that we should go."

"Great. You have a little intestinal distress and now we're heading out to see the murder preacher. Jason, this seems like a bad idea," I said.

"Most of my ideas are," he admitted.

The Tchoupitoulas homeless encampment is a strange place. Situated under the overpass at the intersection of Tchoupitoulas and Calliope streets, somewhere just over one hundred people live in tents and small lean-tos, lined up in relatively neat rows on the mud and gravel ground. There are numerous burn barrels for cooking and warmth and a comparatively stable community of people making do together.

Drug abuse may be rampant, and any variety of crime short of regicide is something the residents need to look out for, but it represents something almost wholesome: a group of the most vulnerable people you could ever possibly meet banding together to help each other in a community. Brother Avery walked among them like he was one of them.

For all the bluster, fire, and brimstone on the pulpit, the tall preacher walked side by side with the residents through the camp. Praying with people. Praying for people. He stepped over used needles on the ground, walked past a barrel fire that smelled of burning feces, and offered his full attention to each person he spoke to, treating them like the most important thing in his world in the moment of their interaction.

Jason and I stood at the edge of the camp watching him. It was surreal to see the man who had been spewing so much hate offering such love and compassion to these people, who literally had nothing to give.

"We need to get closer. Talk to him," Jason suggested.

"Are you sure that's a good idea?" I asked, putting my hands on the side of my head and giving myself fake horns "Not sure he'll appreciate me for who I am. What if he's a willworker?"

"I don't see how he finds out unless you tell him," he said. "Because from here, there's nothing special about the guy."

"Nothing?" I asked, raising my eyebrows.

He shook his head. "Not a thing. His aura is that of a man of faith, who believes in his convictions with all of his being, but nothing magical or supernatural at all."

"So how's he doing the thing with the hearts?" I asked.

Again, he shook his head. "I don't know. Let's go ask him."

"Jason, remember how I said this was fun and interesting?" I asked.

He nodded.

"This is moving it into dangerous and suicidal. We know this guy can kill people just by wishing for them to be dead and your plan is to walk up and irritate him? Do you see how that's counterproductive to the 'being alive' result that we're hoping for?" I said.

"Sort of. We know people die when he names them from the pulpit, but not how he does it. I want to get closer to see if he tips his hand," he said and started walking toward Brother Avery.

We approached while he was kneeling with an African American man wearing a taqiyah. They were grasping hands with their eyes closed as we arrived. As we got closer, I had a growing itch between my shoulder blades. I nervously looked around us.

"Heavenly Father, please bless Your humble child Hassan and give him the strength to cast out his demons. Give him the grace to forgive himself for whatever trespasses he may have committed, for he wishes only to be Your humble servant and to spread Your Word. Amen." His voice was deep and resonant. As impressive as it was in the videos, they seemed to have lost something on the low end of the register. You could feel him talking like a rumbling in your lungs. He slowly came to his feet and smiled as we approached, holding his arms out in greeting

"I see that the Lord has blessed me with two weary travelers. What can I do for you on this fine afternoon, brother and sister?" he asked.

Jason smiled. "Good afternoon, Brother Avery. I'm Paul Bradshaw, and this is my partner Penny Smith. We're reporters with Clarion Herald here in New Orleans. We were hoping we could ask you a few questions, to let our readers know a bit more about you."

Brother Avery offered a guarded smile and regarded us both carefully. I fought down the urge to reach out and cloud his mind or to become more appealing to him. I wasn't certain what his reaction to either of those might be.

"I wasn't aware that the papists paid much attention to a simple tent revivalist like myself," he replied. "I'm afraid you won't find much in the way of pomp and circumstance with us, Mr. Bradshaw and Ms. Smith."

"We completely understand that, Mr. Avery–" Jason replied.

"Brother Avery," the other man quickly corrected him.

"Apologies. Brother Avery," Jason conceded. "We're more interested in the substance of your services than what you say. What you do. That sort of thing. There has been talk of you performing bonafide miracles."

"Ah, and now we're to the quick of it. Tell me, Mr. Bradshaw, are you referring to removing the curses laid upon His children that The Lord has sought fit to grant to those I've prayed with or the deaths of the sinners that I identify from my pulpit?" he asked.

"Five of each, correct?" I asked.

Brother Avery turned his intense gaze to me. For a moment, I was sure he'd sniffed me out. He'd extend an arm and pronounce me a demon. A harlot. Maybe some other old-timey word that men have used to control women over the centuries. I've always been partial to strumpet, myself.

But the denunciation never came, he just forced a smile. "There have been five deaths, certainly, but we've saved far more than five people from the Enemy's curses at my ministry."

"And that's been documented?" I pressed. The itch between my shoulder blades got worse while Jason looked at him, his expression guarded and Brother Avery held his smile, his eyes growing hard.

"How does one document the work of The Lord when He's breaking curses?" he asked.

"Medical records?" I suggested, offering my sweetest, least sincere smile. "Blood work and test results. MRIs for the MS patients?"

"I have nothing to prove, Ms. Smith. Much as I don't seek secular fame, I'm uninterested in subjecting the gifts from on high to the sort of base scrutiny of a medical procedure. The Lord has seen fit to remove the curse of blindness from Brother Owen and little sister Katherine. The curse of cancer from Sister Clara. The curse of addiction from Brother William. The curse of lameness from Brother Edward. Who am I to question that?" Brother Avery said.

I had the overwhelming urge to punch him in his smug mouth. I imagined it: my fist connecting, sending his too-perfect teeth flying everywhere as his body followed them earthward, insensate from the impact.

That's when Jason's eyes went wide. I followed his sightline but didn't see anything. He continued staring, his complexion going pale.

"Understandable," he muttered to Brother Avery and took my hand. "We should–"

"What I find interesting," Brother Avery said, interrupting, "Is that so much concern has been raised about these base sinners facing their final judgment," he said. "I understand the interest in the lame made whole, but in the depraved laid low?"

Bishop nodded, still spooked.

"These individuals whose lives were cut short were the very apotheosis of sin and depravity. A man who stole food from the welfare system to fatten himself. A man who used his elected position to prey upon children. A man who took money from his congregation to purchase mansions and private jets, but when those people needed him the most, he closed his doors to them. A woman who knowingly used a sweatshop, locking her employees inside only to have dozens perish when a fire broke out. A young man so filled with rage that he opened fire on a crowd of believers, but who the courts refused to properly punish. Again and again and again injustice has been allowed to take root and grow in our society because people are too afraid to stand up and say what they know to be right. Is any loss of human life tragic? Of course. Are those who've died after I named them less tragic than any other? Of course. We all know they are. The world is a better place without them in it, and now they face their final judgment before the heavenly gates," Brother Avery said.

"What about forgiveness? Penance?" I asked.

Brother Avery again turned his gaze on me, and again I felt a rush of panic that I struggled to keep down.

"Forgiveness and penance are only granted to those who ask for it. They are only available for people who show true contrition. None of these monsters did," he said.

"Uh, yeah. Thank you for your time," Jason said, nodding to Brother Avery and taking me by the hand and speed walking away. I could feel the preacher's eyes on us until we made it to my car around the corner.

"Things just got more complicated," Jason said.

"How so? We have exactly the same problem now as when we got here," I complained.

"No. When you were pushing Avery, something happened," he said, wiping sweat from his brow.

"I saw. Your eyes went wide, you got sweaty, you went pale. Er. Paler. You start off pretty pale, honestly," I said. "You looked like you'd seen a ghost."

"No. I looked like I saw an angel," he said.

His pronouncement hung heavily in the air between us for longer than was comfortable.

"Come again?" I said.

"I saw an angel. A servant of the Lord. A being who predates the Earth," Jason replied. 'Didn't you? It was right behind him."

I closed my eyes. "It doesn't work that way. I can't see them unless they reveal themselves, just like they can't see me. If they could, I'd be—look, this just officially became more dangerous than it's worth, Jason. I can't cash in a favor from the Order if I'm too dead to use it," I said, not looking at him.

I stared out my SUV's windshield and heard a deep sigh from the passenger seat.

"I don't blame you," he said.

"Look, Jason, you're a great guy–" I started.

"I'm really not," he interrupted, drawing a frown.

I fucking hate it when people talk over me. Hate. It. It makes me crazy. It didn't make me less crazy this time.

"—ish. Great-ish guy," I corrected after a deep breath. "Nothing's worth this. When actual angels get involved and they start smiting people in the name of the Lord, there tends to be a lot of collateral damage. Get out while you can."

He shook his head. "Not an option."

"Why? There's nothing you can gain that'll be worth dealing with that thing. It's a metaphysical nuke," I said.

He closed his eyes and pinched the bridge of his nose. I recognize that move really well now, it means he's frustrated and looking for the right words. Back then it just looked like a weird way to relieve sinus pressure.

To each their own.

"Walking away isn't an option because they knew about my sister in that letter, and who better to get in good with than a servant of the Divine if you need to get someone out of Hell?" he asked, his voice quiet.

I turned to look at him but found he wasn't looking at me. His eyes were still closed. "Get someone out of Hell? Are you nuts?" I asked. "Most people spend their lives trying **not** to end up there. It's supposed to be unpleasant. Famously so," I said gently.

He shook his head, then signed. "I–it was a few years ago. I was in the seminary, studying to be a priest. I was devoted, body, mind, and soul to the idea of serving God. Carrying out His Will, and had shown a level of—aptitude for some less-than-traditional subject matter that my class had been exposed to. Arcane writings, angelic script, and Judeo-Christian esoterica that had been uncovered over the years, had been approached by people who I now know were members of The Ordinis Templi Erinnys. I expressed interest, then they said they'd be in touch.

"I was meant to take my vows and enter the priesthood within the week when the nightmares started. Horrible, bloody dreams centered around my mother, father, and sister. The same thing every night," he said, tears beginning to gather around his closed lids. "The day of my ordination, it all came to a head. I'll never forget it: the storm raging outside. The burning in my chest as I ran to our house in the Garden District. The smell of blood was hanging in the humid air when I opened the door. The crazed look in my father's eyes while he stood over the corpse of my mother and my sister who he'd gutted like a butcher. Him saying it was all for me. That I shouldn't be there. Her pleading eyes. Her voice while she begged me to help her. She could barely speak above a whisper after the way he'd cut her."

He paused to wipe the tears from his eyes, opening them and looking up at the ceiling while taking a deep, shaky breath.

"It sounds like your dad was a real piece of work, but that's not you, Jason. You didn't do that," I said.

"Those dreams were a warning. Clear as day. If I'd have told her. If I would have reached out, Catherine would still be here," he said.

"That's not true. Plus, it doesn't sound like she's the sort of person who would end up in Hell, anyway," I reassured him.

"I tried to contact her. After. To tell her I was sorry. The ritual worked perfectly. I've used it dozens of times before and after. I couldn't reach her," he said, shaking his head and fighting back more tears. "So I went to the crossroads,"

I hissed. "That's never a good idea," I said.

He nodded. "I know. I wanted answers, and I used what I knew to wring them out of the demon who showed up to treat with me. He confirmed: She's in hell. Where and being held by who, I don't know. The demon wouldn't or couldn't tell me."

He took a deep breath once again, trying to bring it all under control.

He failed.

"She was my baby sister, Ava. I was supposed to protect her. That was my job, and I failed. I failed her," he sobbed.

Succubi are good at a lot of things, but comforting people experiencing real trauma and tragedy doesn't tend to fall into that category. We're more famous for things like 'tie this cherry stem into a knot with your tongue'. It's not that we don't, or can't, it's just–

What I'm saying is that's a completely different skill set.

Hands trembling slightly, I reached out, took hold of his shoulders, and pulled Jason Bishop to me for a hug. He grabbed me and hung on like he was drowning, shedding big ugly tears without reservation. We held each other with me stroking his hair for–well–I don't know how long. Long enough for his eyes to be puffy and red. And for his voice to sound raw. "I-I'm sorry," he rasped.

"For what? Being human?" I asked.

He shrugged.

"Jason, being part of this weird, shitty, cut-throat world we're in means never losing track of who you are. It's the most important thing, otherwise, you end up losing yourself a piece at a time, and all too soon, you don't recognize the person staring back at you in the mirror," I said. "You're human. You love your family. You'd do anything for them. That's you. Never lose that,"

He took another deep, shuddering breath and nodded, wiping his eyes once again. "Thank you."

"For what?" I asked.

"Being a decent person," he said. "I wasn't sure who I'd find when I met you. Nothing could have prepared me."

"My infernal wiles are impressive, no doubt," I said, lightly elbowing him.

"No. But you **are** a genuinely decent person, Ava Dufrense, and that's worth way more," he replied.

I stopped, unsure how to respond to something I knew to be patently false, but decided to let him have this one. He'd have a rough day.

Which left one thing. I took a deep breath.

"I'll stay," I whispered.

"What was that?" he asked.

"I'll stay. To help you," I said. "With the whole angel thing."

"You said you were out," he said.

I nodded.

"What changed?" he asked.

"I'm fickle, what do you want?" I said.

He looked at me quietly for a long time. Fucker was probably doing that aura thing. I can only imagine mine was doing loop-de-loops with all the turmoil I was feeling inside.

That angel could kill me. Dead. Easily. There was no judgment for me if that happened. I'm a succubus, which means whatever spirit's left of me when I die goes straight to hell. It does not pass go, it does not collect two hundred dollars. It was absolute insanity for me to stay and help.

But there was no doubt in my mind that he needed help. That he needed **me**. I wasn't used to that.

Don't get me wrong, I'm used to people wanting me. **Very** used to it. But him needing me felt different. Less possessive. Cleaner. It was a feeling that I wasn't used to, and I found myself craving it.

"Right," he said with a shake of his head. "I was that pathetic, huh?"

"Oh, more than pathetic. Just sad. Wait till I spread it around: Jason Bishop cried like a baby. Like a hungry, angry baby. Ruined my shirt with all his tears and snot," I said with a smirk.

"There it goes, rep destroyed before I ever got started," he said.

"We'll have to figure out a way to rehabilitate it," I said.

"Like by killing an angel," he suggested.

I paused, took a breath, then nodded. "Yeah. I think that's the move."

We sat in my car in silence for a while before Jason spoke. "So how the fuck do we do that?" he asked.

"We can't. Angels are immortal. Predate the Earth and all that. It's impossible," I said.

"Right. So we have to kill him, but he's an angel, so we can't. This is actually something from the seminary. Angels are part of Creation itself. You can't kill one. So we change the rules of the game," he said.

"Change the rules? Of Creation? Jason, you were crying five minutes ago." I said. "We might be able to bind it into something, but he'll eventually get out and start that smiting shit.

"No, don't you see? If we can't kill an angel, we have two choices, we find another way to take him out of play that doesn't involve killing him–" he began.

"Meaning he can get out and start smiting the shit out of us once he's loose. And they always get loose," I warned.

"—or we tilt the board. End his immortality," he finished.

"We just said you can't kill an angel," I reminded him. "Remember, you're new to all this. Research or not, there are some rules that can't be changed. One of those is that angels are immortal. You can't kill them."

"I didn't say kill him. I said we end his immortality. We trick him into Falling."

"And how do we do that?" I asked.

"I think we just talk to him," he replied.

I looked at him for a minute. "Your plan is to face down an immortal, indestructible being that's spent most of creation killing by talking to him?

He nodded.

I sighed then shook my head. "Sure. I'm excited to be a part of this plan. Let's do this!"

What followed was a surreal twenty-four hours. I dropped Jason back off at his bar, then went back to The Bayou Review for work that evening and put on a show like nothing was happening. Like I wasn't staring down the barrel of a divine shotgun.

As I was leaving, Zeke pulled me aside.

"Ava?" he rumbled.

"What's up, big guy?" I asked.

"The kid from the other night. You've been spending a lot of time with him?" he said.

"Yeah," I shrugged. "He's fun."

"Hrm," he rumbled.

"What's that for?" I asked.

"Lots of guys that come 'round here are fun. He seems like trouble," he said.

"Trouble is fun, Zeke," I replied with a smile.

"The not-fun kind of trouble," Zeke said. "The kind that gets people hurt."

"You're going somewhere with this?" I asked.

"Why?" he asked.

"Why? You're gonna need to be a bit more specific," I said, quirking an eyebrow.

"Why him? You've had more men and women throw themselves at you than I can count, but you've really taken to this–wannabe. Word is he's looking into something, and whatever he's looking into is dangerous. Order business," he said.

"People talk too much," I said.

"They do. But you didn't say I was wrong," he said.

"You're not," I admitted. "But I'm a big girl, Zeke. I can handle myself."

"I know. I know you, Ava. Something weird is going on with you," he said. "Why him? What makes him worth breaking your rules and getting directly involved instead of trading favors and dealing in secrets?" he asked.

I paused, thinking about it for a long moment, then I sighed.

"Zeke, do you know what it's like to be me? To be a succubus?" I asked.

"No," he admitted.

"Right. Well, I have a sort of background hum in my head that tells me what everyone around me wants me to be. Constantly pushing at me. You wish I were a bit taller, curvier, and had some muscle on me," I said.

"Ava, I don't look at you like–" he stammered.

"It's fine. It's not just you. It's everyone. Everyone is subconsciously telling me what they want me to be. All the time. Whether they mean to or not, and it's in my nature to try to give that to them. I have to resist the urge to change my shape to make myself just a bit more attractive to them. To you. To everyone. To give you what you want so I can get what I want from you. Do you understand?" I said.

"Not really," he said.

"Imagine if your reflex was to make everyone around you happy because it's what let you stay alive. Now imagine that you knew what you could do to make the people around you happy. That even if they didn't mean to, they were making demands of you every time they looked at you. Demands about how you look, about how you act, about who you are. Sounds exhausting, right?" I asked.

He nodded.

"That's why," I said.

"I don't understand," he said.

"Jason is the first and only person whose subconscious mind has made no demands of me from the time we met. He didn't want me to be taller, shorter, skinnier, curvier, nicer, smile more, be funnier. Nothing. For all his faults, Jason Bishop immediately accepted me for who I was. For me. For Ava, and he had no desire to change anything," I said.

Zeke looked at me for a moment, then slowly nodded.

"Okay. I'll hold off on breaking his neck," he said.

"I'd appreciate that. I'm not sure where things are going with him, but I think they're going to be interesting," I said, smiling and walking into the night.

"Interesting gets people killed," he called out as I left.

I woke up the next morning and met Jason at Bishop's Crossing for a late breakfast. He was uncharacteristically awake when I arrived, but looked like he'd had a rough night of it.

"You sure you're up to this, hot stuff?" I asked.

He looked up from his coffee, face unshaven, eyes bloodshot, skin sweaty. The look of a man who'd been on a bender. He forced a smile. "I'm right as the mail, darlin'" he said.

"Sure you are. I brought you something," I said.

"You shouldn't have," he replied.

"I know, but it might come in handy," I said, sliding the long rectangular box across the table to him. He opened it, then frowned.

"You look like a piece of mail that got lost, then run over, then shredded by the sorting machine," I said. "I thought this might cheer you up. A gift from my father."

"You mean?" he asked.

I nodded. "Might find a use for it later today. Assuming you don't turn into the zombie you look like."

"That feels about right. It was a long night," he said. "But I was up bright and early and headed to the park. The tent is already being set up and chairs are being brought in. Looks like they did everything on the up and up."

"Brother Avery doesn't seem like a big paperwork guy," I said.

"No. But broadcast equipment doesn't come for free. I'm guessing he has somebody footing some bills and pulling some strings," he said. "It might be insightful to find out who."

"Paul Marrane," I said.

"Who?" he asked.

"Paul Marrane. He's a small-time player and hedge mage. Little weasel of a man. He showed up in New Orleans about five years ago and has been skulking around in some of the less savory parts of the scene, staying just off of the Church's radar," I said.

"Where's this Marrane guy getting his money and why is he helping Brother Avery?" he asked.

"Dunno. How'd he get an angel killing for him? That's not a 'normal' kinda thing," I said.

We ate in silence for a moment, his bleary eyes roaming around the bar, then settling on me, then repeating the process a half dozen times before I finally set my tea down. "What?" I demanded.

"I just–you look good," he said.

I snorted. "My hair's a mess and I'm not wearing makeup."

"—and you look good," he said with a little smile. "So, thank you."

"For looking good? That comes with the territory," I said.

He shook his head. "No. For helping. For listening yesterday about–you know. For being here this morning. I know you've got options, so–thank you."

I waved him off. "Just doing what anyone would do," I said.

"You're really not," he said seriously, meeting my gaze. I couldn't read what was going on behind those bloodshot blue eyes, but I decided I wasn't ready for whatever this was going to be, so I looked away.

"We should get ready," I said. "Meet up here at four?" I asked, coming to my feet.

"We could. Or–" he trailed off and looked upstairs.

So I stayed.

Four o'clock saw us approaching the large tent along with the gathering attendees. Jason and I took seats in the back left-hand corner, trying to blend in as best we could. It was a true melting pot of a crowd, teeming with people from every race, body type, or other demographic you'd care to name. It seems that the promise of an actual miracle cure would bring out the most unlikely of petitioners, but one stood out from the rest.

He was a well-dressed man of indeterminate age. Tall, but not overly so, he had hair the color of steel and wore a pair of expensive sunglasses to go with his too-expensive suit. I saw his type in the Bayou Review frequently. They're the ones who feel like they have the right to get handsier the more they spend.

But there was something different about this one. Something–off. He moved in a way that felt wrong, like someone moving a marionette, and his skin had a plasticy, too-smooth quality to it, like he had no pores. He reminded me of something. A whisper of a rumor I'd heard.

"Oh shit," I whispered.

He scanned the crowd and broke into a too-bright toothy grin when he saw me and Jason, and walked toward our seats. I shiver ran up my spine.

Jason saw my expression and followed my eyeline to the man. A moment later, he cursed under his breath.

"I think things just got complicated," he whispered.

"Yup. I think that guy coming this way is a dragon," I hissed back.

"He is indeed," the man replied in a rich baritone, sliding gracefully into the seat next to Jason. "But that makes things more interesting than they would have been otherwise. For you see, I, much like yourselves, do not belong here."

"What are you talking about, we're like peas in a pod in this place, right, Jason?" I said, then looked at Jason, whose frown and firm lip showed a level of stress that I hadn't seen on him before.

"Ah, the poor boy probably looked too closely at the unseen around me. It can be disorienting," the man purred. "Don't worry, he'll recover soon."

"What did you do to him?" I asked, balling my fists.

"Nothing. Nothing at all. But sometimes I'm a bit much, my dear. My name is Silene. Eomund Silene, head of the First National Bank of New Orleans," he said.

"That's not all you are," I said.

"Do you think that only the destitute have cause to seek out Brother Avery's unique gifts from on high? On the contrary, I've been afflicted with a terrible condition for longer than I care to remember," he said, with a predatory smile.

"What are you talking about?" I asked.

He opened his mouth to answer, but Jason jumped in. "He's a dragon," he whispered.

"I know," I said.

"A dragon," he repeated.

"Yeah Jason, I heard you the first time," I said. "This big lizard has been hanging around the edges of New Orleans for a long time. But this is the first time I've heard of a confirmed sighting."

"Big lizard isn't quite right," Silene said. "I prefer to think of us as primordial forces. Remnants of a world long forgotten."

"Best forgotten," I said.

"Watch your tone, girl," Silene said.

"He's got some sort of binding on him that's blocking the vast majority of his power. It's wrapped around his aura like a divine muzzle," Jason said, looking at Silene, who nodded.

"Ah yes, the souvenirs of a misspent youth. Who among us hasn't suffered from unfortunately poor decisions at some point? Mine led to me running afoul of a troublesome young man riding around and slaying my kind. Saint George. You've probably heard of him," he said.

"St. George the Dragon Slayer," Jason clarified. "Silene was the town in the myth where he met and defeated–"

"Me," Silene said. "Yes. The story isn't quite right, but it gets the broad strokes correct. The saint bested me and smote down upon me with his God's vengeance, binding me into human form so that I might better serve those I'd terrorized. And so I've remained."

"The bank. That's your hoard," I said.

He smiled. "Clever. Every lizard needs one."

"What do you want here, dragon?" Jason asked, not looking at him.

"I want healing. Or, more specifically, I want Brother Avery to lift the horrible curse that's been placed upon me. I've tried every cure known to man, and quite a few that aren't. Nothing has been able to break that blasted saint's binding, but when I heard of a man who used an angel to cure his flock? That caught my attention. What better to break a divine curse than one of the Divine?" he said with a smile.

I started to stand, but Silene was faster, standing and walking toward the crowd. "I'd suggest against stopping me. Who knows what could happen if I were to become upset?" He looked meaningfully toward the crowd shuffling in and moved toward the front.

"We can't–" I said.

"I don't know how to stop it," Jason replied, scowling. "We have a choice between that thing or dealing with Brother Avery and the angel. Which is more important?"

I thought for a moment, then sighed. "At the moment, Brother Avery and the angel. They're the problem we know about."

"I agree. Brother Avery and the angel are the job. Strange as it is to say, the dragon is a distraction," he said.

And then Brother Avery's voice rang out from the pulpit.

He had begun.

Chapter Seven

"Welcome, my brothers and sisters," Brother Avery announced from the pulpit. "Seeing so many of you gathered together under one roof helps to make the burden I carry feel lighter, for as the Good Book tells us in Nehemiah 3, 'many hands make light work' and the work we have before us is heavy indeed."

I watched the faces in the crowd staring at Brother Avery, devouring each word in rapt attention as he launched into a diatribe about wolves in sheep's clothing. About evil men hiding behind the trappings of faith, and of the monsters among us that allow them to prey on children while avoiding the consequences.

"Here," Jason said, handing me a small bottle of what looked like clear baby food.

"Gerber? Jason, you shouldn't have," I said.

"Rub it on your eyelids, jackass," he said. "It'll let you see things like I do. Auras. Ghosts. Angels. That sort of thing."

I looked down at the dubious contents of the jar and shook my head before rubbing it on my eyelids as instructed, then opened my eyes to a new world.

The tent was bathed in figures surrounded by flickering flames. Reds, oranges, and yellows rolled off of the people around us as Brother Avery's words rained down on them. Closer to the front, Silene sat, the greenish flames rolling off him taking the form of a crouching dragon bound in glowing white chains, its spectral form overlapping the people in the tent in its enormity. Further still, Brother Avery exhorted the crowd, his flames tinged white from his faith.

Behind him floated an angel.

It wore a humanoid form and the light coming from it was painful to look at, washing out whatever features it might have chosen for its face. An odd sigil blazed purple on its chest, looking like a pair of loops with a curved line underneath.

"Angelic script," I whispered. "Like it's wearing a nametag."

"Yeah. I don't recognize it," Jason said.

"Ambriel. A member of Azrael's host. One of the angels of death." I said.

"Well fuck. We have to take on the angel of death?" he asked.

"No, that would be crazy. We're taking on *one of* the angels of death. That's completely different," I whispered. "If it makes you feel better, we're probably going to die," I said.

"I don't think so. Not today," he replied.

Brother Avery reached the crescendo of his sermon. "And so we recognize the evil that is represented by none other than Simon White, the defense attorney that saw to it that those fifty-nine pedophiles were able to walk away, leaving broken lives! Leaving broken spirits! Leaving broken families in their wake! And if there is any justice in this world, Mr. White will feel God's wrath for the horrors that he has allowed to continue to walk upon the face of creation!"

As soon as Simon White's name was out of Brother Avery's mouth, Ambriel's wings had spread and the angel streaked from the tent.

"Here we go," I muttered.

Jason put his hand on mine, giving it a squeeze. "Give it a minute."

I took a deep breath and nodded, looking around the room at the spiritual conflagration surrounding me. The choir had begun to sing an old hymn called "There is Power in the Blood", which seemed all too apt considering what was going to go down at the end of the service.

And we waited. And we watched. Finally, after an agonizing twenty minutes, Ambriel returned, his right hand glowing with reddish light.

"I think that's it," I said.

"Yeah. I think he's pulled the life energy out of that man. Their target," Jason said.

"From what we saw before, now he heals someone," I said.

Ambriel laid his left hand on Brother Avery's right shoulder, and the preacher snapped to attention.

"And now, my brothers and sisters, step forward! Those of you afflicted by one of the many curses that afflict the Children of God, step forward and be healed! Step forward that those curses may be lifted!"

Silene stood immediately and got into line, his herky-jerky movements covered up by the swell of people attempting to do the same. People pushed and shoved until the banker ended up third in line.

"And you, my sister, what favor do you ask of The Lord? Of what curse shall He unburden you?" Avery asked.

The thin African American woman sobbed as Brother Avery touched her forehead. "Alcohol, Brother Avery. I–I can't–" she trailed off crying.

"And so we implore!" Brother Avery cried.

In the spirit world, there was a red flash from Ambriel's hand, which traveled through Brother Avery and into the woman, settling into her head. She fell to the ground, cheeks wet with tears. Deacons quickly carried her away.

Brother Avery came to Silene. "And you, my brother. What curse would you ask The Lord to ease from your shoulders?"

Silene smiled. "My body is wracked and diminished, Brother Avery. I would only ask that He restore to me what I have lost," he said.

"And so we implore!" Brother Avery beseeched to the heavens.

He placed his hand on Silene's forehead and the red glow from the angel streaked through the preacher and into the inhuman monster standing before him. I watched as the bindings placed upon him nearly a millennia ago by St. George the Dragon Slayer were removed by the request of this itinerant preacher. The chains containing his draconic aura shattered, and Silene took a deep, satisfied breath before stepping to the side of the stage.

Next, he came to a painfully thin East Asian man and asked, "What favor do you ask of The Lord? Of what curse shall he unburden you?"

"Cancer, Brother Avery. Colon cancer I don't know how much time–" he cried.

"And so we implore!" the preacher cried.

Brother Avery put his hand on the man's head and the light flashed once again, traveling through the preacher and into the supplicant, causing a red glow deep inside him.

Fine. It was his ass, okay? The supplicant's ass glowed.

Moving on.

Jason was fiddling with some objects in his lap when I turned to him and said "I have an idea," and slunk out to stand near the back exit. It didn't take long for Silene to approach, his business here having concluded. His stride was far more even, no longer having the look of a badly puppeted marionette.

"So that's it?" I called after the dragon.

"My dear child, what other business could I possibly have here? The angel did his duty, the clergyman asked for his miracle, and I received my cure. Quid pro quo."

"Hardly. This may have been a miracle, but doesn't your kind put stock in older traditions? Things like debt and hospitality?" I asked.

The dragon paused and looked at me over his shoulder. "What did you just say?" he asked.

"I asked if your kind followed the traditions around hospitality and debt," I repeated.

"Yesss and?" he said.

I swallowed. "If you do, since Brother Avery removed a curse from you, wouldn't that place you in his debt?"

"No compensation was requested," he hurriedly replied.

"It was implied, wasn't it?" I asked. "It was a service offered in good faith to the followers of his God. For you to have presented yourself to him under false pretenses seems to present a problem there."

The dragon turned to face me, stepping forward and getting into my personal space. "What are you playing at, girl?"

"Contracts. My kind are experts. You've breached the concept of both hospitality and debt to Brother Avery. You owe him," I said.

Silene looked me in the eye for a good thirty seconds, then broke into a smile. "Draconic magic would overwhelm any mortal who had it bestowed upon them."

"Do you have anything else to give?" I asked

"I could send for–" he said.

"No, the breach has occurred now. You need to make it whole now," I said.

He looked at me for a long moment and repeated. "What are you playing at, girl? This won't help you against your angel," he said.

"No, but I think it'll give some closure to the problems this preacher has been causing," I said.

"He could die," Silene said.

"You owe him a debt. Pay it back," I replied. "If he dies from the reward, your debut would still have been paid."

Silene looked at me once again, his eyes confused. Finally, he shrugged.

"Your terms are accepted, succubus," he said. "For the record, not the sort of deal I generally make with your kind."

"Yeah, we're all branching out lately, aren't we?" I said.

Chapter
Eight

I followed Silene in and detoured once inside, re-taking my seat next to Jason.

"What was that about?" he asked.

"I suspected that if he pre-dated Christianity, Silene is probably someone who puts a lot of stock in the 'old ways.' Rights of hospitality, traditions around debts, that sort of thing," I said.

"Go on," he said, his eyes locked on Silene as he worked his way back up through the crowd.

"I pointed out that he'd received a gift from Brother Avery, and that placed Silene in his debt," I said.

"I bet he loved that," he said.

"About as much as you probably think. I said that the debt was due and he needed to make good," I said.

"You don't have the authority to do that," he pointed out.

I waved my hand. "A minor detail that Silene didn't manage to realize before he was marching inside to settle his debt with our dear Brother Avery," I said.

Jason watched the dragon slide gracefully through the crowd, his precise fluid movements were nothing like the mockery of locomotion he'd shown before.

"That kind of power? The kind a dragon wields? I don't know what that'll do to a person," he said

"Me either," I said. "But Avery James knew that every time he named someone during those sermons, those people died, and he kept doing it. The guy's a serial killer."

Jason's eyes stayed on him for a moment, and finally, he nodded. "Yeah. Well, one way or another, the die's been cast," he said.

I turned to watch Silene approach, his draconic aura now fully freed from restraint. The massive reptilian form would more than fill the entire tent, and I marveled at the idea that any single person had been able to stand up to it, much less defeat and bind it.

"Will the angel try to stop him?" I asked.

"Ambriel? Unlikely. I don't think it can see auras that way, otherwise it would have seen the two of us and clocked us as not belonging here right away," he said. "Look at it. It's looking out over the crowd from time to time, but mostly it's just sort of staring at Brother Avery," Jason said.

It was true. The dragon was almost to the steps leading up to the stage where Brother Avery prayed over his supplicants, flashes of light flowing from the angel, through him, and into each individual in turn. The light was dimming, now little more than a shimmer clutched in the angel's grasp

"Brother Avery James?" Silene's voice cut through the crowd, the s at the end of the name was slightly drawn out and dug into my ears unpleasantly

"Yes, my brother? Your curse has been lifted by the grace of God," the preacher said.

"It has indeed, Brother Avery. I am in your debt," Silene said. It wasn't a thank you. It was a statement of fact as if reading numbers out of a ledger

"No, my Brother. The Lord God has seen fit to grant you your prayer. I am but His humble servant. A conduit, if you will. All praise should be given unto His Name," Brother Avery responded.

Silene held out his hand as if to shake with the preacher. "I insist, Brother Avery. In my line of work, and in my culture, debts are to be repaid as quickly and efficiently as possible. Please, take my hand. Accept this small gift. A token of appreciation," he said.

Brother Avery smiled and reached for his hand, willing to accept a handshake from the man he'd healed if it would move him along. Assuming this would end the interaction.

He was oh so very wrong.

Silene's hand grasped his in a vice-like grip, and Brother Avery's eyes shot wide open. His mouth fell into an "o" of anguish, and he gasped for air. To the people in the tent, it appeared he was having a moment of religious ecstasy. Or possibly an orgasm. Those are tough to tell apart sometimes.

To me and Jason, we saw greenish power flowing from Silene into Brother Avery. Lightning strikes of the draconic magic lanced through the preacher's body, striking out at Ambriel's hand where it touched the shoulder and sending the angel tumbling off the stage and into the back wall of the tent.

"I thank you, Brother James Avery, for the gift. For the service that you have rendered unto me. It is our custom to ensure the gift offered matches the gift received in both scope and efficacy. I grant unto you the object of your desire. I grant unto you the golden tongue so fêted in your Enemy. May you use it and remember –" Silene then said something I can't even begin to pronounce. I don't think a human tongue, jaw, and throat can successfully repeat that sound, and I'm not even exactly human.

Brother Avery arched his back and we could see light pour out of his eyes, nose, ears, and mouth, and heard screams from the crowd.

That's when I noticed that the light wasn't just on the spiritual side of things.

Silene wore a massive grin as he continued to grip Brother Avery's hand, and he gripped the preacher's hand.

"Tell your God Silene thanks Him for undoing the curse He placed upon me. Tell Him this is but a taste, little mortal," Silene hissed.

And an eyeblink later, Ambriel had recovered and flown at the dragon, barreling into him and breaking his hold on Brother Avery.

The preacher immediately fell to the ground, his eyes wide and staring, and his mouth moving slightly as if he was trying to say something. Around him, the tent had erupted into pandemonium. The faithful were screaming, heading for any exit, or wall, heedless of those around them in their terrified attempts at flight from whatever horror was unfolding in front of them, as Ambriel had revealed themself in all their glory, and was attacking one of the supplicants that Brother Avery had cured just moments before.

I can see how that would feel like a mixed message.

Silene backhanded the angel, sending Ambriel up into the rafters of the tent, and smoke began to pour out of the dragon's mouth and nostrils.

"You may have the field, little angel. My work here is done. My debt has been paid," he said. The smoke swirled around him as Ambriel roared in challenge and flew, a flaming sword held in their right hand. The angel swung through the smoke, attempting to cleave the dragon in two, but was too late. Flame and blade alike found nothing but smoke. The dragon had vanished.

"No!" Ambriel cried, its voice wracked with pure anguish. "No, Lord! Father! Please!"

A split second later he was back, hovering near Brother Avery, cradling the man's head in their hands as they turned their face up to the heavens and wept.

"Lord, this man is one of Your greatest creations! He sees with such clarity! Such vision! He sees Your design and helps me to improve upon it, just as You intended. In his voice, I hear Yours. Please, undo this evil that has been thrust upon him!" Ambriel cried.

"Ava, it's showtime. Sprout your horns and be ready," Jason said as he rose to his feet.

"How do you know about my horns?" I asked. "I never told you about them."

"They come out when you're sleeping," he said.

"You watched me sleep?" I asked, smiling as I rose to my feet to join him.

"Now's hardly the time," he muttered.

"We're about to face down an angel of death, Jason. I don't know if we're going to get many other times," I said.

He looked at me for a moment, indecision playing out over their features, so I decided to stop waiting. I stepped forward, grabbed him by the hair, and kissed him.

He was surprised at first but seemed to catch on quickly and didn't seem to mind. He enthusiastically returned the kiss, then I stepped back. He blinked.

"Don't want you too distracted, hot stuff. Let's do this," I said with a smirk.

The two of us walked up to the grieving angel, stopping about twenty feet away. I concentrated for a moment, then felt my horns emerge. They come out of my hair at about four inches long and curve slightly toward each other. I've been told they're cute, but it's not exactly my favorite look for me.

"Hey, angel!' Jason called out.

"Ambriel," I corrected.

"Hey, Ambriel!" Jason called out.

"Who?" the angel exclaimed, laying the object of their affection gently down on the stage and turning its gaze toward us.

Now that it was revealed, the shine from its face was diminished. Their features were androgynous and delicate, with lovely, high cheekbones and a pointed chin. Curly golden blond locks tumbled from their scalp to their shoulders, with some partially obstructing their strikingly blue eyes. "Infernal filth," they spat, floating up higher from into the space above us. "Was it you? Was this your doing, demon? You and your mortal thrall?"

"Hey!" Jason objected.

I looked at him and shrugged, looking back at the angel. "Well, I mean this part of it, yes," I said. "Not all of it, mind you. The thrall has a good head for this sort of thing, but the part where we got the dragon to overload your murderous mortal friend was most definitely me."

"It was pretty damned sexy too, not gonna lie," Jason said, his eyes not leaving the demon.

"Aww, thanks, babe," I said, keeping my eyes on the grim servant of death who was slowly becoming more angry.

It flew at us in a flash, proving my assessment of 'slowly' to be painfully, hilariously incorrect. Much like Ambriel had attempted with Silene, it buried its shoulder into my midsection and sent me tumbling through rows of folding chairs, then rose back up to hover over where I lay.

"Well, shit," I groaned.

"Foolish demon. Your kind has ever been but chaff before the sickle when the servants of The Lord bring His wrath down upon you,' Ambriel said down its nose at me.

"But you're not bringing His wrath down, are you? You're bringing 'his' wrath," Jason said, kneeling next to Brother Avery's breathing but nonfunctional body with the dagger I'd given him earlier. The bare blade was held to the preacher's throat. It had an oily, liquid-like quality to it and shone with an unpleasant reddish-black energy in the spirit world.

Ambriel hissed. "Where did you get that, mortal?"

"Oh, this old thing?" Jason said. "Been in the family for generations. Why, what could a quicksilver blade with infernal runes possibly do to you?"

Ambriel stayed very still, its eyes on Jason.

"Oh, I know it won't do anything to you," Jason said with a bitter laugh. "But we both know that's not the case with him, don't we?"

Ambriel stayed still as a statue aside from its steadily beating wings.

"In fact, we both know that this sort of blade was made to send mortal souls straight to Hell, don't we? Ask me how I know, Ambriel. Go ahead. Ask me," Jason said, his voice rising.

"It is the blade that was used on your sister, apostate," they said.

"It was used on my sister," Jason lied. "An innocent. Struck down in her youth by a madman. By her own father."

"What of it?" Ambriel asked.

"Your God took something away from me, Ambriel. His ineffable plan took away my mother and my sister. Through no fault of their own, through no sin, and through no carnal, or venial act, they were struck down and condemned to an eternity in Hell. Your God allowed that to happen. Explain how that was fair to me, angel. Explain the justice in that. Explain it to me now, or your preacher goes to join her, drowning in his own blood," he said, his voice deadly quiet.

Ambriel hovered, waiting.

I came to my feet and made my way over to stand next to Jason.

"This man has sinned in far greater quantity and quality than Catherine ever had, and her life was taken from her. Her soul was damned. Explain to me why this man deserves anything less. Explain why I shouldn't punish God for what He's done," he demanded.

A tense silence filled the tent as Jason and Ambriel stared at each other.

"Tell me, angel. What made you decide to follow the orders of a mortal instead of your Creator? You have no soul. No free will. You're just a tool. An instrument to serve His Will. What made you decide to freelance for this worthless sack of shit?" Jason asked.

Ambriel remained silent.

"I mean, I get that angels have probably served great men from time to time. Men who actually furthered God's will. But for an angel to fall in with someone of utterly no consequence is kinda crazy, isn't it?" he asked me.

"I don't think there's any records of it in all the annals of Hell. The fact is that Brother Avery James isn't even on our radar. He's worthless. An afterthought," I agreed.

Ambriel's perfect blue eyes flashed in anger. Their fist clenched around the hilt of their blade.

"Still not moved to speak? Is it because you're afraid of what I'll do to your boss here, or because you know that the boss you're supposed to be working for is a sick fuck whose actions are completely and utterly indefensible?" Bishop said, nearly spitting the last at the angel. "What is it, Ambriel? Is that why you decided to serve a mortal man instead? I mean, I get that Brother Avery dressed it all up in fancy verse. He pretended it was God's Will he was serving, but when you boil it down to the basics, Avery James had an attack dog that he could turn loose to murder anyone he wanted, and he knew it. He liked the idea of that kind of power. He reveled in it."

"No. Brother Avery was–is a good man," Ambriel said, their voice coming out in a whisper.

"Who decided that? You? You're a being of service, remember? Angels have no soul. No free will. You don't get to decide that, do you?" Jason asked, hammering away at the angel.

"I heard him speak. Heard the Lord's words spill from his lips," Ambriel said.

"Why not just ask God, Ambriel?" I asked. "Instead of depending on a mortal prophet, just go to the source."

"She's right. How is it that a demon has a better feel for how this should work than an actual servant of The Divine?" Jason asked. "Why didn't you just push it up the chain of command and ask The Lord God Almighty for direction? Why take it from a poor preacher? A man?"

"It's not that simple," Ambriel said.

"Of course it is. Would Azrael not let you?" Jason asked.

"The archangel Azrael is–" they began.

"Were you afraid to ask? Afraid of what the answer would be? Were you afraid to be told the thing you felt inside you wasn't part of your design? That'd you'd strayed from the path laid before you at the dawn of time?" he asked.

"Were you afraid your desires were no longer pure?" I asked, putting as much suggestion into the question as I knew how, pushing my infernal aura around the distracted angel, lowering their inhibitions.

Ambriel glared at us both. "No. I know my intentions are–"

"Intentions don't mean shit, Ambriel," Jason interrupted. "Thought and action are as one. If one is corrupt, so is the other. That's basic second-grade Catholicism. Any school child can tell you that."

"No, they don't understand, I'm doing God's–" they tried again.

"How is it that mortals have a better grasp of this than you?" I asked. "How has an angel stooped so low?"

"Enough!" Ambriel roared.

"Demon, you and your pathetic talking ape. Do you think you can speak to me that way? Me? I am Ambriel, a seraphim of the Host of the Archangel Azrael, who mortals refer to as The Angel of Death! I am tasked with ushering the dead to their rightful resting place. Do you think to question me? *Me*? Succubus, you are little more than a plaything for mortals' most base and carnal desires. I know not what hooks you've placed into this hapless thrall, but it matters not! I will cleanse this place of your vile corruption and send you back to the Pit, where you belong," Ambriel raged. "You both attempt to speak to me as if you are my betters? Laughable. The aspiration toward equality is beyond either of you, much less superiority over one such as I, who has watched the ages unfold. I was there when the Lord said 'Let there be Light' and I will be there for the final battle against the Enemy on the fields of Armageddon. I am beyond either of you. Better than either of you. Look upon me and despair, for I am your ending should any harm befall that man!"

I took a step back, worry playing out plainly on my face. Seeing me move, Ambriel sneered and feinted forward. I squeaked and took a step back, hiding behind Jason.

"Are you proud of yourself? Terrorizing a helpless woman just because your feelings are hurt?" Jason said, his face pale.

"That's no woman, but if frightening the Whore of Babylon made flesh is the task required of me, I will happily perform it. No, I will revel in it," Ambriel said. "Lay down the blade and I will see to it that your ends are swifter than you deserve."

"Pride goeth before the fall," Jason whispered, a smile breaking out on his face. I squeezed his shoulder and stood up, dropping the pretense of helpless terror.

Ambriel scowled. "What?"

"I would think you'd recognize your scripture, Ambriel, paraphrased or not," I said. "Maybe the actual verse from Proverbs verse 16: 18-19 will help jog your memory: Pride goeth before destruction, And an haughty spirit before a fall. Better it is to be of a humble spirit with the lowly Than to divide the spoil with the proud."

The angel's expression froze.

"Jason, wasn't Pride the sin that caused the fall of The Morningstar?" I asked.

"Why, I think it might have been, Ava," I replied.

"And hasn't Ambriel very clearly and deliberately stated they are improving upon God's plan?" Jason asked as Ambriel's face morphed from cruel triumph into horror.

"Why, I do believe he did, Jason. Right before they talked about how proud they were to be an angel, which placed them above humans," I said. "That seems like the sort of thing that the Lord would take issue with."

Ambriel slowly sunk to the ground, and for the first time since we first saw them, their feet touched the soil. The moment they did, the soft, divine light that had been emanating from them faded, slowly at first, disappearing from their extremities, then from their body, until finally all that was left was their halo.

"No! What have you done?" they cried.

Then their halo faded away.

Jason rose to his feet, stalking toward Ambriel while the now Fallen Angel wept. He raised the knife he'd been threatening Brother Avery with and brought it down.

I intercepted the stab on the way down.

He looked at me, confused. I gave him a short shake of the head "Please, allow me," I said.

Jason nodded, and I stepped forward, putting my hand under Ambriel's chin and raising their face to mine. "You said some truly hurtful things just now, but I remember reading somewhere that to forgive is divine," I said.

Ambriel looked up at me, their face full of hatred.

"What makes you think I want your forgi–" they began.

They didn't get to finish, because I punched them full in their perfect fucking mouth. I saw a tooth go flying as they skidded back onto the ground, staining their bright white robes.

"But we established that I'm not divine, motherfucker," I announced as I proceeded to smack the formerly invincible being around the tent.

Holy shit did it feel good.

We didn't kill them.

We both sorta wanted to, but honestly, the level of pathetic emanating off the bruised, beaten, and bloodied angel was truly something to behold. We found some loose rope from the tent and I tied them up.

Hey, when you've got the skills, put 'em to use, am I right?

And so we sat, taking a moment to appreciate the impossible deed we'd just accomplished.

"You know," Jason began. "We make a pretty good team."

"You mean when I'm not completely carrying your ass?" I said, winking.

"That's not a completely unpleasant prospect," he said with a laugh. "But I'm serious."

"We kinda do," I agreed. "I mean, I'm not ready to start looking for china patterns or anything, but, yeah. I could do this again."

"That's great because I was thinking–" he said, then paused. The back pocket of his jeans was humming.

"What the fuck?" he asked, coming to his feet and yanking out the glowing letter that had started this entire affair. The paper emitted a soft white-gold radiance that was rapidly increasing in intensity. Jason flung it on the ground and backed up, putting himself between me and the misbehaving stationary.

Adorable.

I moved him beside me and waited uneasily for what came next.

There was a flash, and where the paper had fallen, a robed figure appeared. It was tall. At least six and a half feet tall, wearing black robes and a steel grey skull-like mask under its black cowl. Black wings sprouted from its back, and a large, wicked-looking scythe rested in its left hand.

The mask regarded both of us, who had taken several additional steps back, then toward where Brother Avery and Ambriel lay. A gesture from the right hand and Ambriel was gone, their form floating away like motes of light.

"Well, this just got more interesting," I whispered

"I hate your definition of interesting, Ava," he spat back. "Who is this guy?"

"I think we're looking at Azrael," I said.

"The Angel of Death?" he asked.

"Yeah," I said.

"Shit," he said.

"Yeah," I agreed.

The figure regarded us silently behind the skull mask before reaching up and removing it, then stepping forward and leaving the robes standing empty behind him. The figure that emerged was not what I was expecting. Azrael was an older gentleman of Middle Eastern descent. He had a shaved head, a long white beard, and brown eyes that twinkled when you looked at them. Like they were full of stars. He was wearing a very loud Hawaiian shirt and a pair of khaki cargo shorts.

"Well, you sure did screw the pooch on this one," he declared, shaking their head.

"What now?" I asked.

"The two of you. You didn't do this at all like I thought you would," he said.

"You thought–I'm sorry, I'm confused," Jason said.

"Well, of course you are," Azrael said. "You've gone completely off-book on this one, my boy. Enlisting a succubus was utterly unexpected. Turned a lot of heads in the Holy City. It upset a lot of folks. Had them questioning my judgment. But I had faith in you. Both of you, actually "

"You? Had faith in me?" I asked.

"Sure did," Azreale replied, nodding. "And well-placed, I might add. I admit to a moment of concern at first that you might just feed on him and leave him for dead. I have the distinct impression that's going to be a thing with him sometime."

"I would never–" I objected.

"No, not you. Someone else, but that's not important right now," he said. "Unconventional or not, you got the job done. You found Brother Avery and you stopped Ambriel from doing any more harm. Mostly. Did you have to make them Fall? That's going to result in a lot of shuffling."

"Shuffling?" Jason asked.

"Duty rosters. Portfolios. Have to spread out the workload since they won't be doing it anymore," he said.

"Was he doing it before?" I asked

"Not really since he fell in with Brother Avery," he admitted. "He's been a bit lax on the actual duties and a bit gung ho on murdering people who weren't supposed to die yet. That's why I contacted you, dear boy. You bringing in this lovely young lady as part of the operation was just an added bonus."

"Me?" I asked.

He nodded, smiling.

"I appreciate that, but–uhhh, I'm kind of a demon?" I said.

"Yeah, but only kind of. Not completely," he said with a shrug. "Now, come here, boy. Let's get this over with."

He stepped up to Jason, who stood dumbstruck. "You, Jason Bishop, have performed a great service to Azrael, the Angel of Death. One of the four archangels in the service of the Lord Our God. In recognition of this service, I hereby grant you a piece of the fires of creation."

"Wait, I gave the –gack!" Jason said, protesting as Azrael shoved something silvery into his mouth, sending Jason into a coughing fit.

"Are you going to smite me or something?" I asked.

"Why, do you want to be smited? Smote? Smitten? Blast I never remember how to conjugate that one, no matter what language it's in. No matter. Do you want that?" he asked.

"No?" I said.

"Is that a question or a statement?" he asked

"No. It's a statement," I replied.

"Then no. Don't see any need to," he said.

"But I'm a–" I began.

"Yes. Demon. You said. Seems like it's a real hang-up for you. Okay. I've paid you off for your highly unorthodox service, so if that's all?" he said.

"Wait," Jason croaked. "Ava."

"Yes, we were just talking," Azrael said.

"I gave her the reward in exchange for her help," Jason finished.

Azrael looked from Jason to me and back again, hands on their hips. "Well. This is highly irregular."

"This whole fucking situation was highly unusual," Jason said.

"But I've given you the reward," Azrael said.

"It's hers," Jason demanded "Transfer it or something."

Azrael shook their head. "Once a divine gift has been bestowed it can't be taken away."

"Like Cassandra from the Greek myths," I said.

"Yes! Very good, Ava! Just like that," Azrael replied, delighted. "But if you're owed a reward from Heaven for services rendered, a promise is a promise."

"Will this hurt me?" I asked, remembering Silene's 'gift' to Brother Avery.

"What do you take me for, some sort of cold-blooded lizard?" Azrael laughed. "No, Much like Mr. Bishop, your reward will be perfectly suited to you."

And so Azrael, the Archangel of Death, laid their hand on my forehead. I felt the slightest of tickles where their hand touched, which spread to my chest, then my stomach, and spread out like a small stream of warmth flowing through my body.

I shuddered, then opened my eyes.

"What—" I asked

"You'll see in time," he said.

"Wait. So Jason got some sort of holy flamethrower and I got a 'and future considerations' gift?" I asked. "That seems a bit unbalanced."

"You've both received the gift you'll need the most," he said.

"If you say 'the power of friendship', I swear to–" I said.

"Nuh-uh. No swearing. Not even for demon-girls," Azrael said, stepping back into their robes.

And like that, he was gone.

Jason and I stood there for a moment as police sirens approached in the distance. Looking down, Brother Avery was still lying there, wide-eyed and babbling quietly.

Jason sighed, shook his head, and said, "This is gonna take some explaining."

Epilogue

Ava finished her story, picked up her wine glass, and toasted everyone at the table before downing the whole thing.

"But that's not when the angel gave me my gift," I objected. "You got it wrong, Ava."

"Nope," she said with a smirk.

"It was after the library thing a few months later," I insisted. "You remember? I'm positive."

"Then you're positively wrong, Jason. That was when it happened," she replied, exuding confidence as only Ava can.

I sat and thought, wracking my brain.

"But I distinctly remember—" I continued.

"I distinctly remember you pickling your brain consistently over the next year or so, Jason," she interrupted. "It's possible that errant memory was chemically altered."

"C'mon, I'd like to think I would know when something that important happened," I said.

"So would I, but I'm used to disappointment," she replied with a laugh. *Ouch.*

"What did the angel give you, Ava?" Dave asked, saving me from further brutalization.

Ava shrugged. "No clue. Said it was something I'd need, so it could be anything."

"I-I don't think I've ever heard that story before," Nat said. "Ava, you're a beast!"

"I know I haven't," Dave added.

"I just got bits an' pieces, sugah. Pieced some of it together over the years after some hints an' scraps, but nothing this–complete," Nero said. "But ain't nothing in that story a huge surprise at this point"

"It makes sense, though," Jackie said. "If anyone in the world could talk to an angel and make it so mad that it Fell from grace just to have the opportunity to kill him, it's Jason Bishop."

There was a round of laughter and the table agreed to drink to that. I saw Ava sitting quietly, a smile in her eyes as she scanned the room filled with our friends.

No.

Filled with our family.

I reached under the table and squeezed her leg and got a bright smile from her as a reward.

The conversation around the table had shifted to a round of stories about me being a jerk to a variety of people and others, but I leaned in and gave Ava a peck on the cheek.

"What was that for?" she asked.

"To thank you. I know talking about a lot of stuff can be hard for you, and that you're strangely shy about being the center of attention when you're not at the club," I said.

"Clever boy," she replied, lightly poking my nose. "There are a lot of things from before that I don't like to think about. Things that I don't like to remember," she said.

"They're not all bad," I said.

"You weren't there for 'em, Jason," she said. "Some of it was a real shit show."

"That's probably true, but every time something awful happened, every false start, every time you fell down all led to right here, and right now. If any of it changes, I don't know if we're where we are," I said, taking her hand and kissing the back. "And I wouldn't trade where we are for anything in the world."

"Okay, those were scary, no doubt. Some of that stuff is gonna give me nightmares," Jackie said. "But I've got something that'll top all of 'em."

"I can't wait to hear this!" Nat exclaimed. "Spill the dirt you've got on Bishop, Jacke!

"Are you sure this is a good–" Victor started.

"Zzzzz!" Nero said, waving his hand at Victor. "I want Miss Jackie's dirt on Bishop too. Spill, girl"

Jackie nodded somberly, took a deep breath, and began.

"Have you ever heard him sing karaoke?"

The
End